Praise for the novels of Kristin Rockaway

"Smart, fun, fast-paced. Rockaway seamlessly blends the trials of modern dating with the challenges of being a woman in a male-dominated workplace."

—Helen Hoang, author of *The Kiss Quotient*

"For everyone who has been wronged in the world of online dating! Revenge is a dish best served digitally i
capturing what it's like to pursue ambi
Snappy pacing, a delightful group of b
tech and a workplace love interest mad

—Sally Thorne, *USA TODAY* bests

"Rockaway has masterfully painted the current dating landscape so many are navigating these days."

—Renée Carlino, *USA TODAY* bestselling author of *Blind Kiss*

"Will have readers laughing and celebrating… Perfect for fans of Doree Shafrir's *Startup* and Hannah Orenstein's *Playing with Matches*."

—*Booklist*

"A fun, sexy debut perfect for readers who love exotic settings and a great love story."

—Karma Brown, bestselling author,
on *The Wild Woman's Guide to Traveling the World*

"Brilliantly navigates one woman's quest to let go of what is practical to pursue her passion and surrender to her inner dreamer."

—Kerry Lonsdale, bestselling author,
on *The Wild Woman's Guide to Traveling the World*

"Can a novel be smart *and* loads of fun? Kristin Rockaway's debut is proof that it's possible."

—Camille Pagán, bestselling author,
on *The Wild Woman's Guide to Traveling the World*

Also by Kristin Rockaway

The Wild Woman's Guide to Traveling the World

How to Hack a Heartbreak

KRISTIN ROCKAWAY

GRAYDON
HOUSE

ISBN-13: 978-1-525-83425-7

How to Hack a Heartbreak

For questions and comments about the quality of this book, please contact us at CustomerService@Harlequin.com.

GraydonHouseBooks.com
BookClubbish.com

Printed in U.S.A.

For Emilio.

I'm grateful the internet brought us together.

How to Hack a Heartbreak

1

Never trust anything you read on the internet.

It's sound advice. I'd read it somewhere, possibly on the internet, but I'd never really taken it seriously until the night Brandon, 26, from Brooklyn stood me up.

According to his bio, Brandon was a "thrill seeker who lived for the moment and loved with abandon," which should've been my first clue that he was full of shit.

As I sat alone at the bar, staring at the bottom of my empty cocktail glass, I cursed myself for agreeing to this date in the first place. Normally, I'd never waste a Friday night meeting some random guy I matched with on the internet. First dates were reserved for Tuesday or Wednesday nights only, when there was almost always nothing better going on. But when Brandon's beautiful bearded face slid across my screen asking me to join him for a drink at a bar in the Financial District, I thought there'd be no harm in making an exception to my rule.

That was a rookie mistake.

I tapped my phone and stared at the screen. It was 6:18. The last message I'd received from Brandon was at 4:37: meet u @ the barley house @ 6.

Maybe he was just running late. I messaged him back: Are we still on for tonight? then waited in vain for a response.

"Another vodka soda?" The bartender whisked my glass away and wiped down the lacquered wood countertop. I had a choice: I could escape now with my dignity and go find Whitney, who was likely tearing it up somewhere on the Lower East Side. Or I could give Brandon from Brooklyn the benefit of the doubt, and nurse another drink while I waited for him to arrive. I swiped through his profile photos and felt giddy at the sight of his pouty lips and deep-set eyes.

"Sure, I'll have another." Yeah, he was probably just running late. After all, this was New York. There were a million obstacles that could be preventing him from getting here on time: train malfunctions, traffic snarls, police investigations shutting down major thoroughfares. I needed to stop being so cynical.

Still, Whitney's words echoed in my head: *Don't put all your eggs in one basket*. So I fired up the Fluttr app and checked to see if there were any potential love interests in the immediate vicinity.

Fluttr was the dating app of choice these days. There wasn't anything particularly special about it—it worked just like every other dating app I'd ever used: post a couple of not-terrible photos. Enter your name, age, and location. Then swipe through a seemingly infinite pool of available men. A left swipe meant no, a right swipe meant yes, and if you swiped right on a guy who swiped right on you, you could message each other through the app. Simple, straightforward, and not at all original, but for some reason, it was hugely popular. There were more people signed up for Fluttr than any other dating app in the city.

So far, I hadn't had much luck with it. Most of my matches led to disappointing first dates, endless go-nowhere in-app messaging, or the occasional unsolicited dick pic. But with so many guys to choose from, I was sure Mr. Right was only one swipe away.

"Here you go." The bartender set my drink down on a fresh cocktail napkin. The first sip made my head swim. Time to get to swiping.

Bachelor number one was shirtless. *Swipe left.*

Bachelor number two was slamming a beer bong. *Swipe left.*

Bachelor number three was sandwiched between two bikini-clad women. *Swipe left.*

Finally, hope appeared in the form of Joe, 25, from Murray Hill. Hazel eyes, thick black hair, and the perfect amount of five o'clock shadow. No booze or half-naked babes to be seen. And he was wearing a sweater. *Swipe right.*

Digital confetti rained down from the top of my screen. Fluttr proclaimed: *It's a match!*

"Melanie?"

Aha! My patience and faith were rewarded. I quickly switched off my phone and swiveled toward the sound of his voice. But the guy addressing me wasn't Brandon from Brooklyn. It was Alex Hernandez, the new guy at my office, and a fine specimen of manhood.

"Hi." The word tripped over my vocal chords. I was surprised he even remembered my name. A few weeks earlier, we'd received the briefest of introductions during his orientation tour of the building, but we hadn't spoken since.

He'd left a big impression, though. In an office full of bedraggled computer nerds, Alex's sense of style was an anomaly: hair perfectly mussed, jeans perfectly cuffed, button-down shirt perfectly fitted to his lean, solid torso. I'd wanted to see him again, but there was never a good excuse for me to swing by his cubicle, no good reason for us to strike up an idle chat. If I'd known he hung out at The Barley House, though, I probably would've started coming here sooner.

"Mind if I sit here?" he asked.

"Of course not."

He slung his laptop bag along the back of the barstool and slid into the seat. I fussed with my earring, struggling to act casual. It was difficult, given the fact that Alex Hernandez was mere inches away from me. He smelled like leather and cloves. I bet his skin was warm to the touch.

"How's the help desk been treating you?"

Alex was, of course, referring to my role at Hatch. If any employee had a problem with their personal computer—a broken mouse, an outdated version of Word, a virus they'd accidentally downloaded from an infected website—I was the gal to solve it.

"The usual," I said. "Fine. Busy. Nothing exciting."

"Cool. So, what are you doing here all alone?"

"I'm not alone." Of course, I was obviously alone, but I didn't want Alex thinking I was some loser who hung out in bars by myself on Friday nights. Then I remembered why I was really there: to meet a guy from Fluttr, who was most likely in the process of standing me up. "I'm meeting someone. Maybe."

"Maybe?"

Here was another rookie mistake: arranging an internet date within walking distance of my office building. I worked on

Water Street, right at South Street Seaport, so most of my coworkers grabbed their happy hour drinks at bars along those cobblestone streets surrounding Pier 17. The Barley House was farther west, closer to the Stock Exchange, tucked away in a hidden corner of Maiden Lane, so I figured it was a safe zone. I thought I'd disappear into a sea of off-duty traders celebrating the end of their workweek. I didn't realize the place would be half-empty, or that my secret office crush would roll in and sit down next to me.

Rather than risk embarrassing myself with a truthful answer to Alex's question, I deflected. "Is this bar some hush-hush Hatch hangout I've never heard about?"

"Nah, no one ever comes here except for me. I live down the block. I'm here all the time. And after the day I've had, I need a stiff drink." He flagged down the bartender and ordered a Maker's Mark on the rocks, then turned to me and asked, "Do you need another one?"

"No, thanks." This second vodka soda was already going straight to my head. I doubted I'd be able to finish it. "Why was your day so bad?"

He let out an exasperated groan. "A deployment went totally bonkers. I had to code a last-minute bug fix, but then that introduced another bug." The bartender delivered his whiskey and Alex paused to take an urgent gulp. "I finally got it all sorted out, but by then everyone was pissed."

"That sucks."

"No kidding." He ran a hand through his thick, dark curls. "And it didn't help that Greg dumped a giant cup of coffee all over his brand-new laptop."

"Yeah. That thing was toast."

The coffee incident had taken up most of my morning, actually. Greg had strolled into my cubicle, slack-jawed, holding his four-thousand-dollar laptop by the corner of its cracked screen. "Uh… I spilled," he said, as if it wasn't obvious from the liquid oozing out from under the keys and dripping onto the carpet.

"What's up with the broken screen?" I asked, gently taking the computer from his hands and placing it on my desk.

"Uh… I dropped it."

For a man who was supposed to be the brains behind a burgeoning business, Greg didn't seem particularly bright. Or motivated, for that matter.

"Give me a few hours," I'd said. "I can try to salvage the hard drive and set you up with a new machine."

"Uh-huh." He was already engrossed in his phone, scrolling through something that looked like a Reddit thread. "Just text me when it's done. I'll be…out." And he tripped over my cubicle wall as he walked away.

The whole thing was laughable, honestly. That a man like Greg could secure hundreds of thousands of investor dollars without knowing much of anything or doing any work. But when I saw the anguish on Alex's face, I swallowed my snicker. Of course it wasn't funny to him.

See, even though Alex and I worked in the same office, we had wildly different jobs. I worked for Hatch, a start-up incubator that provided seed funding and temporary office space for app developers with big ideas, also known as Hatchlings. I supported the Hatchlings in their day-to-day activities, and as a full-time employee, I enjoyed a regular salary, two weeks of paid vacation, and a phenomenal dental plan.

Alex, on the other hand, was one of those app developers with the big ideas and Greg was his partner. They were a few weeks into their three-month incubation period, which meant they had only a short amount of time left to perfect their app. At the end of their stint, they'd show off their final project to big-time investors from venture capital firms all over the country. If their demo was a failure, that'd be the end of it. They'd be shooed out of Hatch and would have to start over somewhere else, doing something new. But I'd still be there, collecting my paycheck, replacing busted laptops for a whole new cohort of wannabe start-up founders.

"How are things going with your project?" I asked. "What's the name of your app again? Sorry, I should probably know this."

He waved away my apology. "There are like two dozen start-ups at Hatch right now. I don't blame you for not keeping track. We're Fizz."

"Fizz. And…what does it do?"

"It's a ride-sharing app."

"That's cool." *Even if not totally original.*

"It's all right." He shrugged and took a long sip of bourbon. "To be honest, it's not going so well."

"Oh. I'm sorry."

"It's okay. Even if we fail, being at Hatch is still a foot in the door. A way to make contacts in the start-up community. I'm only twenty-six—there'll be plenty of other opportunities." He frowned slightly, like he was having a hard time convincing himself that failure was an option. "I mean, that's probably why you're working the help desk, right? As a stepping-stone."

"Right." Except not really. I was working at Hatch because they were the first company to offer me a job after graduation, and I didn't want to look a paycheck horse in the mouth. Not when I was drowning in student loans. Plus, rent in New York

City wasn't exactly affordable. I wasn't worried about planning my career path; I was worried about how to pay my bills.

Of course, I'd started at Hatch four years ago. Now, I was the same age as Alex, in the same position as when I first left college, with no goals or dreams beyond my current dead-end job.

Sometimes I thought it'd be nice to be the person with the vision, as opposed to the person who fixed the broken laptops of the visionaries. But it's not like I had any brilliant ideas worth pursuing. So working the help desk was where I had to be.

"So," he said, "where's this someone you're maybe meeting?"

I glanced at my phone, tapping the screen as if I expected to see something there. "I'm not sure."

"Well, I'm glad I ran into you."

My mouth curled into an involuntary smile. "Really?"

"Yeah." He returned the grin. "You know, we only spoke that once and it was so quick. I kept meaning to stop by your desk and say hi, but I could never find a good excuse. Maybe we can grab lunch next week? If you're free."

"Of course." I had to fight to keep myself from squealing. Alex Hernandez was flirting with me. I mean, that's what was happening, right? After a vodka soda and a half, it was hard to tell. The booze might've been playing tricks on my ego. I could be blowing our banter out of proportion.

Still, he didn't break my gaze, even as he brought the bourbon to his lips and took a long-drawn-out drink. He swallowed, licked his lips. My eyes dropped to the movement of his tongue. He was flirting with me, no doubt about it.

Perhaps getting stood up was a blessing in disguise. In fact,

I was glad Brandon from Brooklyn never showed his face. Because Alex was here, in the flesh. That was way better than a virtual Fluttr match.

Just as I started fantasizing about how the rest of our evening would unfold—a candlelit dinner, a romantic stroll by the waterfront, a sexually charged taxi ride back to his place—a nasal voice called his name from across the bar. Instantly, he straightened. I turned and spotted a leggy brunette stalking toward us. Or, rather, toward Alex.

"Hi!" She planted a kiss in the corner of his mouth, leaving behind a smear of berry lipstick.

"Hi." Alex looked sheepish. Of course he did. He was flirting with his coworker behind his girlfriend's back. *Asshole.*

He wiped the lipstick away with his fingertips. "Jenny, this is Melanie. We work together. Melanie, this is Jenny."

She smiled politely and shook my hand. "Hello."

"Hi."

Jenny slipped onto the stool on the other side of Alex, who was downing the rest of his Maker's Mark with closed eyes. She looked past him, at me, a polite yet cold smile on her berry-painted lips. This was probably my cue to leave.

I tapped my phone. It was 6:42. Safe to say Brandon from Brooklyn was officially a no-show. *Asshole.*

"Can I grab the check, please?" I waved my arm like a madwoman, trying to flag down the bartender, then texted Whitney: Where are you?

Meanwhile, Alex whispered something and Jenny giggled maniacally. The bartender delivered my bill and I slapped down my credit card, pretending not to overhear what was surely foreplay.

God, I was an idiot.

My phone lit up with Whitney's reply: Date's over already? Must've been bad. We're at Verlaine. Come!!!

I replied OMW and signed the bill. The feet of the barstool scraped against the slate floor as I slid off my seat. Alex turned his head at the sound. "Are you outta here?" he said, looking somewhat surprised.

"Yup." Unable to meet his eyes, I met Jenny's instead. "It was lovely to meet you, Jenny."

Her smile softened. "You, too."

I'd made it halfway to the door when Alex called out, "See you Monday, Melanie." Too mortified to form a proper response, I waved half-heartedly over my shoulder and fled the scene, all the while thinking, *I am never using Fluttr again.*

2

I spotted them as soon as I walked through the front door of Verlaine. They were huddled together on one end of the large plush sectional that lined the back of the bar. Lia was talking, and from the wistful smile on her face, it was probably something to do with her new boyfriend, Jay. Dani sat on one side of her, leaning forward with her elbows on her thighs and listening intently. Whitney sat on the other side, her gaze wandering around the room in search of something more interesting. When she caught sight of me, she thrust her bangle-covered arm in the air.

"Mel!" Her voice rose above the chatter and music. Dani and Lia looked up and I weaved through the crowd toward them.

"Hey." I squeezed in next to Whit, accidentally bumping a guy sitting beside her. "Sorry," I said.

"No problem," he replied. From the glassy sheen to his eyes, he'd clearly taken full advantage of the happy hour specials. "You can bump me anytime, baby."

Gross.

I angled my body away from him and toward the girls. "What's going on?"

"Lia was just telling us about her upcoming Mexican adventure," Dani said.

"Mexico? Wow."

"Cabo," Lia said. "Jay is taking me to this super exclusive resort right on the beach."

Of course he was. Jay was always showering her with thoughtful, expensive treats. Dinners at trendy restaurants. Orchestra seats at Broadway shows that had been sold out for months. Jewelry worth more than a semester of college tuition. A luxury vacation was the next logical step.

I'd be lying if I said I wasn't the teensiest bit jealous. After spending years dating loser after loser, it was hard not to see the blissed-out look on Lia's face and think: *Why not me?* But her relationship gave me hope, too. A mere two and a half months ago, Lia right-swiped Jay on Fluttr. Now, they were bound for a Mexican beach. If it worked for her, it could work for me. Surely, there was at least one other decent man to be found on that app. *Maybe I shouldn't be so quick to give up on it.*

On the table before us, a lone spring roll withered on a porcelain plate. It looked like it'd been sitting there awhile; the greens were wilted and a skin had formed on the dipping sauce. But seeing as I hadn't eaten anything since my usual noontime peanut butter sandwich, my stomach growled at the sight of it.

"Anybody eating this?" I didn't wait for an answer before scooping it up and cramming it in my mouth. Not the freshest spring roll I'd ever eaten, but the carrots were still somewhat crunchy, and it put a temporary stop to the roiling in my stomach.

As Lia went on about snorkeling and sunset cruises, I wondered if I'd ever get the chance to stay at an exclusive resort in Cabo. Probably not. That would require money, or failing that, a rich guy to pay my way. And the way things were going, I'd likely be single and debt-ridden for the rest of my life.

A server approached and began to clear away the empty glasses and plates. "Another round, ladies?"

Whitney gave an enthusiastic "You bet!" Then she turned to me. "So, you had another shitshow of a date?"

"Kind of. But, not really."

"What does that mean? It either sucked or it didn't."

Three pairs of curious eyes trained on me. I froze, suddenly embarrassed to admit I'd been stood up. I felt like it reflected some kind of unflattering mark on my character, which was ridiculous seeing as Brandon from Brooklyn knew nothing about me besides my name, age, and location. Our brief interaction took place entirely within a virtual world. Saying it out loud would make it real.

Unfortunately, Lia saw right through me. "He never showed, did he?"

I sighed. "Nope."

They all gasped at the same time. Whit shouted, "Fucker!"

Lia reached across her to put a comforting hand on my knee and said, "I'm sorry. If it's any consolation, it's happened to me before."

"Really?"

"Yeah. Just before I met Jay. This guy and I made plans to meet up for a drink in the Village and he totally stood me up."

"Was his name Brandon?"

She shrugged. "Honestly, I can't remember now. It was like it happened in another life."

"Men are the worst," Whit chimed in.

"Not all men," Lia chided. "You know the saying—you've gotta kiss a lot of frogs before you find your prince."

Oh, right. The myth of Prince Charming. The preposterous notion that there was a perfect guy out there who'd fulfill all your desires and dreams. It seemed a little far-fetched to think there were enough of these princes to satisfy every woman in the world. It also seemed unlikely that they'd be hanging around on Fluttr, just waiting for you to stumble upon them with a flick of your thumb.

"No, Whit's right," I said. "Men are the worst."

"It's not just men, though," Dani said. "I'm ghosted by women on Iris all the time."

"What's Iris?" Lia asked.

"A new dating app for queer women."

"So you've given up on Fluttr?"

"No," Dani said. "I just wanted to try something else. Fluttr has a decent interface for LGBTQ users, but my thinking was that maybe a woman-only space would have a different sort of vibe—less bullshit, more tact. But so far I'm not having much luck."

"Why is online dating so horrible?" I moaned.

"I suspect it has something to do with the detachment associated with digital correspondence, and the inability to establish a true connection with someone in the absence of physical cues. Philip Brixton has conducted numerous studies about the importance of nonverbal communication. The results are fascinating."

Only Dani could turn a Friday night bitchfest into an academic analysis of human behavior. Don't get me wrong: I was proud that she was doing so well for herself, but the rest of us weren't getting a PhD in Sociology. Her ten-dollar words and references to obscure research studies were lost on us. But I didn't want to make her feel self-conscious, so I said, "Interesting," even though I had no clue what she was talking about.

Whit was less subtle. "Speak English, nerd."

Dani tossed her braids over one shoulder and pushed her glasses up on her nose. "It means that it's really hard to give a shit about someone unless you can look them in the eye. Body language is crucial to building relationships."

"See? I always say body language is important." Whit adjusted her Bombshell Bra with such vigor that her breasts nearly spilled out of her deep V-neck T-shirt. The drunk guy next to me muttered something lecherous, but Whit ignored him and continued, "I've never had a problem with the guys I've met on Fluttr, though. True, I get the occasional weirdo with an Asian fetish, but that's certainly not a Fluttr-specific phenomenon. So that blows your whole detachment theory out of the water."

"I wouldn't classify what you do on Fluttr as 'building relationships,'" Dani said, as the server delivered our drinks. Lia and I snorted, but Whit smirked triumphantly. She'd had a ton of success with dating apps because she used them purely for hookups. No guy in his right mind would ever left-swipe Whitney Hwang's photo: pouty red lips, silky black hair, cleavage for days. She listed her occupation as "Provocateur," which wasn't completely inaccurate given the fact that she worked in PR. I'd lost count of how many one-night stands she'd racked up thanks to Fluttr.

Which was great for her. But I wanted something that lasted more than a night.

"I just wish there was a way to weed out the profiles of people who aren't interested in a meaningful relationship," I said. "Or people who say they're interested in a meaningful relationship, but really aren't."

"Like people who ghost out of nowhere after weeks of pointless messages," Lia added.

"Or people who stand you up," Dani said, with a swig of her martini.

"Or people who send you dick pics," I said.

Dani cringed. "I've never had that problem."

"Of course you haven't. You only date women."

"I love how they're always non sequiturs, too," Lia said. "Like you're just texting about the weather and out of nowhere—surprise! It's a penis. What's the point?"

"It's pure exhibitionism," Dani said.

"It's borderline abusive."

Whit cocked her head. "You know, I don't really mind the occasional dick pic."

"Men are the worst." I drained the rest of my martini in one dramatic gulp, then slammed the glass down so hard on the table, I was shocked it didn't shatter into a million pieces.

"The problem," Whit said, "is that you're going about it all wrong. Fluttr isn't the place to go looking for a happily-ever-after."

Lia raised her finger. "Well, I did use it to meet Jay."

"We know," Whitney said, with a roll of her eyes.

"I'm not even looking for a happily-ever-after," I said. "I'd be satisfied with a happy-for-now. To meet a guy who actually took the time to get to know me and told me the truth and treated me with respect."

"Well, you're not gonna find that on Fluttr." Whit fished

the lychee from the bottom of her martini glass and popped it in her mouth. Then her eyes got wide and sparkly. "Hey, why don't you write your own dating app?"

Lia and Dani oohed and aahed.

"That's a great idea!"

"Yeah, you can make it super selective. Ban all the losers."

"You could totally put Fluttr out of business."

"Aren't you surrounded by start-up investors all day? I'm sure they'd go crazy for a new dating app."

"It's not that simple," I said.

"Who said anything about simple?" Whitney said. "Just because it's not easy doesn't mean it can't be done."

"I can help you design a front end, if that's what you're worried about," Lia said. It was sweet of her to offer, since she was already swamped with the demands of her day job as a graphic designer for a big ad agency.

But designing a user interface wasn't what worried me. It was everything else. I saw what those founders went through. Months of endless demands and sleepless nights. Disappointment. Failure. Rejection. At the end of a three-month incubation period, only half of all Hatchlings went on to receive additional funding. The rest of the fledgling start-ups just died.

Not to mention, putting an app out there with my name on it was a lot of responsibility to deal with. If it sucked, I had no one to blame but myself. Sure, working the help desk wasn't glamorous, but at five o'clock, I punched out for the day and left the stress of it all in the office. It never followed me home.

"I just can't," I said.

Whitney sighed and steepled her fingertips beneath her chin. I knew what was coming next. Another one of her lectures on "leaning in and claiming my seat at the table." Advice on how to define an action plan for my life, tips on how to see it through.

I didn't want to deal with this now. All I wanted was an uncomplicated Friday night bitchfest. Why was it so hard to make that happen?

Before Whitney could get into it, though, our server came by with a tray full of shots. As he set them down before us, I said, "We didn't order these. Did we?"

"No," he replied, tucking the tray under his arm. "These are compliments of the gentleman to your left."

Great.

I peered cautiously over my shoulder to see the drunk guy leering at Whitney's chest. "Enjoy, ladies," he slurred.

Here was something else I didn't want to deal with: the advances of a shitfaced stranger. If we accepted these, he'd expect us to talk to him, or at the very least, say thanks. And I wasn't about to thank someone who'd been aggressively ogling us all night.

"We don't want them," I told the server. "Send them back."

"Wait a minute," Whitney said. "Why are you turning down a free drink?"

"I don't wanna talk to this guy, do you?"

"No, but we don't have to talk to him just because he bought us drinks. That's not how it works."

The drunk guy leaned over, practically falling into my lap. "A simple thank-you would suffice, ladies."

Whit turned to the server, who looked like he wanted to flee the scene of whatever crime was about to be committed. "On second thought," she said, "we'll send those back."

As the server dutifully placed the shot glasses back on his

tray, the drunk guy glowered. "You girls should show a little gratitude."

"Excuse me?" Lia said.

"You heard me." Spittle flew from his lips as he rounded on Lia. "You're lucky anyone bought *you* a drink. If it wasn't for your friend with her tits hanging out, I wouldn't have looked twice."

Before I could tell what was happening, Whit was on her feet, grabbing two shots off the poor server's tray and flinging them in the drunk guy's face. Amber liquid dripped down his cheeks and onto the front of his slim-fit polo. He sat frozen, shock and alcohol impeding his reflexes. People at neighboring tables stopped their conversations and turned to stare, eager to see what would happen next.

But we knew from experience: when Whit started throwing drinks, it was time to leave. We gathered our purses and jackets and hustled her out the door as she screamed a final "Asshole!" over her shoulder.

Out on the sidewalk, we straightened our skirts and smoothed our hair. "Everyone okay?" Dani asked.

We assured each other we were fine. It wasn't the first time a drunk dude had harassed any of us, and it surely wouldn't be the last.

I hugged my purse to my chest and looked around. Rivington Street was bursting with weekend vibes. People smiling and laughing as they emerged from restaurants and ducked into bars. The party was just getting started, yet all I wanted to do was head home and hide under the covers. To left-swipe this entire night from my memory: Brandon, Alex, all of it.

"I think I'm gonna get going."

"Hell no, you're not." Whit grabbed me by the wrist and

pulled me down the block, toward Ludlow Street. "It's rock 'n' roll karaoke night at Arlene's."

Lia squealed. "Ooh! Let's go. I wanna get there early so we can get our names on the list."

"I don't know if I'm up for it," I said.

"Come on." Dani squeezed my shoulder. "Think of how much better you'll feel after you screech out 'Life on Mars.'"

She had a point. There was no pain a little Bowie couldn't heal. And no better way to forget about the misery men had wrought on my life than by making new memories with my amazing girlfriends.

3

Unfortunately, I didn't remember much of what happened after we left Verlaine. The only thing I could recall with clarity was an abundance of Coors Light.

From the way my throat was burning, though, I'd obviously screeched out my fair share of David Bowie. And I had a vague recollection of wolfing down some mystery meat I'd bought from a cart on Stanton Street. In fact, there was still some garlicky gristle lodged between my teeth. Apparently, I hadn't felt the need to floss before I fell asleep.

Sunlight sliced through the slats of my blinds. I squinted and struggled to sit upright, but the room was spinning way too fast for my liking. So I unplugged my phone from the charger and nestled back beneath the covers.

After we'd said goodbye in the wee small hours of the morning, the girls started a group text message. My ancient phone had died halfway through, so I turned it on now to catch up on the conversation.

DANI 2:25 A.M.

Does anyone know what happened to Whit?

LIA 2:27 A.M.

Last I saw, she was making out with
some hipster in the corner of Arlene's.

DANI 2:28 A.M.

Not that guy with the handlebar mustache????

LIA 2:30 A.M.

Yup.

WHITNEY 3:45 A.M.

For your information, handlebar
mustaches are hot right now.

WHITNEY 3:46 A.M.

Besides he's an actor.

WHITNEY 3:47 A.M.

At least I think he is.

LIA 11:04 A.M.

Did you get his #?

WHITNEY 11:52 A.M.

Why would I do that?

DANI 12:12 P.M.

Is anyone else in a world of pain right now?

LIA 12:15 P.M.

I told you not to do those SoCo shots!

WHITNEY 12:17 P.M.

Blech. SoCo is never a good idea.

DANI 12:18 P.M.

Uuuuuuuggggghhhhh

WHITNEY 12:25 P.M.

Mel what's up with you?

LIA 12:27 P.M.

Yeah, are you feeling okay?

LIA 12:28 P.M.

That kabob you ate before you got in the cab looked pretty sketchy.

Funny, it didn't look sketchy to me. Of course, I was so starved that I would've eaten anything at that point.

MEL 12:40 P.M.

A little hungover but other than that I'm fine.

I closed my eyes as a wave of queasiness sailed through my system. Maybe that street meat wasn't the best idea. I should've listened to Lia.

My phone buzzed and I cracked one eye open to check the reply from the girls. But it wasn't a text message; it was a Fluttr alert.

NEW DIRECT MESSAGE FROM JOE!

Oh, right. The guy I'd matched with last night before the parade of humiliation began. Did I even want to read what he had to say? Whit had warned me: Fluttr was not the place to find a respectable guy.

But I kept coming back to Lia and Jay. Nice guys *were* on Fluttr. It just might take some persistence to find them.

Feeling hopeful, I tapped the notification to bring up the message. And there, in all its swollen, veiny shame, was a blurry close-up of Joe's dick.

Goddammit.

I chucked the phone across my room, where it bounced off the wall and landed with a crash against my dresser. That was going to cost me a pretty penny to fix.

Burying my face in my hands, I took slow, measured breaths, trying to calm my racing pulse. Normally, I would've taken Joe's dick pic in stride. After all, some men can be weird and gross. If I wanted to be active in the online dating world, dick pics were just something I had to learn to deal with.

My usual response was to delete the message and unmatch from the guy, but suddenly, that didn't seem like enough. Even though I would never hear from him again, Joe from Murray Hill would still be on Fluttr, spreading pictures of his penis to other unsuspecting women.

Telling him off was an enticing option. It'd certainly feel cathartic, but I doubt it'd actually make an impact. A man who sent dick pics to strangers already had no shame; if I tore him a new one, he'd probably take some sick satisfaction in knowing he got a rise out of me.

What I really wanted to do was get this guy banned from Fluttr, to take away the platform for his exhibitionism. There were options to flag profiles as offensive or harassing or spam, but as far as I could tell, Fluttr never actually did anything about it.

My train of thought was interrupted by a knock at my bedroom door. *Great.* As if I wasn't feeling crappy enough, now I had to deal with whatever Vanessa wanted.

Another knock. "Melanie? You okay in there?"

"Yes." My voice was unexpectedly raspy. I cleared my throat as I threw back my blanket and, on wobbly legs, took the one and a half steps from my bed to open the door. Vanessa stood in the hallway, hazel eyes shining brightly, not a stray hair in her sleek auburn topknot.

"Are you okay?" She looked me over from head to toe, her expression halfway between disgust and concern. "I thought I heard a crash."

"I'm fine." *I was merely launching a piece of delicate machinery across my room. No biggie.* "What's up?"

"Did you get my email?"

"What email?"

"About the party."

"What party?"

Vanessa rolled her eyes at me. "If you got the email, then you'd know."

"Is the party happening right now?"

She squinted. "No, of course not. It's next weekend."

"Then can this wait?"

"No. I need to make sure the email went through."

Her lash extensions fluttered like a hummingbird's wings. I wiped the crust from the corners of my eyes. "But I'm barely awake."

"Please?" she pleaded. "I just sent it a second ago, but then my computer started acting all wonky so I don't know if it went through. Which reminds me, I need you to take a look at it later."

It was clear she wasn't going anywhere until I answered her question. "Let me check."

She bounced on the balls of her feet. "Thanks."

I picked up my phone from where it had landed facedown

on top of the dresser. To my shock and delight, the damage wasn't nearly as bad as I'd expected it to be. Just a hairline fracture across the bottom right corner of the screen. No shattering, no shards. I lucked out!

"Ooh." Vanessa pursed her lips into a disapproving pucker. "What happened to your phone?"

"Uh... I dropped it."

"That sucks." She clucked her tongue. "There's a place around the corner that fixes them cheap. Like ninety-nine bucks or something."

"Thanks. I'll check it out." As if I would've wasted a hundred dollars on a superficial little crack. The phone still worked. When I pressed the home button, the screen sprang to life, revealing Joe's penis in graphic detail.

Vanessa shrieked and recoiled, like she was afraid it was going to leap out and attack her. "What the hell is that?"

"That is Joe, from Murray Hill." I held it up to her to give her a better view, and she retreated farther into the hallway.

"Why is that on your phone?"

"Well, it's not like I asked for it." From the frown lines forming on Vanessa's forehead, it was clear she didn't believe me. "I didn't! Haven't you ever gotten an unsolicited dick pic?"

"What?" Her topknot jiggled as she fervently shook her head. "No, of course not. What kind of person do you think I am?"

"It has nothing do with the kind of person you are." *Or the kind of person* I *am, for that matter.* "Guys'll just send them out of nowhere after you make a match. Aren't you on Fluttr?"

Her lip curled in revulsion. "Ugh. No. The idea of dating some random creep I meet on the internet is..." She ended her sentence with a dramatic shudder.

"It's really no different than meeting a guy at a party or a bar or waiting on line at Starbucks. Everybody starts out a stranger." Though, admittedly, the odds of a stranger flashing you in the middle of a crowded coffee shop were pretty slim.

"Those all sound like terrible ways to meet men." She folded her long, slender arms across her chest and stuck her chin out. "If I'm gonna let a guy put his tongue in my mouth, I'm gonna need to check some references first."

"References?"

"You wouldn't hire an employee without calling past employers to verify their skills and experience, right? So why would you start dating a guy that you know absolutely nothing about?"

It pained me to admit that Vanessa had a point. Still, the idea seemed sort of crazy. I envisioned her posting a personal ad on Craigslist soliciting résumés from potential suitors. She'd call ex-girlfriends, family members, financial advisors. If the guy's story checked out, only then would she schedule a first date.

Unlike me, who jumped at the chance to meet the first pretty face that flew across my screen.

"But how does that work, exactly?" I asked. "How do you check a guy's references?"

"I go to a matchmaker. She interviews guys, and when she finds someone who's up to my standards, she arranges a meetup."

I'd never seen Vanessa hanging around the apartment with anyone who seemed like a love interest. "Have you met anyone worthwhile?"

She scrunched up her nose. "There've been a couple of second dates, but nothing serious. At least, not yet. I've only been doing it for a year, though."

A year. Seems like her strategy for meeting Mr. Right wasn't any more effective than mine. Then again, I wondered how high her "standards" were.

"Her name's Vilma," she added. "She only takes new clients by referral, but I can put in a good word for you, if you want."

I could only imagine how much Vilma charged for her services. Probably more than we paid for the rent on our dump of an apartment. It seemed nice in theory, but not all of us could afford our own personal Vilma to perform background checks on every guy we met. How did Vanessa have that kind of cash? Did being a freelance virtual assistant pay more than I suspected? If so, I might've considered a career change.

"That's okay. Let me check my email." I swiped away Joe's nether regions and found an unread message from Vanessa at the top of my inbox.

From: Vanessa Pratt
Bcc: Melanie Strickland
Subject: Rooftop Rendezvous!

Hey lads and ladies!
Spring has sprung, which means it's time to indulge in this lovely NYC weather with an outdoor soirée. Come over to my rooftop in Downtown Brooklyn next Saturday night, April 14, at 8PM for drinks, snacks, and views for days.
See you then!
xo
V

"Are we allowed to have parties on the rooftop?" I asked.

"Technically, no. But no one's gonna care."

"Some people might."

"So they complain to the landlord. So what?"

I wish I could've gone through life like Vanessa, oblivious to things like personal bankruptcy and eviction.

"Okay. Well, looks like your email sent just fine."

"Great, thanks. Feel free to invite whoever you want. And let me know if you want me to put you in touch with Vilma." She scuttled off down the hallway without a goodbye.

I closed the door and face-planted back into bed, ready to sleep away the rest of my Saturday afternoon. Seconds later, my phone buzzed.

NEW DIRECT MESSAGE FROM JOE!

I knew I should have ignored it. Nothing Joe from Murray Hill had to say—or show—would be good. But I couldn't help myself. Years of attachment to a digital device had rendered me incapable of letting a message go unread. My fingers were making the decision for me before my brain had a chance to intervene.

And, of course, it was another dick pic. Or, rather, the same exact dick pic he'd sent minutes earlier. As if he was worried I hadn't received it the first time, and wanted to resend it just to make sure.

My thumb hovered over the unmatch button. Erasing Joe from my virtual life would've been the prudent thing to do. Responding would only give him the attention he craved. But I also didn't want him to think that what he was doing was okay.

I'd had enough of the unscrupulous men in this city. Men who flirted shamelessly with their coworkers when their girlfriends weren't looking. Men who made plans they never had any intention to keep. Men who started conversations with women they matched with on the internet, then followed them up immediately with pictures of their dicks.

What's worse is I continually fell for their bullshit. Time and again, I let men toy with my emotions, make a fool of me, telling myself that maybe this guy would be different than all the others. But no guy was ever different. And I never called them out on their behavior. I just let them go quietly about their lives without ever having to answer for their actions.

That ended right here, right now.

I hit the reply button and typed in a single word: Why?

A moment later, I received his response: Why not?

Joe from Murray Hill did not know who he was messing with.

MEL: Because I'm not interested. Because you're a pig. Because your penis is not as impressive as you think it is. Need I go on?

JOE: Chillax babe. It's all in good fun.

MEL: Maybe for you. But I didn't want the first snap of your janky dick, never mind the second one.

At which point, Joe decided to send me a third copy of the same picture.

MEL: You know what? I'm going to tell everyone about you. I'm going to ruin your reputation. And you'll never get another date in this town again.

JOE: LOL good luck with that babe.

I started to type a response, but the app froze, and the whole interaction disappeared from my screen, replaced with the message:

The conversation could not be loaded. Fluttr user has unmatched with you.

That son of a bitch.

If Joe thought this was the end of it, he was sorely mistaken. Because now I was out for revenge. Not just for me, but for every single woman in New York.

It was time to bring reference checking to the masses.

That's how JerkAlert was born.

4

Some people think I made JerkAlert as part of a malicious, premeditated scheme to humiliate men at large. But in truth, it was just a gut reaction to the futility of the status quo. I'd had a few really bad days, featuring a few really bad dudes. So I did what any disgruntled coder would do: I created an anonymous website where women could rate their dating experiences with the guys they met on Fluttr. Kind of like Yelp, but instead of reviewing restaurants or nail salons, you reviewed your dates.

It didn't take me all that long to get it up and running. Too hungover to get out of bed, I spent the rest of my Saturday writing the code. Then on Sunday, I slapped together some quick graphics, uploaded it all to my discount web host, and invested $9.99 in the purchase of JerkAlert.biz. (Unfortunately, JerkAlert.com was already taken, pointing to a site that appeared to be permanently under construction.)

On Sunday night, when it was all finished, I logged my first entry.

Name: Joe
Age: 25
Location: Murray Hill
Review: Sent three consecutive dick pics. Also, used the word chillax.

As soon as I hit the submit button, I felt ten pounds lighter. Like all that rage had dislodged itself from my body and floated away. It was liberating.

And somewhat addictive.

I hit New and logged another man.

Name: Brandon
Age: 26
Location: Brooklyn
Review: Bailed on our first date without warning or explanation.

The simple act of typing their names out, seeing their misdeeds printed in pixels on my screen, was enough to make me feel better. I was putting all my pain out there, into the void of the internet, so it could no longer drag me down.

I spent the next few minutes logging the details of other men I'd encountered on Fluttr who'd flaked out, harassed me, or otherwise screwed me over.

There was Shawn, 27, from Hoboken, who started a very friendly text conversation and then abruptly demanded nudes.

There was Enzo, 30, from Washington Heights, who showed up to our date looking about twenty years older than his profile picture.

There was Pavel, 28, from Astoria, who smashed and dashed after our third date, never to be heard from again.

And then there was Alex.

Technically, he didn't belong on JerkAlert. We hadn't met on Fluttr. We never went on a date. Before our little run-in at The Barley House, we'd barely said two words to each other.

But, still, he'd hurt my feelings. Before his girlfriend showed up, he was definitely flirting with me. He asked me to lunch. He made me think there was a reason to have hope, and then pulled the rug out from under me.

It was humiliating.

Name: Alex

Age: 26

Location: FiDi

Review: Flirted with me hard. Asked me out. Then his girlfriend showed up.

After I hit Submit, I had a pang of conscience. After all, what he did was shitty, but Alex wasn't the *worst* guy in the world. He was still smart and attractive. And at least he didn't show me a picture of his dick.

Besides, it didn't matter what I posted on JerkAlert, because I never had any intention of letting anyone else see what I'd written. Now that I'd purged my disappointment and embarrassment, I realized the site was a terrible idea. It was mean-spirited and dirty, the exact opposite of what I wanted my love life to be. Just because guys—or, more accurately, *some* guys—made my Fluttr experience miserable, it didn't mean I had to stoop down to their level. I could rise above and choose to remain positive. And I would.

As soon as I showed it to the girls.

From: Melanie Strickland
To: Whitney Hwang; Lia Berman; Dani Silva
Subject: Introducing… JerkAlert!

I found the solution to my problem…http://jerkalert.biz

After our bitchfest on Friday night, I figured they'd get a kick out of it. Maybe they'd even review a few men of their own before I took the whole thing offline.

Monday started off as per usual.

"I can't connect to the internet."

Josh Brewster was standing in front of me, nostrils flaring like a pissed-off bull. As if I were the cause of his internet connectivity issue, as opposed to the person who could help him solve it.

"Have you tried—"

"Listen," he said, "I don't have time for this. I got Vijay breathing down my neck right now and this fucking broken piece of shit won't work." He gave his laptop a violent shake. "You're the help desk, right? Give me some goddamn help."

There was no point in engaging him. I knew what these Hatchlings were like. Entitled bros who thought I existed merely to serve them. If I dared to challenge Josh right now, he'd report me to my manager, Bob. Then Bob would say, "Calm down, Mel. Don't take things so personally." He'd tell me these guys were under a lot of pressure, and that it was my job to make their lives easier. Plus, he'd probably be annoyed with me for forcing him to have this conversation in the first place.

I knew because this had happened before, too many times to count. So even though I hated having to grin and bear this verbal abuse, in the long run, it was far easier to suck it up and play nice.

"Let's take a look," I said, forcing a smile as Josh thrust the laptop into my hands. A quick peek at the proxy settings confirmed my suspicions. "You're infected with malware."

"What?"

"Did you shut down the local firewall?"

"No, why?"

"There's a virus on your laptop. It's blocking your internet access." This was the second time I'd had to clear malware from Josh's computer in as many weeks. The first time, his desktop had become overrun with pop-up ads for adult chat rooms and discount designer sunglasses. "What kinds of websites have you been visiting?"

He snorted. "You know, I don't like what you're implying. Don't go accusing me of shit. Ever think that maybe you just didn't fix the problem the first time around?"

Stay calm. Don't engage.

"I'm gonna need a couple of hours to fix this. I can drop it off at your desk before lunch."

"Un-fucking-real." He threw his hands up in frustration. "I can't meet my deadline without a working laptop. What the hell am I supposed to tell Vijay?"

That you've been surfing porn sites instead of doing your job.

"I'll get it done as quickly as possible, Josh."

"Make sure you actually fix it this time."

With a swivel of my office chair, I turned my back to him, pretending not to hear the swearing as he stormed away.

The nerve of this guy, trying to pin his shady web-browsing habits on me. Then again, I'm not sure why I expected better behavior from someone who had a "Free Mustache Rides" sticker on the cover of his laptop. Which was most definitely in violation of Hatch's Code of Conduct, but I wasn't going to be the hysterical bitch who pointed that out.

Instead, I calmly closed each one of the dozen programs Josh had open and rebooted the system in safe mode to prepare for yet another round of virus removal.

While I waited, I pulled out my phone and saw a text from Whitney: That JerkAlert thing you sent last night is amazing. Where did you find it?

Funny. She thought it was an actual website.

MEL:

I made it myself. Hilarious, no?

WHITNEY:

More like brilliant!

Josh's laptop flickered on, and I began the tedious process of scanning for vulnerabilities and deleting infected files. Between this incident and Greg's coffee spill, I was basically a high-tech janitor, cleaning up the messes the Hatchlings so carelessly left behind. What a perfectly good waste of my eighty-thousand-dollar computer science degree.

It constantly amazed me, how these irresponsible guys scored sought-after spots in one of the most reputable start-up incubation programs in the country. Maybe that explained why such a high percentage of them failed. Maybe they were really good at pitching their ideas during the application process, but when it came to following through on what they promised, they couldn't deliver. Maybe all it took to succeed in this business was the balls to finish what you started.

In that case, I'd have made a kick-ass start-up founder.

"Knock knock."

I swiveled around to see Bob standing in the doorway of my cubicle, his arms folded across his chest, his face all scrunched up. He looked like he had indigestion.

"Hey. What's up?"

"Just had a little visit from Josh Brewster. He wasn't too happy."

"Is he ever happy?"

"Not that I've seen," he said. "But he told me he's been having an ongoing problem with his laptop and that you haven't been able to provide a fix."

"The ongoing problem is that he keeps downloading viruses onto his computer."

"Didn't you install security software?"

"Yes, and I have no idea how these things keep getting around it. He's probably disabling his virus scanners so he can surf around some shady corner of the deep web."

Bob sighed and ran a hand along his bald head. "Look, that's the other thing, Melanie. You can't go around accusing people of stuff you can't prove."

"I didn't accuse him of anything. I was only speculating. It's my job to fix his broken laptop, right? In order to do that, I need to know what's causing the problem."

"Do you have any evidence?"

"No."

"Then you have no idea if that's what he's doing."

"Well, what kind of app is his team developing?"

"You should already know this." Bob scowled. "They've got Blitz. It's a fantasy football app."

"There you go. He's probably into gambling, and that means—"

"Enough!" Bob's sharp tone cut my conspiracy theory off at the root. "Stop with the Nancy Drew routine and just do your job. Which, if you've forgotten, is to clean up his laptop and get it back to him as soon as possible." He turned to leave, then stopped abruptly, adding, "The guys are under a lot of pressure here. Stop giving them such a hard time."

I stared at the empty space he left behind, his final sentiment echoing in my brain.

The guys.

Yup, that was a pretty accurate description of the Hatch population. In the four years I'd been here, only a handful of women had walked through the door. My workdays were devoted to serving men. And not only did I need to keep their tech devices working, but, apparently, I was also responsible for protecting their fragile egos.

Infuriating.

I resumed my scan of Josh's laptop, deleting suspicious registry entries and replacing hacked files. With each passing minute, my keystrokes grew more forceful. At one point, I smacked the keyboard so hard that I dislodged the space bar.

Then, when I was sure his system was free from any and all traces of malicious software, I installed a little insurance policy: a keylogger. It'd run silently in the background while Josh did his work, recording each one of his keystrokes and storing them in an encrypted file. This way, if he disabled his virus scanner and went to a shady website, I'd have evidence.

He'd never know it was there. But the next time he came

into my cubicle, screaming his head off about my inability to fix his laptop, I'd show him my receipts. That'd shut him up.

It was noon when I finished. I tucked his laptop under my arm and headed toward the Blitz work area, steeling myself for what would undoubtedly be a torrent of insults and four-letter words. But Josh wasn't there, and his team members didn't bother to look up from their screens as I gingerly placed the repaired laptop on his desk and ran off.

I took the long way back to my cubicle, skirting the window-lined perimeter of the office space, so I could enjoy the views. From up here on the twenty-ninth floor, New York looked divine. Sunlight sparkled off the East River. Boats glided beneath the Brooklyn Bridge, leaving frothy white wakes. It was the ideal afternoon for an alfresco lunch.

And by that, I meant sitting at one of those picnic tables on Fulton Street and snarfing down the peanut butter sandwich I'd thrown in my purse this morning. Not especially glamorous, but with my budget being what it was, I'd take what I could get. All I had to do was grab my stuff from my desk drawer and—

"Melanie?"

I spun around, and there was Alex, looking characteristically dapper in fitted chinos and a cotton oxford. The top two buttons of his shirt were undone, revealing the tiniest tuft of black hair.

Stop looking at his chest.

"What's up?" I asked, completely calm, completely cool.

"I'm waiting on a database build, so I've got nothing to do for the next hour or so. Are you free for lunch? We can go to a restaurant at the Seaport."

Unbelievable. After that debacle on Friday night, you'd think he'd have the decency to be contrite.

"I don't think so," I sniffed, my gaze floating out the window.

"You sure? It's my treat." He leaned in slightly, lowered his voice. "I've been looking forward to it all weekend."

"Have you?"

I fixed with him an icy glare. He drew back, his expression halfway between confusion and terror. "Did I do something wrong?"

"Why don't you ask your girlfriend?"

"I don't have a girlfriend."

Does he think I'm a total idiot? "I met her, remember? Jenny."

His brow relaxed as he released a sigh of nervous laughter. "Jenny's not my girlfriend. She's just a girl I met on Fluttr. That was our first date. And, uh...it didn't go so well."

"Oh." Turns out, I actually *was* a total idiot. My face must have flushed a dozen shades of crimson. I could feel the heat radiating from my cheeks. "I'm sorry."

"It's fine," he said. "I can see why you would've thought that. But now that we've cleared up that little misunderstanding, are you interested in getting lunch?"

One side of his mouth quirked up in an adorable little half smile. There was no way I could say no.

My peanut butter sandwich would stay good until tomorrow. Probably.

"Let's do it."

5

We settled on Fresh Salt, a café on Beekman Street with outdoor seating. As I sipped my ice water, I took a moment to bask in how perfect everything was. A mild breeze floated off the river, and the snippet of sky visible between the surrounding buildings was blue and cloudless. For once, there were no construction vehicles spewing exhaust, no jackhammers clobbering the asphalt, no open bags of garbage festering on the pavement. The usual noises and odors of a New York City street were absent. It was simply a beautiful Monday afternoon.

And the most beautiful part of this beautiful scene? Alex Hernandez, smiling at me from across the weathered wooden table. Tousled hair, tawny skin, the perfect amount of five o'clock shadow shading his jawline. Somehow, he was equal parts scruffy and tailored, and it suited him.

"I have a question for you," he said.

"Go for it."

"Were you really meeting someone on Friday night?"

"Yes. A Fluttr date, actually."

"Then why'd you bolt out of there so fast?" His eyes went all wide and disbelieving. "Wait a minute, did you stand him up?"

"No! I would never do that." I ran a finger through the condensation on my water glass. I wasn't particularly keen on rehashing how I'd been blown off by some Fluttr rando, but there was no other choice but to tell the truth. "He stood *me* up."

"Ouch." The look of pity on his face was unbearable. "Sorry."

"It happens." I shrugged one shoulder, trying desperately to evoke a sense of indifference. "Getting jilted is just one of many risks you take when you decide to meet a stranger from the internet."

He chuckled. "Fluttr is the worst, isn't it?"

"The worst."

"I should just delete my profile. I'm convinced no one ever meets anyone worthwhile on that app."

"Actually, one of my best friends met her boyfriend on Fluttr, and they're pretty serious."

"Is he a nice guy?"

"I mean, he seems nice," I said, realizing the only things I knew about Jay were the things Lia told me about him. They'd been dating for almost three months, but I still hadn't met him. From the photos she posted on her Instagram account, it looked like they had a genuine mutual affection. But there was always some excuse why he could never meet us for a drink: late nights at the office, last-minute emergencies, business trips that sent him out of town for days at a time. I didn't even know what kind of job he had that kept him so busy.

What I did know was that Lia was the happiest I'd ever seen her.

"He makes her happy," I said.

"They're definitely one in a million. I've never hit it off with anyone I've matched with."

I smiled in solidarity. "Me neither."

"See what I mean? No one I know has. Which begs the question of why people keep going back for more."

"It's those ads on the subway. They get inside your head."

Fluttr had recently launched a marketing campaign aimed at New York City straphangers. They featured photos of radiant couples embracing against breathtaking backdrops, like rain forests and white sand beaches. Big, bold letters across the top screamed Fluttr: Don't Let the *One* Get Away.

And though I knew damn well there wasn't some male model impatiently waiting to whisk me away on a fantasy vacation, these ads always stirred an urgency inside of me that was hard to suppress. If I wasn't swiping through Fluttr this very instant, I might miss the man of my dreams and never see him again.

Alex nodded. "That's true. Those ads always make me feel bummed out about being single."

"It's just so hard to meet people."

"But it doesn't seem like Fluttr is making it any easier. We have too many choices, too much information. It's paralyzing."

"So you think we should go back in time to the days of... What were those called? When people would print dating profiles in the newspaper?"

"Personal ads."

"Right."

"No," he said, carefully. "But I feel like we don't take the time to get to know our potential partners anymore. We spend maybe two seconds looking at someone's picture before—" he whistled and mimicked a swiping motion, flicking his finger through the air between us "—writing them off forever. I can't help but think we'd be better off meeting people in person."

"Like at speed dating events."

Alex laughed, an infectious rumble. "Maybe."

"Or in bars."

"Or in the office."

After he said that, he looked right at me, biting his bottom lip like he was suppressing a smile. My stomach did a little somersault when I saw his dark eyes dancing with mischief.

Was this a *date*?

As I tried to discern wishful thinking from sad delusions, the server came along and placed a platter in the center of the table. "Here's your antipasto."

"Looks great," Alex said.

I nodded in silent agreement and the server took off with a polite smile.

The platter *did* look heavenly. There were plump green olives, slick with oil. Great hunks of hard Italian cheese. Thin slices of prosciutto and thick rounds of salami. Crusty bread and crispy crackers. A dollop of jam and a honeycomb.

This was so much better than a lukewarm peanut butter sandwich.

Before I could decide which delicacy to sample first, someone behind me yelled out, "Yo!" and Alex released a string of curses under his breath. When I glanced over my shoulder, I saw Greg crossing the cobblestone street, headed directly toward us.

"I apologize in advance for anything he says," Alex uttered, then gave Greg a sharp little wave.

"S'up, man?" Without asking if he could join us, Greg yanked a chair from the adjacent table and pulled it up to our tiny little two-top. "That database finished or what?"

"It should be soon." Alex rubbed the back of his neck. "I started the build before I left. That was, like, twenty minutes ago. I'm sure by the time I get back we'll be ready to roll."

"Cool." Greg reached for an olive and tossed it in his mouth, then reclined, swinging a casual arm over the back of his bistro chair. "You catch the fight last night?"

Alex threw me a feeble smile of apology. "Nope."

"It was sick. Austin jammed Hammill with these crazy kicks to the middle, so when he fell down, I was like, okay, this shit's over. And then out of nowhere, Hammill popped up with these hammer fists like an animal."

As Greg went on and on about what I assumed was some sort of cage fighting match, he helped himself to a slice of baguette, piling it high with prosciutto and cheese. Alex looked on in bewilderment, before blocking Greg's outstretched hand from grabbing the salami.

"What're you doing?"

Greg gave him that same dopey look he'd given me last week, when he destroyed his laptop. "What?"

"That's our lunch, man. Hands off. And, by the way—" Alex gestured toward me "—this is Melanie. Mel, this is Greg. Not that you need any introductions, since I know you two have already met."

I could tell by his frown lines that Greg had absolutely no idea who I was. I'd spent hours salvaging data from his coffee-drenched hard drive, and he hadn't bothered to commit my face to long-term memory.

"Anyway," Alex continued, "we're kind of in the middle of something here. Can you give us some space?"

"Uh…okay." Greg stood, jamming his pilfered food into his mouth before ambling away. He left his chair jutting out into the middle of the sidewalk. Alex replaced it at the neighboring table.

"Sorry about that," he said.

I forced a laugh. "It's okay. Totally not your fault."

"It kinda is. Greg's my partner, after all." He raked a hand through his hair, tugging at his curls. "Which is something I regret more with each passing day. I wish I'd never signed on to this project with him."

"That's awful. I'm sorry." Though, truth be told, I was a little relieved. If Alex had actually felt like Greg—slack-jawed, tactless, dim-witted Greg—was an ideal business partner, I would've questioned his judgment. As it was, I couldn't figure out why he'd teamed up with him in the first place. Or how they'd managed to score a spot at Hatch.

"Greg talked a big game when we first met," he said, snapping a cracker in two.

"Did he?" Skepticism oozed from my pores.

"He seems stupid, I know, but he's just really good at playing dumb to get out of things. When it comes to sales pitches and presentations, he's a rock star."

I tried to picture Greg standing in front of a room full of suits, delivering an articulate speech, gesturing to a polished PowerPoint presentation. The vision was incongruous with the Greg I knew, the guy who spoke only in sentence fragments and never looked me in the eye.

"How did you meet him?"

"At a tech meetup in Brooklyn. I was working this corporate

job and hating it and wanted to try to get into the start-up world. Greg was there and we got to talking and he said he was super close to securing funding for Fizz. All he needed was a strong engineer. So I helped him with some specs and a mock-up to finish his application to Hatch. A few weeks later, I quit my job."

"And now here you are."

"Here I am. Except it's not what I was expecting it to be."

"What were you expecting it to be?"

He nibbled his cracker and shrugged a shoulder. "I don't know. Not like this, though. Half the time, it's like I'm working in a frat house."

I could relate to that. Testosterone levels in the office were off the charts. Of course Josh Brewster got away with his "Free Mustache Rides" sticker. Any guy who complained about it would be seen as a traitor to his gender.

"Plus," Alex continued, "I'm shouldering most of the workload right now. Greg's not really holding up his end of the deal. He makes a lot of promises, but he's not so good with the follow-through."

"Can you complain to someone about it?"

"There's no one to complain to. The investors don't wanna hear it. Now's the time when we're supposed to be proving we can run a business independently. But honestly, I don't think we can."

Disappointment settled in the grooves etched across his forehead. And who could blame him? Imagine quitting your stable, if soul-sucking, job to take a chance on a fledgling start-up, only to discover your partner was a fraud and a flake. It made my gig at the help desk seem downright tolerable.

Alex shook his head, clearing away the furrows. "Anyway,

like we were talking about on Friday, this is just a stepping-stone to bigger and better things."

I swirled a bread crust in honey and took a sweet, crispy bite. "Totally."

"How long have you been working at Hatch now?"

"About four years. I started right out of college."

"Wow. You've probably learned so much about the start-up world. What works, what doesn't. What investors look for in potential founders."

I nodded. From my experience, there were two main requirements most start-up founders needed to secure seed funding: being a guy, and being a jerk. Of course, Alex only fulfilled the first of those two, but his partner more than compensated for the second with his obnoxious behavior.

"And I bet you've made a ton of contacts in the industry, too," he said. "Especially with a new set of Hatchlings coming in every three months."

"Not really. I work the help desk. Hatchlings aren't really interested in discussing the business with me. They only ever acknowledge my existence when they have some laptop emergency, and then they come into my cubicle screaming their heads off and lobbing insults. Present company excluded, of course."

His mouth hung open in shock. "That's awful."

Poor, naive Alex. So unaware of the inequities of the tech world.

"Look," I said, "to be honest, all I want out of Hatch is a paycheck. And the health insurance is pretty sweet, too."

"So, you're not interested in launching your own start-up?"

"Of course I am." The words burst forth with conviction. Because if I dug down deep into the softest parts of my core, I'd find this truth buried there: I *did* want a piece of the start-up pie. And not just a tiny sliver. I wanted a big, fat, decadent hunk of it. I wanted to create something of value, something that would make people's lives better. To have a vision and to bring it to life.

I didn't want to coast. I wanted to speed down the runway and take flight.

The problem was, my accelerator seemed to be jammed.

"Hatch just isn't a good fit for me," I said, grossly oversimplifying a complex and sexist situation.

"Have you ever been to any of the tech meetups around town? They have happy hours at least once a week. That's where I connected with Greg." He grimaced. "Though I realize that's not a ringing endorsement."

"Yeah, I've been to a couple of those."

Actually, I'd been to only one. Two years earlier, and it was not the inspirational networking event I'd been promised.

I'd certainly had high hopes. Eager to make a good impression on potential collaborators, I designed business cards with a link to my programming portfolio, and bought a chic blazer on clearance to conform with the professional dress code. When I strolled into the vast conference space that night, I was feeling calm and confident, ready to reach out and grab entrepreneurship by the balls.

Unfortunately, there weren't many balls to grab at this event. Oh, there were plenty of men there—in fact, it was a veritable sausagefest. But any time I struck up a conversation with a guy who seemed halfway decent, he'd invariably prove me wrong.

More than once, a guy gaped at me in astonishment and said, "You don't *look* like a software developer." Some guys hit on me; others avoided me like the plague. I didn't have any worthwhile discussions and left feeling completely discouraged.

I did give out two business cards, though. Which was a huge mistake, because for weeks on end, I kept getting anonymous text messages containing—what else?—dick pics. After that, I threw the rest of my cards in the trash and swore off tech meetups for good.

"They haven't been very constructive," I said.

"That's a shame," Alex said. "So much of this business is about making contacts and networking and putting yourself out there."

"Well, I'm sort of hoping that the right opportunity will come along when I least expect it."

"The right opportunities are the ones you create yourself."

He beamed at me, and my insides melted to warm goo. God, he was gorgeous. But his beauty went beyond good looks. It went far deeper, into his brain and his heart. He was a rare breed of man, one who didn't see a woman as an objective or a threat. Sure, he might've been a little clueless, but he seemed like he was open to listening and learning. Most important, he was kind and supportive, and damn if I didn't need some positivity in my world right then.

"I like that idea," I said, a smile tugging at my lips. "Creating my own opportunities."

"Absolutely. You're in charge of your own life. You've got the power."

"I've got the power."

Just saying it made me feel powerful. It seemed so obvious, but I'd never considered it before: I didn't need to play nice with the guys to get ahead. Playing nice was for chumps. All those obnoxious brogrammers and disparaging douchebags and sexual deviants? Screw them.

If I wanted to launch a start-up, I didn't need to lean in and claim a seat at the table. I could stand up and do it by myself. Because I was in charge of my own life.

And that included my love life.

"What are you up to this weekend?" I asked.

"No plans as of yet. How about you?"

"My roommate is throwing a party on the roof of our building. She said I could invite whoever I wanted. Some of my girlfriends will be there. I'd love it if you came."

His eyes sparkled in the afternoon sun. "Thanks. I'd love to go."

"Great."

With a satisfied grin, I sunk my teeth into a fat slice of salami.

I was going to get what I wanted out of life, I was sure of it. And nothing would stand in my way.

6

It's amazing how a small shift in perspective can make a monumental difference in your quality of life.

After that lunchtime chat with Alex, I returned to the office with a spring in my step. And though I wouldn't go so far as to say I was eager to resume my afternoon shift at the help desk, I certainly wasn't dreading it the way I normally did. The mind-numbing tasks were the same as always—installing software updates, clearing paper jams, resetting passwords for people who accidentally left their caps lock on—but completing them no longer drained me of my will to live.

Because now I knew: this job at Hatch was a means to an end, not the end in and of itself.

Of course, I didn't have a clue what the actual end was, but it had to be out there waiting for me somewhere. I'd find it eventually.

Probably.

In the meantime, I had a steady salary and eight paid holidays a year.

And I had Alex.

My secret office crush was now my plus-one to Saturday night's shindig, and I was counting the minutes until it arrived. I couldn't remember the last time I'd looked forward to a date like this, or the last time a guy had made me feel this hopeful and happy. To think we might never have been brought together if it weren't for a couple of shitty Fluttr dates. Brandon from Brooklyn sure did me a solid.

With visions of Alex's broad chest and dazzling smile swirling through my head, the hours in my cubicle sailed by. The next thing I knew, it was way past five—almost six o'clock. Time to head home, where I could unwind with my favorite pastime: snarfing junk food and binge-watching Netflix. If my commute went smoothly, I could be snuggled up in bed with a bag of Doritos in under twenty-five minutes.

But, naturally, my commute did not go smoothly.

Commuting on the A train was never a pleasant experience. Every day, there was some sort of signal problem or system failure, and it was always so crowded, snagging a seat was out of the question. So it didn't strike me as odd when the train pulled into the station packed from window to wall. The doors opened, and I dropped a shoulder to shove my way on, wedging myself beneath the arm of a man who was holding the overhead handrail.

It was a precarious position—my face jammed into one guy's armpit, my hips skillfully twisted to avoid the crotch of another guy behind me, my arm stretched skyward to grasp the remaining three inches of available subway pole, my whole body trying desperately not to lurch into the lap of the woman seated directly below.

But the trip was supposed to be only twenty-five minutes. I could deal.

Then, somewhere between Jay Street and Hoyt-Schermerhorn, things went south. The conductor's voice, muffled and apathetic, came over the loudspeaker.

"We're experiencing congestion up ahead. We should be moving shortly."

Congestion was their code word for everything. A chorus of teeth-sucking and sighs echoed throughout the car, but I took solace in knowing the next stop was mine. When the doors opened at Hoyt-Schermerhorn, I'd be free.

Ten minutes later, we still hadn't budged an inch, and the comforting whir of the AC ground to a halt. Shortly thereafter, the lights went out. Neither event seemed to warrant an update from the conductor, though. As we waited in the dim, sweltering train car, the murmurs among my fellow straphangers grew increasingly agitated and profanity-laced. Without proper ventilation, the air grew thick and funky. People took off their jackets and fanned themselves with their *New Yorkers*.

Soon, fury set in. Men and women alike started cursing and screaming.

"What the hell is going on?"

"I need to get out of here."

"Why aren't they telling us what's wrong?"

"This fucking subway!"

A cramp seized my shoulder. Even though the train wasn't in motion, I still had a firm grip on the handrail over my head. Partially because I wanted to brace myself—you never knew when we might start up again, unexpectedly—but also, because it was next-to-impossible to move. We were crammed together in this insufferably small space, like a joyless, foul-smelling clown car.

Finally, the pain grew unbearable, and when my fingertips started to tingle from lack of circulation, I had no choice but to let go. Ever so slowly, I lowered my right arm, turning slightly to reach for the open space with my left hand. As I shifted my weight from one foot to the other, my ass brushed up against something narrow and stiff.

Shit. It was the crotch I'd been trying to avoid.

Quickly, I pivoted away, but the crotch followed me, quite literally on my tail. My heart smashed against my rib cage like an unhinged prisoner trying to break through the bars of her jail cell. Beads of sweat dotted my hairline. There was nowhere to go. I was trapped in a tube underground with a stranger's erection pressed against my ass cheek.

I had a choice: I could pretend it wasn't happening, and passively allow this pervert to grind against me. Or I could make a big stink. Tell everyone in the subway what he was doing. Publicly shame him for his depraved and disgusting behavior.

In the past, I'd always chosen the former. Whenever I happened across some masturbating weirdo on the street or handsy bro in a bar, I merely turned the other way, hoping that if I ignored them, these guys would simply vaporize into thin air. It required a healthy dose of self-delusion, and the ability to instantaneously incite an out-of-body experience. But the alternative—speaking up—was always too terrifying to consider.

Now, as I stood there getting dry-humped by this sicko, I realized I had nothing to be afraid of. What could he possibly do to me? He was stuck, just like I was, just like everyone else was, on this godforsaken subway. There was nowhere for him to hide, and if he tried to hurt me, I had a hundred angry commuters here to back me up.

This guy was doing this because he didn't think I had the

courage to call him out. He figured he'd get away with it. He'd undoubtedly gotten away with it before.

Well, fuck him.

"Excuse me!" A voice boomed through the darkness—confident, commanding, and totally badass.

To my surprise, the voice belonged to me.

"May I have everyone's attention?" I paused for effect, took a deep breath, and continued. "I'm sorry to bother everyone, but I just needed to let you all know that the man behind me is rubbing his dick against my backside."

Immediately, the crotch retreated. I turned my head as far as it would go, finally getting a close-up look at my molester. He was shorter than I'd envisioned, with greasy hair and thick glasses. An angry pimple flared pink against his pasty chin.

What a sad little acne-ridden man.

"It's this guy." I jerked my head back toward him. "Right here."

Snickers of disgust rose from the crowd, followed by loud reprimands.

"Leave that young lady alone!"

"The fuck is wrong with you, man?"

"Can somebody alert the conductor?"

Flashes went off as people whipped out their phones to snap pictures of him. He looked panic-stricken, eyes darting around the car at the irate mob. "I didn't do anything—she's making it up."

"No, I'm not."

"We believe you," said the woman sitting below me.

The guy next to her moved to stand. "Here. Sit down. Get away from this guy." I squeezed past him and lowered myself into his seat. He stood in my place, easily a foot taller than the perv, who was now cowering beneath his hostile stare.

"Go ahead," he said. "Try that shit on me and it'll be the last thing you ever do."

The energy in the car seemed to pulse and swell. Some people continued to scream at the offender, while others asked me if I was okay. "Thank you so much for your concern, but I'm fine," I said.

And I meant it. In fact, I felt great. Exposing this shithead was empowering. Maybe next time, he'd think twice before jamming his hard-on against an unsuspecting commuter.

Suddenly, the lights came back on. Cheers erupted from the crowd as the train lurched forward without an explanation. We inched along, intermittently stopping and starting, until we finally arrived at Hoyt-Schermerhorn. When the doors opened, a flood of passengers streamed out, carrying the subway pervert with them on the tide.

I followed closely behind, feeling significantly less invincible than I had a few moments ago. My squad of protectors was dispersing, walking up the stairs toward the G train or the exit. Now I was alone, and if he wanted to, this guy could follow me home and get his revenge.

Then I saw the cop. He was standing against a pillar, his eyes scanning the crowd as he mumbled into his walkie-talkie. A small but raucous group of people headed his way: the woman who told me she believed me, the man who gave me his seat, and, in the middle of it all, the perv, who was being manhandled by the others and appeared to be on the verge of tears.

"This is him, Officer," one of them said, thrusting him forward into the arms of the law.

New Yorkers get a bad rap, but in a time of crisis, they will rally to your side without a second thought.

A hand rested softly on my shoulder, and I turned to see

an older woman with a furrow of concern in her brow. "Are you sure you're okay, honey?"

"Yes, I'm okay."

"That was a brave thing you did, putting him on the spot like that," she said. "Lord knows I've dealt with my share of unwanted willies. If you ask me, they should cut it right off."

Her gnarled fingers sliced through the air like a pair of dick-snipping scissors.

"Uh...thanks so much."

She smiled warmly, revealing a mouth full of yellowed dentures, the last person on earth you'd ever suspect of advocating for penile amputation. Women are often a lot tougher than they look.

After giving the police a brief statement, I politely declined their offer of an escort home. The pervert was going with them, so I was no longer afraid of being hunted through the streets of Downtown Brooklyn.

Instead, I enjoyed a leisurely stroll back to my place, feeling safe and free and brave. On the way, I decided to treat myself to an extra-special dinner, loading up on all my favorites at the corner bodega: Sno Balls, Cool Ranch, Chubby Hubby, and, purely for nutritional balance, some coconut water and a bruised banana. I couldn't wait to throw on my pj's, crawl into bed, pig out, and watch *Jane the Virgin* until my eyes were sore.

But when I stepped inside the apartment, I realized getting to bed wasn't going to be so easy. Not with fifty tin cans blocking the path from the foyer to my bedroom. And in the middle of the mess sat Vanessa, wearing safety goggles and wielding a cordless drill.

"Hey," she said, totally casual, as if our apartment always looked like the sorting room at a recycling plant.

"What's going on here?" I asked.

"I'm making lanterns for Saturday night." She held up a can with a pattern of holes punched in it. "You pop a little tealight in there and it glows. Put enough of them out and they'll make the whole space twinkle."

This must've been another one of her Pinterest projects. Last month, she'd dragged a raggedy dresser drawer in off the curb and upcycled it into a wall-mounted wine rack for our kitchen. It sounded wacky, but it looked cool. She was a pretty talented crafter.

"Do you own that drill?"

"No, Ray loaned it to me."

"Does he know what you're using it for?"

She answered with a shrug, but I knew she'd kept him in the dark. Ray was our super. If he knew his drill was going to be used to create decorations for an unsanctioned rooftop party, he never would've given it to her, since he's the one that was going to have to deal with all the complaints.

"Can I help with anything?" I asked.

"No, thanks. I've got it covered." She lowered her head and resumed her work, the room echoing with the sounds of shredding metal and spinning gears.

I carefully maneuvered around the tin can obstacle course to get to my bedroom, where I shut the door against the racket.

Alone, at last. I couldn't jettison my bra fast enough.

After changing into my favorite sweatpants and a hole-ridden T-shirt, I busted open that bag of bodega goodies and woke my laptop from its peaceful slumber. Lines of code filled the screen, a reminder of how I'd spent my weekend: getting digital revenge on the guys who did me dirty. I'd almost forgotten about that.

By now, the cathartic effects of JerkAlert had worn off, and it was time to free up some space on my web server. I signed into my dashboard, ready to take the whole thing down. But when I looked at the activity log, I did a double take.

Over a hundred new records had been added to the JerkAlert database. Overnight.

For a moment, I thought there was some sort of glitch. Like the hosting service had linked my login to a different account. Or I'd been hacked by some cyberpunk with low ambition.

Reading the entries, though, they were clearly legit. Dozens of tales of women who'd been jilted by guys they'd met on Fluttr.

My friends had apparently been busy.

I texted Lia, Whit, and Dani: Did you 3 stay up all night adding guys to JerkAlert?

A few minutes later, the responses started rolling in:

DANI:

What are you talking about?

LIA:

I didn't add anything...

DANI:

Neither did I. I mean, hello? Look who you're asking.

MEL:

Don't tell me Whit entered all of these herself. There are over 100!

And then, in a separate text, without copying Lia or Dani, Whit asked me: Got a sec?

This could not be good.

She answered on the first ring. "Don't be mad."

Which meant I was about to be really, really mad.

"What did you do?"

"I shared JerkAlert with a couple of contacts."

In Whit-speak, "a couple of contacts" could mean hundreds of people. Working in PR meant she had endless connections. Not to mention a skewed sense of the meaning of "a couple."

"I didn't want anyone else to see this," I said. "It was just a joke."

"Well, how was I supposed to know? You didn't say that."

She was right, I guess. I didn't tell her not to send it around. Besides, if I was concerned about discretion, I shouldn't have sent it to Whit in the first place.

"It certainly doesn't *look* like a joke," she continued. "It's really well-done, Mel."

"Thanks." An unfamiliar tingle bloomed in my chest. Pride. It had been so long since I'd felt it. "I'm taking it down, though."

"What? No!"

"Yes. It made me feel better for a minute, but it's not like it's gonna fix anything. Dating is depressing enough without putting more negative energy out there into the world."

"Look, I'm all for spreading positive vibes," she said, "but you've obviously struck a chord here. Women are having a hard time on Fluttr. At JerkAlert, they can connect and share their experiences. Plus, it's a way for them to protect themselves against shady guys. Before you swipe right, you can check their JerkAlert profile to make sure they're not gonna send you a dick pic."

"I thought you didn't mind dick pics."

"Only sometimes," she said. "The point is, most women

do mind. And it's not just dick pics you're saving them from, either. Women are logging all kinds of shady shit. Guys who ghost, who stand you up… Did you see that one guy who was actually *married*?"

My stomach clenched. "No."

"Yes! He was dating a girl for like a month before she found out. I guess he'd stuffed his wedding ring in the pocket of his pants and when he took them off it went flying across her bedroom floor. How stupid could he be?"

"Wow."

"See? You're doing a real service with this site." Whitney cleared her throat, shifting to a more subtle, serious tone of voice. Her no-nonsense, get-shit-done, businesswoman voice. "And beyond that, this could be a step in the right direction for your career."

I snorted. "Yes, I'm sure this would look great on my résumé. Melanie Strickland—Founder of JerkAlert.biz, because JerkAlert.com was already taken."

"I'm serious. The concept is original and compelling. You could really turn this into something big."

"It's not the kind of thing I want to go public with, Whit. Do you know how pissed guys would be if they knew I was the woman behind it? Especially that married guy. Who knows what they'd do?"

"So stay anonymous. The public doesn't need to know who you are. That actually makes it more interesting."

My initial instinct was to tell her she was crazy, hang up the phone, and continue with my plan to delete the site. But then I remembered Alex's words: *The right opportunities are the ones you create yourself.*

What if this was my opportunity?

JerkAlert was my vision, and I'd already brought it to life. Maybe it would be the ticket to a brand-new phase of my career.

"Okay. I'll keep it."

"Great! There's just one thing."

There was always just one thing with her. "What?"

"I have a few minor suggestions for improvement."

7

Whit's "suggestions for improvement" weren't exactly minor. They were huge changes to the basic functionality of JerkAlert.

Like adding a login system, to prevent people from spamming the site with fake profiles. And a search feature, so users could easily find the men they were looking to review.

Plus, I had to figure out a way to make sure the right guys were receiving the right reviews. For example, there was surely more than one Brandon from Brooklyn, but only one of them had stood me up. I couldn't go slandering an entire borough's worth of Brandons just because one of them happened to be a jerk.

At first, the thought of revamping JerkAlert was overwhelming. These changes would take hours. Days, even. Was it really going to be worth all the time and effort I'd have to put in to make it better?

Then I remembered: this was *my opportunity*. My opportunity to demonstrate my prowess. To take something kind of cool and make it even cooler. If I nailed this, the help desk might soon be a distant, unpleasant memory. So even though I couldn't be sure all this work was going to pay off in the end, the only way to find out was to try.

That's why, instead of watching *Jane the Virgin* for six hours that night, I coded. I coded until my eyes were bloodshot, until my knuckles cramped, until my thoughts became garbled and mushy. At three thirty in the morning, I didn't so much fall asleep as lose consciousness.

The next two days went something like this: wake up in a panic, having slept through my alarm; get ready in under fifteen minutes before heading to work, groggy and disheveled; spend the next eight hours enduring an endless stream of so-called "techies" who can't figure out how to fix their own computers; finally, race home to work on JerkAlert until I pass out.

It was an exhausting routine, but the satisfaction I felt from those late-night code-athons made the struggle worth it. I'd never worked on a project like this before, something original and challenging, something that had sprung from my own imagination and that people responded to. Creating JerkAlert made me feel inspired for the first time in… Well, it was the first time I could remember feeling inspired.

Though I did have an additional source of inspiration: while all this web development was going down, things with Alex were heating up. Every so often, he'd drop by my cubicle, just to say hi. We synchronized our runs to the coffee machine, and then lingered a little too long stirring milk and sweetener into our mugs. We shared secret smiles as we passed in the hallway. Working the help desk was somewhat tolerable now, knowing he was simply a DM away.

To think I'd almost written him off because of a simple

misunderstanding. I made sure to delete that JerkAlert entry I'd entered on Sunday night, where I accused him of flirting with me behind his nonexistent girlfriend's back. All record of my idiocy had been scrubbed from the internet forever.

On Wednesday evening, shortly before midnight, I typed out my final closing curly brace and deployed the whole updated JerkAlert site to my server. It looked fantastic. By cross-referencing the JerkAlert database with profiles I pulled from the Fluttr app, I could display photos, improve searches, and reduce the chance of mistaken identities.

God, I was a genius.

I spent a few minutes poking around the site, clicking links and searching for random phrases, just to make sure everything was working as expected. Then I texted Whit and told her to give it a whirl.

Her response: Will get to it 2morrow. Out in the Village rite now and SUPER LIT. Wanna join?

No thanks, I wrote back, have fun, then continued surfing JerkAlert, taking obscene pride in the fruits of my labor. The speed with which the pages loaded, the slickness of the UI. It looked totally professional. Not at all like it'd been hastily coded in a few harried, Dorito-fueled nights.

The database had tripled in size since Monday night. There were now over three hundred unique men who'd been logged to the site, some of whom had more than one review. Like Nate, 35, from Tribeca, who sent four women the same dick pic. And Hakim, 23, from Sunnyside, who started at least a dozen different text conversations with the charming opening line, RU horny?

When I came upon Eddie, 38, from Staten Island, I stopped clicking. His review read:

Total effing scumbag. Dated him for six weeks last summer before his wife called me on the phone telling me to stay away from her husband. Swipe left on this one, ladies. HE'S MARRIED.

This couldn't have been the same married guy that Whitney had been talking about, could it? She'd told me a whole different story involving a wedding ring popping out of his pants pocket. Out of curiosity, I typed the word *married* in the search box at the top of the screen.

Twelve records came up, each one representing a different married guy who'd been trawling Fluttr for a side piece. From their pictures, they looked like decent guys. Guys I might've even swiped right on if I'd seen them in the app. You'd never suspect them of being shameless cheats.

Then again, my dad looked like a decent guy, too.

I didn't know every detail of how my parents' marriage came undone. I'm not sure how long Dad had been unfaithful or exactly when Mom found out about it. All I remember is the defiant glimmer in her eyes when she told me the news.

"Dad's moving out tomorrow." Her voice was flat, matter-of-fact.

"What?" I looked up from my SAT vocabulary list to see her looming in the kitchen doorway. I'll never forget the word I was trying to memorize at that moment: *aberration*. "What are you talking about?"

"I'm sorry to spring this on you, sweetie." She approached the table and sat down next to me. "But there's no way to sugarcoat it. Your dad's been cheating on me and I told him to leave."

"What?"

Her words weren't making sense. My dad was an accountant. He wore sweater-vests and collected vintage Star Wars figurines. He drove five miles under the speed limit at all times. Surely, I thought, a man this seemingly wholesome and cautious would never cheat on his wife.

But I was wrong. He left the next day, just like Mom had said he would. As he rolled the last of his suitcases out the front door, he shot me this woebegone look and said, "I'm sorry, pumpkin." As if saying he was sorry made up for the nightmare my fifteen-year-old life had suddenly become.

After dinner, Mom drained a bottle of white zin and I retreated to my room with my SAT study guide tucked under my arm. Not like I could concentrate. I stared at the pages, unseeing, the sentences blurring together through my tears. A few hours later, Mom stumbled in without knocking.

"How are you doing?" she asked.

There were so many ways to answer that question. Terrified, confused, furious, sad. But I settled on, "Fine."

Her eyes slid to the floor. She knew I wasn't fine. "I'm sorry for this, sweetie."

"It's not your fault," I said. "I just can't believe it. I mean, it's *Dad*."

She let out a shaky breath. "I didn't wanna believe it, either. But looking back on it, all the signs were there. As soon as he started working those late nights at the office, I should've known something was up."

I'd noticed he'd been working late a lot, but I didn't think anything of it. I just figured he had a lot of tax returns to file. Now I realized I was a fool for assuming my dad was an honest guy.

Mom looked so sad sitting at the edge of my bed, half-drunk, her liquid liner smudged beneath her watery eyes. I knew I never wanted to end up like that, but it seemed impossible to prevent. Sometimes the greatest man in the world could turn out to be a dirty, dirty cheat.

In a way, maybe the seed for JerkAlert had been planted that night. Maybe, subconsciously, this site *was* a premeditated scheme to humiliate men who behaved shamefully. But that's not what I was thinking as I scrolled through the profiles of those twelve philandering assholes. What I was thinking was how happy I was Alex wasn't one of them.

I knew this gushy, smitten feeling wouldn't last forever. I knew he'd eventually disappoint me, in some way or another. But right now, he made me feel fantastic. And I wanted to ride that wave for as long as it would hold me up.

My gaze dropped to the clock in the corner of my computer screen. 1:04 a.m. An early night for me! I shut down my laptop and headed to the bathroom to brush my teeth. When I returned, the blue light on my phone was flashing. Alex had texted.

> I don't know if you're up, but I just finished working, and in case you are, I wanted to say good night. 😚

Fireworks went off in my chest. Not those simple one-burst wonders, either. These were flaring fountains, the kind that whistle and pop as they spurt every color of the rainbow in a constant stream of exploding light and energy.

Maybe, I thought, hopefully, naively. *Maybe I've found myself one of the good ones.*

I returned his kissy-face with some heart-eyes and crawled beneath the covers, cheeks straining from my hundred-watt smile. When the phone buzzed again, I grabbed it with glee, hoping Alex had returned my heart-eyes with an actual heart. But it was from Whit. She'd sent a link to a YouTube video with the message:

This is you, rite? I can barely make out the picture, it's so fucking dark, but I would recognize your voice anywhere.

She must've been wasted, because this text was totally nonsensical. Confused, I tapped the play button. Shadows moved around the screen, silhouettes of people in a dimly lit crowd. There were no distinguishable faces, just hints of movement. The light from someone's phone screen, the flash of an earring as a head shook.

Wait, that earring looked familiar.

A tinny voice rang through my speaker, garbled at first, then clear as day: "The man behind me is rubbing his dick against my backside."

Oh, shit.

With shaky thumbs, I texted back: Where did you find this?

Twitter, she replied. You've gone viral!

Against my better judgment, I opened the Twitter app. Right there, under "Trends for You," was the hashtag #DickInTheDark.

I was internet famous, all because of an unwanted willy.

8

I'd never been so grateful for a lack of proper lighting.

I mean, I wasn't feeling particularly grateful at the time, when we were trapped in a tunnel with no fresh air and no personal space. And frankly, the power outage was to blame for the very existence of the video; if we hadn't been stuck there in the dark for so long, that perv wouldn't have had the opportunity to grind against me, and I wouldn't have screamed the word *dick* in the middle of a crowded subway car.

But at least the darkness concealed my face. So even though my voice may have been internet famous, my identity was still largely a mystery. Only people who knew me really well could listen to a five-second snippet of shouting on a low-res cell phone video and know it came from me. To everyone else, that person with the flashy earring and loud mouth was merely an angry, anonymous shadow.

An angry, anonymous shadow that had been turned into a meme.

It seemed bored basement boys everywhere were having a

blast creating their own versions of #DickInTheDark. Taking stills from the video, they Photoshopped cartoon penises, cylindrical vegetables, and a whole host of other phallic objects into the space behind my silhouette. One budding videographer had added a soundtrack to the original clip, auto-tuning my voice and dubbing it the "#DickInTheDark Remix." It had been posted to YouTube less than twelve hours ago, and had over fifty thousand views.

Needless to say, I was humiliated. On the plus side, it was a relatively private humiliation. My name wasn't popping up in any online comments, I didn't get any double takes on the street, and, as far as I could tell, nobody besides Whit, Lia, and Dani knew it was me.

At first, I was afraid the Hatchlings might know, too. When I arrived to work on Thursday morning, I half expected to find my cubicle wallpapered with meme printouts, or the "#DickInTheDark Remix" blaring over the loudspeaker.

Obviously, though, that was a ridiculous notion. My colleagues never listened to a word I said, so of course they didn't recognize my voice in the video. When I skittered into the office that morning, no one looked up from his computer screen. I was my usual invisible self.

At eleven o'clock, everyone gathered in the large conference room for our monthly all-hands meeting, where the management team spent an hour boring us to tears. We heard from Charles in Accounting, who assured us we were solvent. Then our chief innovation officer, Arnaud, blathered on about "radical breakthroughs in bleeding-edge technology" for thirty minutes. Finally, our HR manager, Benny, took the mic to remind us of all the things we had to do to remain in compliance with New York's labor laws.

"Just a reminder, people—you need to have your annual workplace harassment training modules completed by the end of the month."

Sighs of annoyance filled the room.

"Yeah, I know, I know." Benny put his hands up. "Don't shoot the messenger. Our attorneys make us do it to mitigate potential liability. It takes ten minutes. Just get it done so I don't have to come after you."

"Wouldn't that be considered harassment?" one of the Hatchlings yelled out, setting off a ripple of laughter through the audience.

Benny chuckled. "You'll have to take the training to find out. Okay, that's all from my end. I'm gonna hand it off to Vijay to close out the meeting."

The crowd clapped as Vijay shook Benny's hand and took his place behind the podium. As the founder and managing partner of Hatch, Vijay was the most powerful person in the room. But with his plaid shirt and oversize glasses, he came across as an ordinary guy. Nothing about him screamed "millionaire," which he was, several times over, thanks to those fifteen years he put in at Google developing search algorithms.

Now, he was taking all that money he'd amassed and investing it in start-ups he believed in. Every Hatchling who walked through the door had Vijay's personal stamp of approval. And at the end of each incubation period, his influence helped decide which Hatchlings received Series A funding and which ones fizzled into obsolescence.

"Today," he said, "I'd like to take a moment to chat about the Hatch philosophy. What we come to this office every day to do. And, more importantly, why we do it."

I slumped down in my chair, preparing to tune out until

Vijay was done talking. Every month, I sat through some version of this same speech, and it was never relevant to me. These were rah-rah pep talks meant specifically for the Hatchlings. Praise for their innovation, encouragement for their effort, and enthusiasm for their future success.

All I did was fix their broken laptops. Vijay had no clue who I was.

"Three years ago, I started Hatch with a purpose—to provide a supportive environment for entrepreneurs to nurture and develop their ideas. And not just any ideas. I was on the hunt for ideas that would make a significant impact. Ideas that would revolutionize the way we do business, the way we interact, and the way we live our lives."

Was he serious with this? The current crop of Hatchlings were developing apps for fantasy football and ridesharing, ideas that had been executed a million times before, in a million different ways. There wasn't anything revolutionary or impactful about them.

You know what *was* revolutionary? JerkAlert. Nothing else like it existed. It was the first public forum where women could easily band together to rise up against the tyranny of dick pics. With one little website, I was making the world a safer place.

And those changes I'd added last night considerably improved the JerkAlert experience. On my way to work this morning, Whitney texted to tell me she loved them.

Perfect! she'd said. You killed it! I'm gonna send it to a few more people, ok?

Great! I'd responded, and practically skipped the rest of the way to the office. When I arrived at my cubicle, not even the sight of Bob stacking desktops on the floor behind my chair could bring my spirits down.

"These need to be upgraded by the end of the day," he said, and I cheerfully obliged. After all, my days at Hatch were numbered. Soon, I'd be able to strike out on my own, and then I'd never have to sit in one of these tedious all-hands meetings again.

Vijay continued his sermon, his hands peacefully clasped upon the podium. "While there are many start-up incubators running successfully in the United States today, I believe the key characteristic setting Hatch apart from the rest is our unyielding commitment to our core values—integrity, decency, and respect."

I thought of the "Free Mustache Rides" sticker on Josh's laptop. Or the barrage of curses and insults the Hatchlings regularly threw my way. Or how Bob expected me to grin and bear it all without complaint.

These core values were a joke.

Surely, I wasn't the only one who realized this. Sitting up, I stole a few discreet glances around the conference room. Guys perched on the edges of their seats, hungrily devouring every word rolling off Vijay's lips. Eyes focused, heads nodding, their attentiveness on full display.

It was all an act, put on for Vijay's benefit. It had to be. Because these Hatchlings sure as hell weren't committed to living their professional lives with anything close to integrity, decency, or respect.

"In conclusion," Vijay said, "I want to say that I'm proud of the work we do here. Hatch start-ups have the power to change the world."

The room erupted in another round of applause, a few hoots

arising from the back, before everyone stood up and filed into the hallway. My stomach rumbled. It was lunchtime, and there was a peanut butter sandwich with my name on it waiting for me in my purse.

But during my earlier scan of the conference room, I'd noticed Alex was MIA. So instead of heading right back to my desk, I casually veered to the left, toward the Fizz work area. There, I found him hunched over his keyboard, shoving heaping forkfuls of salad into his mouth between frantic fits of typing.

Clearly, he was drowning in code. Not wanting to interrupt his flow, I stopped short, ready to double back toward my cubicle. Then suddenly he sat up, stretching his arms way over his head. His shirt lifted away from his waistband, and my eyes dropped to the sliver of abdomen peeking out. Hard, tan, toned.

"Hey, Mel."

I jumped at the sound of his voice. When I looked up, his mouth was twisted in that mischievous little half smile. I'd been caught gawking. Oops.

"Hey," I said. "Sorry, I didn't mean to bother you."

"No bother." He wiped his lips with a napkin and spun his chair around to face me. "What's up?"

"Just dropped by to say hi. I didn't see you at the all-hands meeting."

"Oh, yeah. I forgot about that. I've been so wrapped up in this." He waved his hand over his laptop, reference books, sticky notes, crumpled-up pieces of paper. "Did I miss anything good?"

"Nope. They're always boring and pointless."

"So, basically, they're Fluttr dates."

"Basically." I broke out in a belly laugh, happy for the comic relief after the tragedy of that miserable meeting. Alex laughed, too, our eyes like opposing tractor beams drawing each other in. For a split second, we were the only two people on the entire twenty-ninth floor.

Then Greg materialized, seemingly out of thin air. He was looking at my face, studying me, almost as if he was seeing me for the very first time.

"Wassup?" he said.

"Uh...nothing."

I turned to Alex, wondering if he noticed these creepy vibes Greg was giving off. But his gaze was already sliding back to his computer screen, the wheels turning in his brain as he tried to solve some programming problem.

"I'm gonna get back to work," I said.

Alex grinned and glanced my way. "Talk to you later."

"Later," added Greg. He simpered, his tongue touching the tip of his front teeth.

So gross.

I returned to my desk, to the peanut butter sandwich and the stack of desktops awaiting upgrades. By 4:59, I'd finished them all. At five o'clock, I was in a bathroom stall, changing into my sweats. Five minutes later, I was already headed out the door, toward the uptown 4 train, on my way to meet Lia for our weekly workout.

Every Thursday after work, Lia and I had a fitness date. We started planning them a few months back, after one particularly gluttonous all-you-can-eat happy hour experience at El Cantinero. The two of us drooped over our supersized margaritas, struggling to digest the countless flautas and enchiladas we'd inhaled.

"I feel unhealthy," she said. "Like I've got refried beans and tequila pumping through my veins."

"In a way, you do."

She groaned. "I need to start working out."

"Me, too," I said, cramming another salsa-laden chip in my face.

"Hey, wait." She straightened, brightening. "I just remembered I have this Groupon for a kickboxing class."

"Why do you have that?"

"I think I bought it after the last time we came here and stuffed ourselves." She pulled out her phone and started swiping. "It looks like they've still got some available. Wanna get one and go with me? They've got a class open this Thursday after work."

"Sure. Sounds fun."

And it was fun. It was also grueling and excruciating. I left with bruises all over my body. The next morning, each step I took was torture.

By the weekend, I started feeling better. Stronger. Healthier. But on my meager budget, paying full price for these classes was out of the question. That's when we decided to scour Groupon for fitness deals, switching up our workout routines based on whatever was cheap. We committed to Thursday nights, and hadn't missed a single week since.

Tonight's class was in Union Square at a rowing studio, which was essentially a small room packed from wall to wall with rowing machines. When I walked through the door, Lia was already there, decked out in mesh-panel leggings and a sports bra. She'd plopped her purse onto the machine beside her.

"Saved this for you," she said.

"Thanks." I carefully lowered myself into the sliding seat and looked around. "What do you think a rowing class will be like?"

"I watched a YouTube video last night. It seems pretty intense."

"Ugh." I moaned, not because of the intensity of the upcoming workout, but because the mention of YouTube sent me spiraling into a vivid flashback: cartoon penises. Autotune. #DickInTheDark.

Lia knew exactly what I was thinking. She squeezed my forearm and gave me a sad smile. "Are you doing okay?"

"Yeah," I said. "It's really not that bad. Nobody knows it's me in that video, besides you guys."

"I'd love to find out who started the whole meme thing. These people are losers with too much time on their hands."

"In their defense, some of them do have good Photoshop skills."

Our conversation was cut off by three sharp claps. A woman with massive traps and a velociraptor tattooed on her bulging thigh stalked into the room, yelling, "Are we ready to go, people, or are we ready to go?"

The question was hypothetical, obviously, because thirty seconds later, the small space resounded with the zip and whoosh of a dozen rowing machines in motion. Five minutes in, I was short of breath; ten minutes in, I could no longer feel my feet.

Whenever I got to this point in a strenuous workout, panting and snuffling like a dehydrated dog, I'd usually start half-assing it. Go a little slower, ease up on the weight. Stop pushing myself so hard. Give myself a chance to catch my breath.

Today was different. Today, rather than giving up, I conjured images of reasons why giving up wasn't an option. Reasons I needed to grow stronger, to build stamina, to show the world I was not to be fucked with.

Each yank on those handlebars had a meaning.

Yank. I was going to make it someday, on my own.

Yank. These Hatchlings would be sorry they ever crossed me.

Yank. The same goes for that subway perv and the jerks who turned it into a giant internet joke.

Before I knew it, we were in our final sprint. Our instructor screeched at us, "Go as fast you can! Give it your all!" I yanked and pulled and heaved, sweat pouring off my forehead and splattering onto the parquet floor.

These men will not break me.

A buzzer rang out, sudden and terrifying.

"That's it, everyone! Good work!" She clapped again, then added, "Make sure you get your stretches in," before disappearing behind a door marked Employees Only.

My whole body throbbed. I leaned forward, head in hands, willing my heart rate to return to normal. All my worry and anger were gone, replaced by fire, passion, and, inexplicably, burning sexual desire. I pictured Alex, his sliver of stomach, the tuft of hair on his chest beneath his shirt, my hands exploring—

"That was weird, wasn't it?" Lia said, busting apart my fantasy. "Good, but weird."

I sat up and huffed out a breath. "Yeah. Weird."

"What are you smiling about?"

"Huh?"

"You're grinning like an idiot."

"Am I?" My hand flew to my face, patting my cheeks, my lips. Yup, that was a smile. "I guess I'm just feeling good."

"Good! If this place ever does another Groupon, we'll have to get in on it."

We gathered our belongings and walked down the stairs to the street. Out on Fifth Avenue, we exchanged sweaty hugs.

"Are you headed to Jay's now?" I asked.

"Nah, he's working late."

"What does he do again?"

"He's in finance."

"Doing what?"

She gave me a funny look. "Honestly, I don't even know. He's explained it a few times, but I always zone out when he talks about it. Something to do with trading. All I know is it's boring as hell."

We laughed, then she added, "Actually, you can ask him yourself on Saturday night."

"Is he coming to the party?"

"Yup. We've been together almost three months now. I told him it's way past time for him to meet my best friends."

"Awesome. I can't wait." I looked down at my feet, hesitant to say the next words. As if admitting it might jinx me. "I'm bringing someone, too."

"Who?" Her eyes bulged, fingers wiggling in excitement. "Did you meet someone?"

"Yeah."

"On Fluttr?"

"No, at work. His name's Alex. He's a Hatchling. Super nice and funny." *And hot.*

She grabbed my hand and squeezed, squealing in delight. That was one of the things I loved most about Lia: when her friends had good news to share, she always reacted with unfettered joy. There was never any pettiness or jealousy with her. Just genuine delight.

If anyone deserved happiness, it was her.

"That's so exciting! Congrats!"

"Thanks. Here's hoping."

Squeezing my hand one more time, she smiled. "I have a good feeling about this one, Mel."

And though the words were on the tip of my tongue, I was too afraid to say them out loud.

I have a good feeling about this one, too.

9

In my time as a single woman, I'd been on a lot of dates.

A lot of dates.

But it had been a while since I'd been on a date that I actually cared about.

I mean, in a way I cared about all of them. If I didn't think there was some tiny fragment of a chance that a guy could become my happily-ever-after, I never would've bothered to swipe right on him in the first place.

The problem was, I'd encountered so many terrible men, suffered through so much disappointment and humiliation, that I'd stopped looking forward to dating. It had become a chore, a burdensome task I had to check off my to-do list: *Don't wanna die alone? Better go have a drink with this random guy from the internet!*

So while I remained vaguely hopeful and remarkably persistent, my enthusiasm for dating had waned. I stopped investing myself emotionally. I stopped caring.

Which is why it took some time for me to identify the

source of that funny feeling in my stomach. It started as a little twinge on Saturday morning. By afternoon, it had morphed into a full-blown tremor. When I checked the clock at half past five and realized Alex would be arriving in less than three hours, my belly was churning like a stormy sea.

Only then did it hit me: I was nervous.

And I was nervous because I actually cared.

See, Alex wasn't some random guy from the internet. Our flirtation had not been restricted to skillfully angled selfies and text bubbles; it was real life, in person. Whether or not I liked it, I was already emotionally invested. I wanted tonight to be amazing.

In other words, I wanted Alex to take one look at me and develop a sudden urge to whisk me off to the bedroom.

After giving my reflection a once-over, though, I decided I had a lot of work to do.

A quick Google of the phrase "date night beauty tips" brought up a treasure trove of advice on "how to knock his socks off." I picked a link at random and began working my way through the items on "The Ultimate Pre-Date Checklist."

For the next hour, I primped and preened, tweezing my eyebrows, filing my nails, shaving everything south of my collarbones. At item number seven, I hit a dead end:

> Get Glowing: Brighten your complexion with a hydrating and restorative face mask.

There were no face masks in my limited arsenal of beauty supplies, and it was too late to pop out to the store to get one. But judging by the number of empty Sephora shopping bags we had crammed under the sink, Vanessa must've had *some-*

thing I could use to "clarify tone and improve texture." Whatever that meant.

I emerged from my bedroom to look for her and, instead, found our entire shared living space covered in party paraphernalia. Flowers, streamers, and strings of fairy lights littered the couch. Silver tubs filled with bags of ice and bottles of rosé were strewn around the kitchen. Our counters overflowed with all manner of snacks and serving trays. And, of course, there were fifty tin-can lanterns in the foyer.

It was like a Pinterest board exploded inside the apartment.

Vanessa popped up from behind the breakfast bar with a giant bag of marshmallows in her hand. "Hey," she said.

"Hey." Instantly, I felt a pang of guilt. I'd been so consumed by beauty prep that I hadn't considered asking her if she needed any help with party prep. Even though this was technically her shindig, and I wasn't thrilled about the idea of getting in trouble with the landlord, it's not like I'd tried to talk her out of hosting it. Our rooftop did have incredible views of the city. It would be the perfect backdrop for a springtime get-together.

Or, say, a first kiss.

"There's a lot of stuff going on here," I said. "How can I help?"

She tore open the bag and waved away my offer. "Don't worry. I've got it covered."

With a meaningful glance toward the cluster of tin cans blocking the front door, I asked, "Are you sure?"

"Yeah, it's totally fine. I have a system." One by one, she plucked the marshmallows from the bag and placed them gingerly on a tray, aligning them flawlessly, discarding those with surface imperfections. "Oh, I meant to ask you—how many of your friends are coming? So I know how much food to put out."

"Just Dani, Whitney, and Lia. And Lia's bringing her boyfriend." I paused, swallowing a squee. "And I invited a guy, too."

"A guy?" She cocked her head, intrigued. "Tell me more."

"His name's Alex. I met him at work."

"How old is he?"

"Twenty-six."

"What does he do for a living?"

"I told you, I know him from work. He's with one of the start-ups there."

"Hmm." She pursed her lips and squinted. "That could go either way."

"What does that mean?"

"Well, if all goes well, he could be making a ton of money in a few years. But if he can't find a good investor, he's one step away from bankruptcy."

"I don't really care about how much money he makes."

"Okay, sure." She winked, like we were sharing some secret. "What about his family?"

"What about them?"

"Who are they? Where do they live?"

"I have no idea. Why does that even matter?"

"His relationship with his parents can influence so much about how he acts toward you. A clingy mom, a domineering dad—these things can cause problems down the line. It's important to know what you're dealing with up front."

Geez. If this was the kind of background check Vanessa put all her first dates through, it was no wonder she was still single.

It was one thing to screen prospective partners for assholish behavior, like sending dick pics or committing adultery. But it was quite another to research their family history and calculate their earning potential. Not only was it bonkers, it was putting the cart before the horse. First see if there's any chemistry, *then* start inquiring about messed-up parents.

Though having messed-up parents seemed irrelevant. After all, I didn't want to be judged by *my* dysfunctional family.

Eager to change the subject, I said, "I was wondering if you had a face mask I could use."

"Of course." She dropped the empty marshmallow bag on the counter and rubbed her palms together. "What kind do you want?"

"Uh…something to clarify tone and improve texture?"

She nodded sharply. "I've got just the thing. GlimmerGlam makes this colloidal silver mask with algae plasma. Let me go grab it for you."

After Vanessa disappeared into her bedroom, I leaned in for a closer look at the tray she was putting together. The marshmallows were on the top level of a three-tier stand. The second tier held an artfully arranged stack of graham crackers, while squares of chocolate took up the bottom. A hand-lettered sign beside it read S'mores Station.

Super cute, but it's not like we could have a campfire on the roof. Could we?

A knock came at the door. I gently kicked the tin cans aside, clearing a pathway to answer it. I flung it open to see Ray standing in the hallway, a ladder slung over one of his burly shoulders.

He smiled politely. "Hi, Melanie, how you doin'?"

Oh, shit.

My first instinct was to shove him forward and close the

door, hiding the evidence of the forthcoming crime from his view. But the man was twice my size. I could lean all my body weight against his broad, brawny chest and he wouldn't budge an inch.

Instead, I shimmied to my right, forming a human shield between his eyes and the catastrophe going on behind me. Of course, as I did that, I completely forgot about the tin can collection on the floor. Pretending not to hear them crash and clatter around my feet, I said, "I'm great! Totally great. How can I help you?"

He opened his mouth to answer, but fell silent when his gaze drifted over my shoulder to see inside.

Shit. Shit, shit, shit.

I panicked, grasping for a plausible lie that would explain away the existence of a S'mores Station in the middle of our apartment. Then his face broke out in a goofy grin. "Hey, Vee."

Vee?

I spun around and saw Vanessa strolling toward us, entirely untroubled, jar of GlimmerGlam in hand. "Hi, Ray."

"You ready for me to hang up those lights?"

She nodded, grabbing a tangle of wires from the couch and foisting them into his arms. "If you can string them diagonally from the chimney to the access door in a symmetrical crosshatch pattern, that'd be great."

"I remember the pictures you showed me." He looked at me and said, "You believe this girl's got me surfin' Pinterest?"

So that's why Vanessa wasn't worried about getting in trouble with the landlord. Ray had a thing for her. If anyone complained about the party, he wouldn't turn her in. Not with that lovestruck look on his face.

"Hurry up," she said. "The party starts in two hours. When you're done, I need you to set up the tables and bring the rest of this stuff upstairs."

"All right, all right. I'm on it, boss."

With that, he lugged his ladder and the lights down the hall and disappeared into the stairwell.

Vanessa closed the door and saw my mouth hanging open. "What?"

"Are you dating Ray?"

She scowled, scandalized by my question. "Of course not!"

"Well, he's obviously in love with you."

"No, he isn't."

"Yeah, he is. Why else would he be helping you with all of this?"

"Because it's his job."

"It's not his job to string up fairy lights for your illicit rooftop party. In fact, I'm pretty sure this could be putting his job at risk."

She flinched, like she hadn't yet considered this possibility. But the concern quickly faded from her face. "You worry too much."

This coming from the woman who conducted an investigative report on every guy she'd ever considered dating.

"Here." She handed me the cosmetic jar. "Apply a thin coat, leave it on for fifteen minutes, and your face will be taut as a drum skin."

"Thanks a lot."

Vanessa returned to her spot behind the kitchen counter, and I retreated to my room to resume my groom-athon. Kneeling in front of the mirror, I smeared the pearly white gel onto my face, which promptly hardened into a shiny, silver mask. When it was done, I looked like one of those living statue street performers that hung out at the Seaport.

I replaced the lid and inspected the label. GlimmerGlam made some bold claims about the efficacy of their product. Was this truly going to "infuse my cells with energy and empower my skin"? Not likely.

Turning the jar over in my hands, my eyeballs nearly popped out of my skull when I read the price tag on the bottom: a hundred and nineteen dollars. How could Vanessa afford this stuff? And she was so quick to share it with me. This single serving of face mask must've cost at least twenty bucks, probably more. I'd have to throw in a little more toward our grocery bill next month to make up for it.

While waiting for the mask to do its magic, I signed into the JerkAlert dashboard to check up on the current stats. Ever since Whit sent the upgraded link to "a few more people," hundreds of new records had been added to the database. The site had even found an audience beyond New York City. As I scrolled through the latest additions, I found a ghoster from LA, a con man from Austin, and a guy from Washington, DC, who liked to call women he matched with on Fluttr "whores."

JerkAlert was rapidly turning into a nationwide directory of douchebags.

I got so wrapped up in reading profiles that I lost track of time and left the mask on for a full half hour. It didn't seem to matter, though. After I peeled it off, my skin looked fine. Holding my face close to the mirror, I searched for signs of empowerment or energy infusion, but came up empty. I looked pretty much the same as I always did. This mask was a rip-off.

After that, I lost steam on the whole beauty checklist thing. I wanted to look good—jaw-dropping, even—but the truth was, there was no hiding who I really was from Alex. He'd already seen me in the office, with my drab business attire and disempowered skin and, despite that, he was still interested. Besides, did I really want to run through this checklist every time we had a date?

So rather than squeeze into Spanx and stilettos, I plucked my favorite maxi dress from the closet. It was flowing and gauzy, with a flattering empire waist and a plunging back. I slipped on some comfy flats and let my hair fall over my shoulders in natural waves. My only makeup consisted of smudged eyeliner and a sheer shimmery lip gloss.

Without meaning to sound like a total egomaniac, I thought I looked pretty damn hot. Hopefully, Alex would feel the same way.

By the time I emerged from my bedroom, it was a little after eight. The mess in our common area had been cleaned up, and there was no trace of Vanessa or Ray. With festivities presumably underway, I grabbed my phone and headed upstairs to the roof. The access door was ajar, so I pushed it open and stepped directly into a party stylist's wet dream.

The first thing I noticed was the lighting. Vanessa was right: those tin can lanterns made the whole space twinkle. Coupled with the fairy lights sparkling overhead, and the Manhattan skyline in the distance, the rooftop had an otherworldly feel.

At the same time, the decor made it homey. Distressed area rugs and oversize pillows covered the ground. There were ultralow tables constructed from wooden pallets, adorned with lacy tablecloths and flower arrangements. Off to the side was a bar area featuring pitchers of something pink and a snack table with a spread of finger foods.

But the pièce de résistance was the infamous S'mores Station. It was set back against the redbrick chimney, the hand-lettered sign hanging from the wall. And beside it was a makeshift fire pit, constructed from a metal bucket and a heaping pile of lava rock. A few early arrivals were already roasting marshmallows over the flames.

"Whaddya think?" Vanessa had sidled up behind me. "Did I go over the top?"

"No." *Well, maybe a little.* "It looks incredible."

"Thanks." She led me to the bar and filled a mason jar with pink liquid. "Try this sangria."

The first sip was sweet and tangy on my tongue. "Yum."

"I made it with rosé and raspberries."

"Delicious." I scanned the growing crowd, looking for familiar faces. Specifically, I was looking for Alex, but he was nowhere to be seen.

There was a group of guys in the corner, big, beefy dudes in Dickies and tight T-shirts. Not really my type, but pleasant to look at.

"Those are Ray's friends," Vanessa said, following my gaze. "See? He didn't do any of this because he's in love with me. He did it because he wanted to have a rooftop party, too."

"So, you guys are, like, cohosting this?"

She shrugged one shoulder. "Sort of."

"Where is he now?"

"Hooking up speakers. We need music here, desperately." Waggling her fingers at someone behind me, she patted my arm and said, "I'll catch up with you later," before sashaying away.

I took a long, slow sip of sangria and walked toward the parapet at the edge of the rooftop. This view of the city was postcard-perfect. Before I moved to New York, this was how

I'd pictured it: flashy, flawless, highly romanticized. I never considered the reality of day-to-day living in this town. How I'd have to keep a job I hated just to pay my rent. How I'd have to fend off erections in a crowded subway car.

Then again, it wasn't all bad. I'd made some great friends here. Like Whit and Dani, who were striding through the roof access door now, smiling at me.

"Hey, girl!" Whit bellowed, arms outstretched for a hug. "You look super hot."

"Thanks, so do you. Where's Lia?"

"She's coming with Jay," Dani said.

"Oh. I'm excited to finally meet him—aren't you?"

"Yeah, I'm really curious to see what he's like in person."

"Whatever." Whit motioned toward the bar. "I need a drink."

She poured two mason jars full of sangria and handed one to Dani before topping off my half-empty glass. "What's new with you two?"

"I had a shitty date last night," Dani said.

"Where'd you meet her?" Whit asked.

"Iris."

"So why was it shitty?"

"We had nothing in common. She's a fashion blogger living off a trust fund. Meanwhile, I've been wearing these—" Dani pointed to her well-worn motorcycle boots "—since I was an undergrad."

"So what? You're supposed to be sharing a bed, not a closet."

"It wasn't about the clothes. It was about what the clothes represented. Our disparate backgrounds. Our divergent values."

Whit popped a raspberry in her mouth. "She was dumb, wasn't she?"

"As a rock. Our conversation stalled before we'd even ordered our drinks." Dani sighed and stared into her mason jar. "I'm so tired of dating. Part of me just wants to give up, and I might as well. Studies show the stigmatization of singlehood is waning, anyway."

"Have you tried Instabang?" Whit asked. Dani opened her mouth to protest but Whit quickly said, "I'm serious. Sometimes an NSA hookup can reinvigorate you. Think of it as a pit stop for fuel on a long-haul flight."

"That's repulsive."

"Don't be so judgmental."

"I'm not being judgmental, I'm simply—" Dani stopped midsentence and pointed toward the door. "Oh, there's Lia."

I turned around and spotted her weaving our way.

"Hey, guys!" Her voice was a high-pitched trill. She seemed excessively chipper, like a cheerleader who'd downed a case of Red Bull. "Sorry I'm late, but Jay was taking forever so I told him I'd just meet him here."

"Why was he taking forever?" Whit asked.

"He's working." Lia threw up her hands. "I know, who works on a Saturday night, right? At this rate, I'm half expecting him to bail on Cabo." Her smile faltered a bit.

"I'm sure he's not gonna bail on Cabo," Dani said.

"Of course he's not," I added. "He's probably working all these extra hours so he can afford to take the time off."

"I know. You're right." Lia let out a shrill laugh. "I'm being dramatic. He'll be here soon." She turned to me and asked, "Where's your man?"

Whit scowled. "What man?"

"Just this guy from work I've been flirting with. Alex. I invited him tonight." I stole a glance down at my phone. 8:22.

Maybe he was gonna pull a Jay and bail, too. "It's totally casual, though. Like, he might show, he might not."

God, I was an idiot. I'd used that stupid silver face mask for nothing. Didn't I know better by now than to let myself get emotionally invested in some guy who was only going to disappoint me in the end?

Men are the worst.

Suddenly, the music started up, a sexy swell of bass and synth. I felt warm all over, as if someone had switched on a heat lamp and aimed it directly at my body. It must've been the alcohol coursing through my veins. One glance at my empty mason jar confirmed my suspicion.

The bass thumped, the synth pulsed, the heat continued to rise. Maybe it was more than the alcohol. I raised my head, searching for the source of the unexpected warmth.

Then I saw him standing in the doorway, backlit, curls fluttering in the breeze, looking like a well-dressed demigod.

He was here. Alex hadn't disappointed me.

Yet.

10

The look in his eyes made me feel more beautiful than any overpriced face mask ever could. It was sultry and hungry and a little dazed. Like perhaps he'd developed a sudden urge to whisk me off to the bedroom.

"You're gorgeous," he said.

"Thanks." I tingled all over.

"I'm sorry I'm late. The subway on the weekend, you know? It's always a disaster."

"Don't worry about it," I said, totally relaxed, as if I hadn't been on the verge of a meltdown thirty seconds ago. "Let me introduce you to my friends."

Pointing to them in turn, I said, "This is Whitney, Lia, and Dani."

He smiled and shook each of their hands. "It's so nice to meet you."

Whit gestured to the bottle he was holding. "Is that Moët?"

"Yeah. I hope it's okay."

"Uh, it's better than okay." She chugged the remainder of her pink sangria and said, "Let's pop that bad boy open."

"Sure thing."

As he untangled the gold foil and wire cage, I stole a quick glance at my friends, checking to see their initial reactions. Dani shot me a discreet thumbs-up, mouthing, "He's cute." Whit impatiently eyed the champagne, while Lia stared off into the distance.

The bottle popped open with a *thwop* and white foam bubbled up and over the neck. He filled our glasses to the rim, then grabbed an empty mason jar from the bar and poured one for himself.

"Cheers, everyone," he said, then looked me in the eyes. "To new friends."

"Cheers." We echoed, clinking glasses and taking our first fizzy sips.

Alex surveyed the surroundings. "This place looks great. The lights, the food, the fire pit. Did you do all this, Mel?"

"No, I didn't do anything. This was all my roommate, Vanessa."

"Is she a party planner or something?"

I shook my head. "She's a virtual assistant."

"Well, there's a lot of planning involved in that line of work, I guess." He turned to the girls. "What about you all? What do you do for a living?"

Lia went first. "I'm a graphic designer at the Golden Group."

"Wow, the Golden Group is a big deal. Good on you for scoring that gig."

"Thanks," she said, visibly warming to his words. "It's kind of a dream job."

"I bet." Next, he turned to Dani. "And you?"

"I'm pursuing my PhD in Sociology at The New School."

He addressed me with laughter in his voice. "I didn't realize your friends were all geniuses."

Dani blushed a little. "I wouldn't call myself a genius, but I'm certainly no slouch."

Finally, he flashed that dazzling smile over to Whit. "And what about you?"

Instead of answering his question, she flipped it back on him. "Aren't you a Hatchling?"

"Um..." He shifted his weight from one leg to the other, thrown by the sudden change in conversational direction. "Yeah. I am."

"You're not one of those assholes that gives Mel a hard time all day, are you?"

"Whitney!" I hissed, "Of course he isn't."

"Well, you're always saying the Hatchlings are such dicks to you."

Alex winced. This was so awkward. I wanted to crawl under the snack table with a pitcher of sangria and that entire tray of marshmallows.

"Obviously, Alex is different," I said. "Why would I invite someone here who wasn't nice to me?"

"Look, it's okay," he said, his voice steady and gentle. "I get it, Whitney. Melanie's your friend, and you're worried about her. Men can be manipulative jerks, I see that at work every day. I try my best not to be one of them."

"You're not," I said, shooting a meaningful look at Whit.

He licked his lips and continued, "For what it's worth, I don't enjoy being around the other Hatchlings, either. Like I told Mel, sometimes it feels like I'm working in a frat house. And if it's that uncomfortable for me, I can't even imagine how uncomfortable it must be for her, one of the only women in the office."

For once, Whitney didn't interject with a snarky comment. My friends were rapt, all eyes trained on Alex as he reached for my hand, linked his fingers through mine, and said, "Honestly, Mel makes being at Hatch way more bearable. I used to dread going to work in the mornings but now..." He swung his gaze over to me. "Just knowing I'll get to spend a few minutes with her is reason enough for me to get out of bed."

Oh, he was good. Even Whitney looked impressed, which was a feat, considering she enjoyed shredding arguments like a slow-cooked pork shoulder.

"That's beautiful," Lia said, her voice warbly and threatening to crack. Dani and I exchanged a brief, troubled look.

"You okay?" Dani asked.

Lia nodded. "Yeah. That was just a really nice thing to say, Alex. Mel means a lot to us and I'm glad to see there's someone else looking out for her." With a sniffle, she added, "I could use some more champagne."

"Of course," he said, and quickly refilled her cup.

With my friends sufficiently charmed, the tension dissipated, and the conversation flowed. Alex asked thoughtful questions and listened attentively to their answers. He established eye contact and laughed at their jokes, replenishing drinks whenever they were needed. The whole time, he held tight to my hand. My fingers quivered.

Could he have been any more perfect?

Just as I started to float away on a cloud of pure joy, I heard it. It was faint and low quality, but I'd recognize those autotuned lyrics anywhere. Some asshole behind me was playing the "#DickInTheDark Remix" on his phone.

Alex didn't seem to notice. He was too busy having a lively chat with the girls. But all I could hear was my digitally processed voice singing, "rubbing his dick against my backside," over and over again.

The more I tried to block it out, the louder it seemed to get. It might as well have been playing over the speaker system. The girls didn't acknowledge it, though, and I certainly didn't feel like telling Alex the whole backstory of how I became a Twitter hashtag. I put on my best poker face and pretended like I was engrossed in our conversation, completely oblivious to these people behind me who were laughing at one of my most humiliating moments.

Finally, the video ended. I could breathe again! But no sooner had I filled my lungs with oxygen than this guy pressed the replay button and listened to the whole damn thing a second time.

"Honestly," Whit said, a little too loudly, "can this guy turn off his fucking phone?"

Anxious not to cause a scene, I shushed her. "Don't start, please."

"Well, it's ridiculous."

"Yeah, I agree," Alex said. "I don't understand what people find so funny about this whole thing."

I felt the blood drain from my face. "You've seen that video?"

"Not the original one, just the remix. Someone was playing it at work the other day."

No surprise there. Truthfully, I wouldn't have been surprised if some of the Hatchlings had been responsible for spreading a few of those memes.

Again, the video ended. And again, the guy pressed Replay.

"For fuck's sake!" Whit whipped around and grabbed the phone out of the guy's hand, jabbing the stop button with one lacquered nail. "Enough with this shit."

Oh, God. My desire to hide out under the snack table returned with a vengeance. I shielded my face with one hand. Not because I was afraid someone might recognize me, but because Whit was about to start a brawl in a place with a million cell phones, and I did *not* want to wind up in another viral video.

Surprisingly, though, the guy behind us backed off. He huffed out an uninspired "Whatever," and meandered over to the other side of the roof.

Lia patted my shoulder blade. "You okay?"

"Yes, of course. Why wouldn't I be okay?" I was smiling, putting on an act for Alex, hoping to avoid this particular topic of conversation. Or, at the very least, postpone it until our second date.

But he was annoyingly perceptive. "That video bothers you."

"Yes." I nodded, grasping for an excuse. "It's very bothersome."

"It is." His face was serious, a storm brewing above his brow. "I can't believe the amount of shit women have to put up with from men all the time. You're constantly harassed, from all angles. At work, on the street, on the subway."

"Amen," Whitney said.

"Don't forget the internet," Dani added.

"Is it that bad on the internet?" he asked, causing us to burst out in peals of laughter.

"Yes," I said. "On Fluttr, in particular."

"How? Like what do guys do that's so bad?"

"I got two words for you, Alex." Whit counted off her fingers. *"Dick. Pic."*

"Yeah, but that can't happen very often, right? Like, every once in a while some weirdo sends you one and then you report him and he gets thrown off Fluttr, right?"

"I get at least one a day," Whit said. "Sometimes two. Sometimes more."

"And reporting them is pointless," I added. "Those messages probably go to some unmanned mailbox that's never read."

"Whoa." He looked shell-shocked. The reality of being a woman had blown his mind. "Why does any woman ever use Fluttr, then?"

"Because there *are* good guys on there," Lia said. "It's how I met my boyfriend." Suddenly, her face drooped, and she pulled out her phone. "Speaking of which, I should probably call him to see where he's at."

She wandered away, toward an empty corner of the roof. We watched her in silence as she tapped at her phone screen, held it to her ear, and slowly lowered it again.

"Whether her boyfriend's a good guy remains to be seen," Whit said.

"I don't understand why you've never liked him," Dani said.

"How could I like him or not like him? I've never met him. If it wasn't for all those photos she posts on Instagram, I'd question his very existence. She doesn't even tag him so who knows what his deal is."

"Supposedly, he has to keep a low profile on social media because of his job."

Whit sniffed. "Sounds like bullshit to me."

"Okay, but regardless, there definitely are some good guys on Fluttr." I turned to Alex. "I mean, you're on there, right?"

"I *was* on there."

"Oh," I squeaked.

What did he mean by that? At lunch the other day, he'd talked about deleting his profile. I thought it was a joke, but maybe he was serious.

Or maybe…

No, there was no way he deleted his profile because of me.

Was there?

While I internally obsessed over the reason for his Fluttr hiatus, the conversation continued around me.

"I think what Mel is trying to say is that the good guys are few and far between," Dani said.

"Yes. Exactly."

"So every time you right-swipe," he said, "you just have to cross your fingers and hope that you're not gonna get a dick pic?"

"Pretty much." I smiled, feeling saucy from all that champagne. "But there's this new website out there that's trying to help women avoid matching with losers."

"Oh, yeah?"

"Yeah." I could hardly contain my excitement. "Remember the other day, when you told me the right opportunities are the ones you create yourself? Well, I kind of took that to heart."

"No!" Whit cried. Champagne flew from her cup, soaking the front of Alex's crisp blue shirt.

The rest of us gasped.

"Oh my God," Dani said.

"Are you okay?" I asked. "What happened?"

"I'm fine," Whit said. "I'm fine. I thought I saw some stalker I used to hook up with but I was wrong. I'm so sorry about your shirt."

"No worries," Alex said, glancing down at his chest in dismay. "Shit happens."

"You can wash up in my bathroom," I said. "I'll show you where it is."

"He can find it himself," Whit said briskly.

"That's okay," he said. "It's just a little spill. Let me grab some napkins—I'll be right back."

Alex threaded his way through the crowd, careful to avoid getting anyone wet. When he was out of earshot, I whipped my head around and glared at Whit. "What the hell was that?"

"You cannot tell him about JerkAlert."

"Why not?"

"Because you're keeping your identity a secret, remember?"

"I'm keeping it a secret from the general public. Not from the guy that I'm dating."

"This is only your first date."

"Technically, it's our second." If you counted that lunch we'd had Monday as a date. Which I was.

"The point is, you're not serious with him yet, right? You're still getting to know him. Who knows if he's trustworthy or not? He could ghost on you next week and spill the beans."

"He can't exactly ghost," I said. "We work together. We'll run into each other all the time."

"Even more of a reason to keep your mouth shut. You don't want the other Hatchlings to find out you're doing this, do you? I'm sure half those assholes are already logged on JerkAlert. If they know you're the one who runs it, they'll make your life even more miserable than they do now."

She had a point. Did I really want to go into work every day with a bunch of guys who had a vendetta against me?

Still, I could never imagine Alex ratting me out. Not to the Hatchlings. He couldn't stand them. "But he's so different."

"I have to agree," Dani said. "He seems really wonderful."

"Look," Whit said, "if things get serious between you two, then you can tell him. For now, keep it quiet. Besides, I have this really great idea for getting the JerkAlert name out there. And I think you've got the potential to blow up, big-time."

"Really?"

"Yes, if you play your cards right."

Blowing up big-time meant I'd never have to deal with the Hatchlings again. I'd never have to fix another broken computer, or smile my way through a barrage of insults. I'd run my own business. I'd be in charge.

Just then, Alex returned, wiping his shirt with a stack of pink cocktail napkins.

"Is it okay?" I asked. "I'm sure we've got some stain remover lying around somewhere if you need it."

"Nah, I'm good." He wadded the napkins in his hand and looked from me to Whit to Dani and back again. "So, what were we talking about?"

"Um…" I bit my lip, pretending to think.

"Wait," he said, "we were talking about Fluttr, and then you said something about creating opportunities."

Scrunching up my face, I stared at the sky, as if I was searching for the answer up there in the blackness. In reality, I was desperately trying to avoid eye contact, lest Alex see right through my ruse. Finally, I shrugged. "You know, I can't remember. It mustn't have been that important if I forgot so easily."

Thankfully, Lia returned, distracting us all with her ruddy cheeks and watery eyes.

"What's wrong?" I said, knowing full well what was likely to be wrong.

"Oh, nothing. It's just...Jay's not coming."

"Wow. He's still working?" I stole a glimpse at my phone. "It's almost ten o'clock."

Her lower lip trembled, and I knew I'd said the wrong thing.

"I'm gonna head out," she said.

We all groaned in disappointment.

"Don't leave just because he's not coming," Whit said. "Stay and have a good time with us."

She sniffled and said, "No, I'm really tired. I should go."

"You know what," Dani said, "I'm gonna go, too. Lemme walk to the train with you."

Lia didn't protest. They put their mason jars down on the nearest table and we said our goodbyes. As Dani leaned in for a hug, she whispered, "I'll see if she wants to talk about it."

"You're a good friend," I said. "Thanks for coming."

After they left, Whit said, "Well, that seals it. Jay is officially on my shit list."

"As if he wasn't already."

"Fifty bucks says he bails on Cabo."

"Ugh, I don't even want to think about that."

"I'll fucking destroy him if he does."

Alex gave a nervous little laugh. "Man, I hope you never put me on your shit list."

Whit fixed him with a savage stare, her eyes two poison arrows pulled taut against their bows. "Don't give me a reason to."

With that, she sauntered away, leaving Alex to gawk in her wake.

"Don't mind her," I said. "She's prickly."

He gulped, and I grabbed his hand, eager to end all the drama and have some fun. The music had kicked up, and I was feeling that sangria. A makeshift dance floor had formed in the center of the roof. "Come on," I said, pulling him toward the crowd of people bobbing and swaying.

We started off innocently, keeping a respectful distance between our bodies as we sidestepped to the beat. Eventually, he reached out, pulling me closer, little by little, until we were pressed together. His hands went to my waist, my hips, to the small of my back. My fingers sank into the lush tangle of curls at the nape of his neck. Our lips were mere inches apart. I could taste the champagne on his breath.

My skin hummed. My muscles throbbed. My mouth ached with desire. I wanted this kiss more than any kiss I could ever remember wanting.

Then someone yelled, "Fire!"

11

Suffice it to say, the mood was ruined. A rooftop kiss was not to be.

It was kind of a tiny fire, though. Some hipster was screwing around while roasting his marshmallow and wound up singeing the end of his foot-long beard. He panicked, like anyone would if part of their body caught fire, and when he screamed, Ray leaped into action. Zipping across the rooftop, our fearless super ripped the fire extinguisher off the wall, aimed it in the general direction of the kerfuffle, and let the foam fly.

Everything within a four-foot radius was promptly doused in a thick coat of flame-squelching froth. The fire pit, the S'mores Station, the hipster. Fortunately, no one was seriously injured, although the hipster guy was in tears.

"I spent three years growing my shit out," he cried, wiping foam out of his eyes. His girlfriend consoled him with a regretful expression, though it was unclear whether she was mourning the loss of his beard or questioning her relationship choices.

There wasn't any property damage, either; just a hell of a gloopy white mess to clean up. But once a fire starts, that's the beginning of the end for a party. The music cut off abruptly, and Vanessa pushed her way to the center of the rooftop, clapping her hands.

"Can I have your attention?" A hush fell on the crowd, and she said, "Thank you so much for coming. It's been wonderful having everyone here on this beautiful spring evening. Unfortunately, with the unexpected turn of events—" she motioned to the fire pit and S'mores Station, which were now toast "—I'm afraid we're going to have to shut down the festivities a little early."

A collective groan broke out and Vanessa quickly added, "I'm so sorry, again. Thank you."

I looked up at Alex, who still held me close, but in a way that was less seductive, more protective. "Are you okay?" he asked.

"Yeah. It wasn't my beard that went up in flames."

"Right." He furrowed his brow, watching Ray as he dragged a giant trash can out of a utility shed. "I should go see if he needs some help with that," he said, and walked away.

While Vanessa began ushering people toward the roof access door in an orderly fashion, I craned my neck searching for Whitney. Finally, I spotted her in the corner, flirting with one of those big, beefy dudes in Dickies. He looked completely titillated. I shuddered to think of what she was whispering in his ear.

"Yo, Sal!" Ray called across the rooftop, to where Whitney was sitting. Her companion winced, then flashed Whit a pained look before running to Ray.

She stood up, smoothed the front of her skirt, and ambled over to me. "That guy is hot."

"He's a friend of our super."

"Your super is also hot." After surveying the dwindling crowd, she said, "Looks like this party's over."

"Nothing'll kill a party faster than a beard fire."

"There's a new club in Greenpoint that's spinning G-house on Saturdays. I've been meaning to check it out. Wanna come with? You can bring your boy toy, if you want."

"Nah. I should stay and help Vanessa clean up."

"Suit yourself." She kissed me on the cheek. "Love you. Use a condom."

I giggled, giddy, but then that weird sensation in my stomach returned, and I felt a little nauseous. There was a good chance Alex and I were gonna get it on tonight. And while part of me couldn't wait to jump his bones, there was another, more insidious part of me that was terrified of screwing things up.

That age-old advice ricocheted around my skull: *make him wait*. At this point in history, when women were fully independent and autonomous individuals, this directive seemed totally antiquated and even a little conniving. Why wouldn't I sleep with a guy who I really liked, who treated me well, and who made me quiver every time we touched?

Because of that other age-old advice: *Why buy the cow, when you can get the milk for free?* Deep down, I knew this was bullshit, but the theory was persistent, and everywhere. I'd even read an article (on the Fluttr blog, of all places) that suggested "taking it slow" helps a woman earn a guy's respect. Sex on the first date, however, earns a woman a one-way ticket to Ho-Town. (They actually used the term *Ho-Town*.)

It was all ass-backward, though. Whit never followed this advice, mostly because she wasn't interested in guys sticking around. But it always seemed to backfire on her, resulting in one-night stands who never went away. Lia, on the other hand, made Jay wait until their fifth date—which, frankly, I find insane—but after that, they grew serious quite quickly. Although, who knew what was going on with them now.

Finally, I thought, *fuck it*, and decided to let my loins lead me where they may. Alex wasn't gonna ghost on me. Like I told Whit, it'd be pretty much impossible, considering we shared a workspace.

Beyond that, he just didn't seem like the type. As I picked up empty mason jars and dirty paper plates, I watched him hose down the fire pit, rinsing each lava rock individually to ensure no traces of flame retardant were left behind. Every move he made was so cautious and thoughtful. If he was that gentle when handling a broken piece of rock, imagine how gentle he'd be with my heart.

Between Alex, Ray, his buddies, Vanessa, and me, it took only twenty minutes to clean up the rooftop. The lights were stripped, the tables were folded, and all the empty mason jars and serving trays had been returned to our apartment. When Ray's buddies bumped fists and left, only the four of us remained.

"Is there anything else I can do?" Alex asked.

"Nah," Ray said, fiddling with the speakers. "All I gotta do is unhook this thing and then we're done. Something's caught back here, though."

"Let me take a look at it," Vanessa said, crouching down beside him.

I glanced at Alex. It was now or never. Because I sure as hell wasn't waiting until the fifth date.

"Wanna come hang at my place for a bit?"

There was no pretense. No sitting on the couch and turning on the TV. No pouring of drinks. We both headed straight for my bedroom, with a purpose. And that purpose was to get it on.

Clothes went flying, hands went searching. When our mouths met, I felt like a long-standing thirst had been quenched. Three orgasms later, I was a paralyzed puddle of pleasure, and the idea that I'd ever considered "making him wait" seemed not only ludicrous but masochistic. There was no valid reason to ever deprive myself of this ecstasy.

At some point after our sex-athon, I passed out, then woke at dawn with an urgent need to pee. Alex was curled up beside me, his chest rising and falling with steady breaths. God, he was even more gorgeous when he slept.

As quietly as possible, I rolled out of bed, threw on an oversize T-shirt, and poked my head into the hallway. No signs of life; that was good. A quick glance into the living room revealed a disaster of epic proportions; that was bad, but a problem to be solved in the morning. For now, I tiptoed into the bathroom and flicked on the light.

The first thing I saw were two tan sculpted butt cheeks, followed immediately by Ray's horrified expression in the mirror.

"Oh, shit!" he cried.

I shrieked. Not out of fear; Ray had always been a nice, polite, completely nonthreatening guy. I was simply shocked—

by the fact that he was here, in my bathroom, in the middle of the night, bare-ass naked.

And, if I'm being honest, I was also shocked at how buff he was. Who knew his Dickies had been concealing such wonder?

Actually, I already knew the answer to that question: Vanessa.

"Melanie, I am so sorry." He grasped desperately at a washcloth, holding it over his groin in a vain attempt to cover his modesty. I ducked into the hall, hiding behind the bathroom door to spare us both the embarrassment of eye contact. "I didn't mean to scare you."

"It's okay," I called. "I just wasn't expecting you to be there. No biggie."

"If I knew you were here, I never would've been walking around naked. I thought you were over at your boyfriend's house."

He thinks Alex is my boyfriend.

I stifled a fit of giddy giggles.

Suddenly, my not-boyfriend came bounding out of my bedroom, a sheet wrapped around his waist. "Is everything okay?" He stopped short when he saw me standing with my back to the bathroom door, sporting what I presumed to be a dreamy smile. "I thought I heard you scream. What's going on?"

Before I could answer, Ray emerged from the bathroom, his nether regions draped in a generous bath towel. "Hiya," he said.

Alex's eyes darted from Ray to me and back again. "Uh… hi."

Then, as if three wasn't enough of a crowd, Vanessa appeared in the doorway of her bedroom. She wore a satin kimono that fell off one shoulder. Her makeup was smudged, her hair was sticking out in twelve directions. I don't think I'd ever seen her so disheveled.

Or so radiant, for that matter.

But her rosy complexion went pale when she saw me and Alex. She stiffened, righting her kimono and crossing her arms across her chest.

"What's going on?" She barked the question, but her voice was shaky around the edges.

"Nothing, baby." Ray moved toward her, one hand gripping his towel. When he touched her, she flinched. "I scared Melanie, that's all. Sorry again, Mel." He flashed an apologetic smile in my direction, then nodded toward Alex. "Take care, man."

"Later."

The door clicked shut behind them, and I clasped my hand tightly over my mouth to keep from howling with laughter.

Alex whispered, "What?"

I held up one finger, then pointed to the bathroom. "Give me one second. I'll tell you when I'm done."

After I finished my business, I returned to my room to find him lounging on top of my rumpled covers, paging through my dog-eared copy of *The Web Development Bible.*

"Doing some early morning research?" I asked.

"Gotta keep my skills sharp. The start-up world is cutthroat, you know." As he turned the page, a sheet of notepaper fell onto his chest. "What's this?"

I slid into bed beside him and froze. That paper he was holding? A note I'd written to myself last week, while I was trying to work out a problem with JerkAlert. It was covered in words like *profile* and *review* and *Fluttr.*

Uh-oh.

In an instant, I snatched it from his hands, crumpled it in one fist, and tossed it behind my headboard. "It's nothing," I said. "Just some scrap paper. Probably a million years old by now. It could've even been in the book when I bought it. I got it used. Online."

Shut up, shut up, shut up.

Alex narrowed his eyes. "Are you okay?"

"Fine. I'm totally fine." I needed to change the subject, fast. "Oh! Let me explain why I was laughing in the hallway."

"Oh, right." He took the bait without a second thought. "I didn't realize Vanessa was dating your building super."

"She's not. Or, at least, she wasn't. He's had a huge crush on her and she was totally in denial about it, but I guess she finally gave in."

"That explains how she got roof access."

"Exactly. She literally slept her way to the top."

He laughed, crinkling his nose. "Hey, whatever works. I don't judge her. Lots of people use sex to get what they want."

I gave him a look of mock suspicion. "And is that the reason you're sleeping with me? For the free computer repair?"

"No." He traced his finger down the curve of my hip. "I mean, don't get me wrong, that's a definite perk. But the only reason I'm here right now is because I really like you."

He punctuated the word *you* with a soft tap in the center of my chest, and the singular motion turned my heart to gelatinous goop.

"I hope that doesn't freak you out," he said.

"Why would that freak me out? Trust me, after all the dating nightmares I've endured, hearing you tell me you like me is... It's special. It's different. *You're* different. And I really like you, too."

Then I leaned forward and kissed him. Slowly, tenderly, thoroughly. As if his lips were the most decadent delicacy I'd ever tasted. And when he pulled me in close and wrapped his strong arms around me, that familiar feeling returned.

Ecstasy.

As far as I was concerned, he could have all the free milk he wanted.

12

I awoke to a rustling. Like someone was folding clean clothes. Perhaps a laundry fairy had arrived in the middle of the night to deliver me from my self-made squalor.

No, it was just Alex, turning his pants right side out and shaking away the wrinkles. He was wearing underwear and socks… Wait a minute. Was he planning to smash and dash?

In an instant, I bolted upright. "Are you leaving already?"

God, that sounded desperate. I mean, the sun was out. It had to have been late morning, possibly even early afternoon. Time to get on with our days, separately. After all, we weren't a couple. He was my not-boyfriend.

Still, if he'd wanted to grab brunch or something, I wouldn't have said no. Even a cup of coffee would've been nice.

Clearly, that wasn't gonna happen, though. When he heard my voice, he gave me this panicky look. A look that said, "My attempt at a smash-and-dash has failed."

"Is everything okay?" I asked.

"Yeah, I'm good. I just…" He spun in circles in the center

of my tiny bedroom, his eyes darting across the messy floor. "What did I do with my shirt?"

I plucked it from the tangle of sheets and tossed it at him. "Here."

"Thanks."

As he fastened his buttons, I seethed. After the night we'd just experienced—a night filled with passion and laughter and multiple orgasms—he was simply going to take off while I was still asleep. He hadn't even been planning to say goodbye. *Asshole.*

I thought he was different. I told him I liked him. I gave away the milk, and now he was breaking free.

God, I was an idiot.

"I'm sorry," he said. "I didn't mean to wake you up."

"Yes," I said, through gritted teeth. "I'm sure you're very sorry."

Worry lines formed on his forehead. "What's wrong?"

Seriously? I couldn't believe he was going to make me spell this out for him. In that case, I wanted to be crystal clear.

"We fucked all night, and you were just about to take off without saying goodbye."

"No!" He looked horrified. "No, that's not… Oh, shit, I'm sorry." At once, he was next to me, on the bed, his hands grasping at mine. "I am so sorry. I can see why it would seem that way, but I didn't want to wake you up. You looked so peaceful and happy lying there. For what it's worth, I wrote you a note." He pointed to my nightstand, where a piece of paper sat on top of the clutter.

Reluctantly, I reached for it. A note was better than nothing, I guess, but I certainly wasn't thrilled about it. It read:

Mel,

Headed to work now. Had an amazing time last night.

Thanks for everything.

Text you later,

A

"You're working on a Sunday?"

"I work every Sunday. Every Saturday, too. There's no such thing as weekends when you're trying to launch a start-up. And I didn't want to leave in such a rush, but I accidentally overslept, and I promised Vijay I'd get him the results of this load test today, and I've got so much to do before I can make that happen."

He raked his hand through his hair, that panicky look returning to his eyes. And I realized that look had nothing to do with getting caught in a smash-and-dash. He was legit terrified of losing his funding.

"I get it," I said, squeezing his hand.

"Thanks." He smiled, visibly relieved. "I had such a great time last night."

"Me, too. Sorry for freaking out on you."

"Don't be. I'm sorry I made you freak out." He slid his hands around the back of my neck, rubbing his thumbs along my jawline. "But I'm glad I get the chance to say a proper goodbye now."

I was so hungry for his kiss that the thought of morning breath didn't cross my mind. It didn't seem to bother him, either. Not from the way he consumed me, his eager mouth enveloping mine, making my whole body tremble.

He broke off abruptly, with a dazed sort of look in his eye. "I'll text you later."

"Okay."

I moved to stand, but he said, "You don't have to get up. Stay. Relax. I can see myself out."

And then he was gone.

After the intensity of that kiss, there was no way I could relax. Maybe I'd have a go with my magic bullet, instead. Reclining in bed, I closed my eyes, licking the remnants of his flavor off my lips. But my plan for self-fulfillment was rudely interrupted when my phone beeped with a text from Whitney.

WHITNEY:

Have you checked Twitter?

MEL:

No, why?

WHITNEY:

You're trending again. ☺

Goddammit.

MEL:

I don't care.

WHITNEY:

No, it's not the #DickInTheDark thing.

It's something else. Something waaay better.

MEL:

WTF does that mean?

She replied with a link. At first, I didn't understand what I was scrolling through. It seemed to be a Twitter feed about bad Fluttr dates or something. Then I noticed all the tweets had the same hashtag: #JerkAlert.

MEL:
Holy shit!

WHITNEY:
I know!

MEL:
How did you find this?

WHITNEY:
Walking into SoulCycle rn,
will tell you later.

WHITNEY:
BTW are you free for dinner tomorrow?
Happy hour @ Stanton Social.

MEL:
Sure.

WHITNEY:
Cool. I'll text Dani and
Lia to see if they're in.

WHITNEY:
And get ready, baby.
You're about to blow up. Big time!

My stomach gurgled, possibly a gut reaction to the idea of blowing up big-time. Which didn't make a whole lot of sense. Just last night, the idea of blowing up was exciting. This was what I wanted, wasn't it? For people to spread the word about my product. A trending hashtag was like a ticket on the express train to success. The stuff start-up dreams were made of.

Technically, though, I didn't have a start-up. I was merely

a woman, running a website from her bedroom, hoping that someday it might turn a profit. I truly believed JerkAlert could be financially rewarding one day. I even believed it could be revolutionary. But at the moment, I was having second thoughts about whether I wanted to lead this particular revolution.

If JerkAlert went viral, there's no way I could maintain my anonymity. Not in this day and age, when everyone carried GPS and a video camera on them at all times. People would be curious. They'd unmask me. Then they'd put two and two together and realize I was the same woman from #DickInTheDark. Imagine the memes they'd make then.

There was also the whole Alex factor. If he found out I was the brains behind JerkAlert from some internet meme, he'd undoubtedly wonder why I didn't just tell him myself. He'd question my motives, become suspicious, and lose faith in me. A wedge would form between us. Our relationship would be over before it even began.

All this anxiety was making me thirsty, so I rolled out of bed and headed to the kitchen for a glass of water. Vanessa was there, standing over the sink, scrubbing out mason jars. She didn't look up when I entered the room.

"Hey," I said.

"Hey." Her scrubbing became more vigorous.

"Do you need any help cleaning?" I asked.

"No. I've got it under control."

A quick survey of the apartment confirmed that she did, indeed, have it under control. The mess I'd spotted in the early morning hours was long gone. All that was left were some dishes, but she was flying through them at an extraordinary rate.

Vanessa herself was cleaned up, too. No more smudged eye makeup, no more tousled hair. It was like our hallway meeting in the middle of the night had never happened. And since she refused to look at me, I assumed she wished it hadn't.

Without a word, I moved toward the cupboard and reached for a glass.

"I know what you're thinking," she said.

Oh, boy.

"I'm not thinking anything."

"It was a mistake," she said, never once looking up from her scrub job. "I drank way too much sangria, and I made a stupid decision."

"Okay."

Vanessa didn't need to justify her romp with Ray to me; honestly, I was the last person to judge someone for making a bad man-related decision. But she seemed intent on explaining herself, anyway.

"Really, I've never done anything like this before. It's so not like me to jump into bed with someone I'm not seriously involved with. I always wait until at least the third date to have sex, usually longer."

"It's really not that big of a deal," I said.

"Yes, it is." She turned off the water and threw the sponge in the sink. "I am so embarrassed. I mean, *Ray*, of all people."

"You could've done worse."

She snorted. "Not likely."

"He's a really nice guy." *With a really nice ass.*

"He's the super."

"Well, think of it this way—if you're dating the building super, you'll be allowed to have rooftop parties whenever you want."

Her face twisted in disgust. "That is so not funny. Anyway, I think after that fire, we won't be allowed on the rooftop anytime soon."

"Ray didn't get in trouble, did he?"

"No. Only one neighbor complained, but Ray managed to keep him from calling the landlord. We were all really lucky that nothing seriously bad happened, though, so he's putting the kibosh on future rooftop parties."

"That's probably for the best." I filled my glass with water, regarding Vanessa out of the corner of my eye. "When that fire broke out, Ray jumped into action fast."

"Yeah. He was so on top of things."

"He seems like a dependable guy."

She smiled wistfully. "He is."

"Plus, he's super handy."

"Oh my God, did you see how flawlessly he strung up those lights? Perfectly symmetrical."

"He's definite boyfriend material."

Vanessa's wistful smile hardened to a scowl. "No."

"Why not?"

"He lives in Bensonhurst."

"So?"

"With his *mother*."

"Oh." Granted, I wouldn't be too thrilled about the idea of having sex with a guy under his mother's roof. But I thought of how radiant she looked, emerging from her bedroom in that silk kimono. "He's obviously smitten with you, though. And it seemed like you were really happy last night."

"I wasn't happy—I was drunk." She peeled off her rubber gloves and slapped them down on the kitchen counter. "Besides, lots of people are happy when they first meet someone, when everything's new and the sex is hot and they have no idea what it is they're getting into. Happiness is irrelevant."

Everything's new. The sex is hot. That sounded a lot like me and Alex.

"You're talking about choosing a partner," I said. "How could happiness be irrelevant? What could possibly be more important than being happy?"

"Like-mindedness. Compatibility. And you figure all that out by doing your research beforehand." She tapped her temple. "Knowledge is power. That's why I go to Vilma. The more you know about a guy beforehand, the less likely you are to suffer some horrible breakup that leaves you shattered into a million pieces." Her lower lip twitched, then she took a deep breath. "Speaking of which, Vilma arranged a date for me on Tuesday night. I've gotta go call my stylist now and see if she can squeeze me in later today. This balayage is starting to look dull."

With that, Vanessa retreated to her bedroom and shut the door behind her. I stood there, staring at the empty space she left behind, marveling at how quickly she was able to dismiss a future with Ray. Living with his mom was an issue, but surely, he couldn't live with her forever.

Then again, was Vanessa's process of elimination really any different from the way I'd filtered out potential mates using Fluttr? I often made my decisions in under two seconds, based on factors that were far more superficial. Who knows how many potentially good dates I'd left-swiped because of a goofy smile or a bad camera angle?

Not that any of that mattered now. Because now I had Alex. And if things continued to go well with the two of us, I'd never have to use Fluttr again. In fact, I was going to go back to my room and deactivate my profile immediately.

And that's just what I did.

When it was done, I scrolled through my Instagram feed, catching up on everything that had happened while I'd been sexing and sleeping. Whit had clearly had a late night, posting a 3:00 a.m. selfie in front of a DJ booth at that club in Greenpoint. Dani, on the other hand, had gotten up early and posted a photo of her coffee cup next to her laptop, with the caption: Sunday morning torture session #dissertating.

And then there was Lia's photo: a bouquet of lavender roses, arranged in a crystal vase. She'd posted it twenty minutes ago and captioned it: Flowers from bae. Apparently, Jay had apologized.

I clicked on Lia's profile and swiped through her most recent photos, stopping when I got to a selfie she'd taken last week. A close-up of their faces, their cheeks pressed together. He was average-looking; a little on the old side, but he wore it well. Salt-and-pepper hair, a couple of distinguished wrinkles around the eyes. He looked decent.

But looks could be deceiving.

Just to be safe, I loaded JerkAlert and searched for "Jay, 41, Midtown." When the page displayed NO MATCHING PROFILES, I realized how silly I was being. Couples had disagreements all the time. Guys flaked, girls cried. Flowers were sent as apologies. It didn't mean Jay was a bad guy.

It didn't mean he was a good guy, either, but the absence of a JerkAlert profile was encouraging nonetheless. As nutty as I'd thought Vanessa sounded with all her talk of matchmaking, there was some truth to be found in her words. Having knowledge made me feel powerful. Maybe JerkAlert could be a useful tool for avoiding not only dick pics, but heartbreak, too.

A twinge seized my chest as I remembered the panicky look on Alex's face when I'd caught him getting dressed in a hurry. He'd had a perfectly reasonable explanation. He'd even written a note. He was a decent guy. But who knew if he was telling the truth?

Like Vanessa said, the more you know about someone beforehand, the less likely you are to suffer afterward.

I typed "Alex, 26, FiDi" in the search box. And when I saw Alex's dazzling smile shining back at me from the screen, my heart shattered into a million pieces.

Review: typical fluttr douche. super hot, but a smooth talker. says all the right things at all the right times. don't trust a word that comes out of his mouth.

13

I was not going to freak out.

This was only one review. Sure, it was scathing, but it was also sort of vague. "Typical Fluttr douche" could mean just about anything.

Well, not *anything*. It definitely meant something bad. Still, I had no idea who actually posted it. Why should I trust the words of some anonymous internet reviewer?

Of course, that begged the question of how useful JerkAlert really was if the reviews were unreliable.

But Alex had been perfect last night, in every single way. Holding me close as we danced under fairy lights. Rushing to help Ray in the aftermath of the fire. Charming my friends with his sweet, thoughtful commentary.

Which, I supposed, could be construed as smooth talk.

I didn't realize your friends were all geniuses…

I used to dread going to work in the mornings…

Just knowing I'll get to spend a few minutes with her…

No! That wasn't smooth talk. When Alex said all those things, he was being totally sincere.

Wasn't he?

Maybe not.

I needed to distract myself from this subject, immediately, so I popped open my laptop and fired up Netflix, then spent the rest of my Sunday in bed, bingeing on junk food and *Jessica Jones*. As I was drawn out of reality and into a fictional world, I dreamed of opening my own superhero detective agency, where I'd investigate secret shady behaviors of men who did women dirty and expose them for the liars they were. Kind of like JerkAlert, only more badass.

Between episodes, I checked my phone in vain for a text from Alex. When I inevitably found nothing, I refreshed my Twitter feed to see if any new tweets had been added to the #JerkAlert hashtag. As the night wore on, activity seemed to die down, so I signed into the JerkAlert dashboard to check current stats and found that, over the past twenty-four hours, web traffic had remained largely unchanged.

This Twitter trend wasn't turning into the big marketing blowout Whit had predicted it'd be. There'd been more buzz over #DickInTheDark, for God's sake.

Which should've eased my mind, right? When Whit told me I was gonna blow up, I'd been so worried about being found out.

Now, all I could think was: Who cared? Who cared if a bunch of basement boys turned me into a sexist meme? Who cared if they exposed and humiliated me? My entire life was a series of humiliations at the hands of men, anyway, and I was still standing. I might as well try to make a buck off it.

Since no one gave a damn about JerkAlert, though, the

point was moot. It looked like I'd be stuck working the help desk for the foreseeable future.

By the time I'd burned through the entire first season of *Jessica Jones*, it was close to midnight. I checked my phone one last time before I turned out the light, hoping to see a message from Alex. But, of course, there wasn't one.

He never texted like he said he would. And frankly, I was beginning to suspect he never had any intention of texting me at all. He probably didn't even have to work on Sundays. It was merely an excuse he'd conjured up when I'd caught him trying to make his escape. Because he knew how to say all the right things at all the right times.

That's when the truth hit me like a runaway freight train: Alex Hernandez had smooth-talked me into the sack.

"The same shit is happening again."

Josh Brewster's voice boomed through my cubicle. I spun around in my chair to find him standing in the doorway, shoulders squared, chest heaving, gripping his laptop in one meaty pink fist. For a second, I was afraid he was going to hurl it at my head.

Instinctively, I smiled. "Good morning, Josh. Can I help you?"

Instead of defusing the situation, my pleasant attitude only seemed to deepen his scowl.

"I don't know. Can you?" He shook the laptop in my direction. "Every time I ask you to fix this piece of shit, it comes back even more broken than when I dropped it off."

Stay calm. Don't engage.

"Let me see what's going on," I said, coating my voice in so much syrup I could taste the sweetness on my tongue.

With a grimace, he handed it over, and I flipped it open to look at the screen. "Hmm. Looks like you're infected with malware again."

"Yeah, that's what you said last time, so obviously, that's not the problem."

I cleared my throat, counting to three in my head before I said something rash that I'd later regret.

Josh took my silence as an opportunity to continue his rant. "The only reason I even brought this to you was because I couldn't find Bob. He's the only one around here who knows what he's doing."

God, this guy was such a dick.

"Well, why don't you leave it with me, and I'll bring it to Bob when I see him? I'm sure he'll be able to fix this right away."

He hissed, sneaking in one final sneer before stalking away. As soon as he was gone, I pulled up the keylogger and started scrolling through the sea of data it had collected on Josh's activity. There was plenty of innocuous stuff in there: emails he'd composed in Outlook; Slack messages between him and the other members of his team; lots of really poorly written code.

But there was a lot more of the not-so-innocuous stuff. Like the hours he spent at a website called FreeBigBoobs.com, or the myriad visits he made to the Sexy Beautiful Women board on 4Chan. Also, as suspected, Josh frequented many a gambling site. If it had the words *fantasy*, *bet*, or *casino* in the URL, chances are Josh had been there.

The logger also showed that before every session, he'd disable the virus scanner. Afterward, he'd restart it, then delete his browser history—the man hadn't even heard of incognito mode!—but by then, his computer was already infected.

I couldn't wait to show Bob the evidence. Tucking Josh's laptop under my arm, I hopped to my feet and headed toward Bob's favorite hiding place: the server room. Whenever he went missing, I knew he was simply holed up somewhere among the racks of computers, seeking solace in the whir of their cooling fans. In there, no one would bother him.

As the boss, he could get away with that. As the underling, I couldn't. I had to stay out on the office floor, acting as the face of the help desk and dealing with the wrath of the Hatchlings. When Bob was in the server room, I was supposed to leave him alone to work in peace, unless there was some sort of urgent crisis.

Technically, the discovery of Josh's internet activity was neither urgent nor a crisis, but I felt it warranted an interruption, anyway. I needed vindication, and I needed it now. These logs were irrefutable proof that the Hatchlings were egregiously irresponsible, and that I was right about it all along. Maybe now Bob would realize I shouldn't have to endure their insults and abuse. Maybe now he'd tell *them* to stop giving *me* such a hard time, instead of the other way around.

I swiped my access card to disengage the dead bolt, and as soon as it clicked, I pushed open the heavy metal door to the server room. Rows and rows of black shelves contrasted with white walls and fluorescent high bays. Hundreds of fans spinning simultaneously created an otherworldly hum. I tiptoed along the corridor, peering around each corner until I spotted Bob sitting on the floor, hunched over his laptop, eyes narrowed in deep concentration. When he heard my footsteps approaching, he shot me a look halfway between fury and dread.

"Why are you in here?" he barked.

"Remember when I said Josh was probably surfing around gambling sites?"

Bob let out an exasperated breath. "Not this again."

"It's different this time. I have proof!" I sat down beside him and whipped out the laptop. "Look."

As I scrolled through the logs of Josh's guilt, Bob looked confused. "What is this?"

"I installed a keylogger on his machine."

His eyes bulged. "You *what*?"

"You told me that I couldn't accuse him of anything without logs of his activity."

"I didn't tell you to install a keylogger. This isn't Hatch-sanctioned software. It's against company policy." Bob grabbed the laptop from my hands, commanding control of the touch pad and inspecting the evidence. "Does Josh know you did this?"

"No."

"Good. Let's keep it that way."

"Do you see what this shows?" I leaned over and pointed out the damning evidence. "He turns off the virus scanner so he can go surfing around shady websites. *That's* against company policy."

"Look at the dates and times. It's always on a weekend or late at night. He's not in the office when this happens. Our firewall would block him from doing it on our office network, anyway."

"So?"

"So, what he does on his own time is his own business."

"Even on a Hatch-issued laptop?"

"Yes. You have to uninstall this immediately."

"But he keeps downloading viruses."

"That's what you're here for."

Anger threaded through my veins so forcefully I began to shake. "That's my job? To let him screw things up and speak to me like garbage, then clean up his mess with a smile on my face?"

Bob spread his hands and lowered his voice, like he was trying to stave off an approaching wolf. "Let's not get hysterical, okay? He's only gonna be here for another few weeks. Then he'll be gone, and you'll never see him again."

I knew he was talking about Josh Brewster. I knew he was referring to the way Hatch worked, bringing in a new cohort of start-up founders every three months. But my mind went straight to one question: Is this what Alex was thinking? *Another few weeks, then she'll be gone, and I'll never see her again.*

I'd been so convinced he wouldn't ghost on me because we worked together, not even considering that our time as coworkers was extremely limited. Sure, avoiding me around the office would be awkward, but he'd only have to do it for a few more weeks. Then he'd be gone, on to the next one, and I'd still be sitting here at Hatch, dealing with a brand-new horrible round of Hatchlings.

Because the next round would be just as horrible as this one was. The Hatchlings were always the same: entitled, ungrateful, and abusive. I was going to be trapped here with an endless rotation of them, forever, and my boss wouldn't even come to my defense.

My face suddenly felt very hot. My eyes stung and my throat swelled and oh, God I was about to do the worst possible thing I could ever do. I was about to cry in front of my boss.

Bob's face contorted in horror. "Are you okay?"

Shit. Shit, shit, shit.

Rule number one in the woman techie playbook: never, ever, *ever* cry in front of your boss. It's hard enough being taken seriously in this industry without wearing your emotions on your sleeve. If I cried now, any hint of respect he had for me would promptly vanish without a trace.

So I swallowed that lump in my throat, blinked back those tears, and forced myself to put on an agreeable smile. "Of course." I took back the laptop and said, "I'll go clean up the virus and remove the keylogger now."

He narrowed his eyes, wary of my sudden willingness to comply, but ultimately, relieved not to have to deal with a weepy woman. "Good."

Without looking back, I fled the server room, speed-walking down the hall to the privacy of my cubicle. My eyes ached from the pressure of holding back tears. I needed to let them flow in peace.

But as I rounded a corner, I careened face-first into a crisp button-down shirt contoured perfectly around a broad, solid chest.

"Whoa. You okay?" Alex grabbed my shoulders, steadying me. The heat from his palms penetrated the thin cotton of my sleeves, sending warm waves across my collarbones that pooled in the hollow of my throat. He flashed me that dazzling smile.

No. Don't fall for it again.

I withdrew from his grip, standing tall, smoothing the front of my shirt. "I'm fine."

His smile faded a bit. Less dazzling, more contrite. "Look, I'm sorry I didn't text you last night. I wound up staying here until two in the morning trying to get the load tests right, then went home to sleep for two hours before coming back here again at six. It's been a nightmare."

"You say that a lot."

He furrowed his brow. "What do I say a lot?"

"That you're sorry."

"Oh." His mouth opened and closed as he struggled for words. "Did I… I mean… Is there something you want to tell me?"

There was a lot I wanted to tell him, actually: that I'd read all about his smooth-talking past on JerkAlert. That I was terrified of letting him get close enough to hurt me. That he looked so good standing there in the middle of the hallway, I just wished he would give me a reason to trust him so we could be sharing a secret kiss right now.

But I didn't say anything like that. Rule number two in the woman techie playbook: never make a scene in the office.

Instead, I gave him my standard pleasant smile. The one I gave all the Hatchlings. "No, I'm just really busy. Need to fix this thing again." I patted Josh's laptop, the "Free Mustache Rides" sticker making a mockery of us all. "I've gotta go."

There was hurt in Alex's eyes. Or maybe that was wishful thinking on my part, to imagine that he cared enough about me to feel hurt by my snub.

I brushed past him, practically running back to my cubicle, the tears already welling in my eyes. As soon as I flopped into my chair, I was filled with regret. I should've told him what I was really thinking, asked him flat out if he thought we had a future together or if I was just another fling. I should've given him a chance to explain.

Eager for distraction, I checked my phone, and was delighted to see a text from Whit awaiting me. She'd sent me a link to a BuzzFeed article; she did this all the time. Usually, it was one of those ridiculous quizzes, like "Which Kardashian Are You?" or "Order a Starbucks Drink and We'll Guess Your Favorite Sex Position." Normally, I'd ignore it, but in that moment, there was nothing I needed more than a mindless diversion from reality.

When I clicked on the link, though, it was not at all what I was expecting.

14

7 JerkAlert Profiles That Have Us Saying "WTF?"

By Kirra Boyce, BuzzFeed Staff
Posted: Monday, April 16, 8:57 a.m.

Ladies, we've all been there: you right-swipe some dude on Fluttr who seems halfway normal, and then five minutes later, he sends you a picture of his dick. It sucks, but if you wanna play the dating game in this day and age, unsolicited dick pics are just something you have to learn to deal with, right?

Wrong.

Now there's JerkAlert, a website that helps take the guesswork out of online dating. Powered by a fast-growing collection of crowdsourced info, JerkAlert (that's .biz, not .com) lets you research a guy before you swipe right. Enter his name, age, and location into the sleek and speedy search engine, and you'll instantly find out the answers to all your burning pre-date questions: Does he have a history of sending dick pics? Is he a serial ghoster? Has he ever been caught cheating? JerkAlert knows.

With over a thousand men profiled (and counting), JerkAlert is a virtual treasure trove of dirt on the worst that Fluttr has to offer. From the guy who's hiding a secret family in New Jersey to the dude who wants to be every woman's "foot slave," these are the top seven profiles that had us going, "WTF?"

With a quivering thumb, I scrolled through the article, dumbstruck, reading the same sentences over and over again. It was unbelievable, really, that something I'd created on a whim was now being profiled on a website like BuzzFeed. Their readership was in the hundreds of millions. According to the stats at the bottom of the page, the article had been emailed, tweeted and shared on Facebook over five hundred times. And it had been published only a few hours ago.

Maybe Whit was right about the whole "blowing up big-time" thing, after all.

I texted her back: Omg.

WHITNEY:

MEL:

How did this happen?

WHITNEY:

Will explain over dinner.

This was amazing. A feature on the front page of BuzzFeed! Whit must've pulled some real strings to score it.

I read through the article yet again, taking pleasure in words like *fast-growing* and *sleek and speedy*. My efforts were being acknowledged; my hard work was paying off. This website was actually going to go somewhere, wasn't it? It was going to save me from the hell of the help desk.

At least, that's what I thought until I read the comments:

Vlad Popov—Philadelphia, PA
This is definitely an elaborate marketing scam by Fluttr themselves.

Gene Steinbach—Irvine, CA
Nah, seems like they'd be shooting themselves in the foot with this one.

Vlad Popov—Philadelphia, PA
No way it could be done by anyone else. Interface works so seamlessly with the app. Impossible to replicate externally.

Michael McCarthy—Seattle, WA
Hate to break it to you but there's no way Fluttr would do this. They employ the best of the best in terms of coders. This JerkAlert website is a slow and clunky POS.

Gene Steinbach—Irvine, CA
+1, Michael. "Sleek and speedy," my ass.

My heart thudded in my ears. I should've known better than to read these; nothing good ever comes from spending time in the comments section. But I couldn't unsee them, and now I was furious. How dare this internet rando call JerkAlert "slow and clunky"? As if Gene Steinbach or Michael McCarthy could do any better.

Though it's not like I knew them. Maybe they *could* code a better website than the one I'd put together. Maybe I was deluding myself, and JerkAlert really *was* a POS.

To be certain, I pulled the site up in my browser, only to find that it was indeed loading slowly, taking forever to perform searches and display images. But when I signed into the dashboard, it all made sense: traffic had more than quadrupled overnight, with thousands of new records added to the database and hundreds of new registered users. Visitors came from places as far away as London and Sydney, Hong Kong and Paris. JerkAlert had gone international.

So, naturally, the site was behaving sluggishly. When I built it, I'd never in my wildest dreams imagined it would reach this scope of influence, with thousands of people from all over the world interacting with it at once. If I wanted people to be impressed by how sleek and speedy my website was, I needed to make some changes. And I needed to do it now, before JerkAlert got a reputation as a "slow and clunky POS."

Josh would have to wait a little while longer for his laptop.

From: Melanie Strickland
To: Joshua Brewster
Subject: Minor Delay

Hi Josh,
I've hit a tiny snag while restoring your laptop. It's going to take a little while longer than normal to fix it, but you'll definitely have it back before the end of the day.
Thanks,
Melanie

Usually, I hated to send out emails like this. Being late made it seem like I was incompetent or couldn't deliver on my promises. But I was beginning to realize that it didn't really matter how well I performed at work. Whether I completed my tasks flawlessly or consistently screwed up, the Hatchlings would always treat me like trash. Case in point, Josh's response:

From: Joshua Brewster
To: Melanie Strickland
Subject: re: Minor Delay

Fucking figures.

Why should I continue to kill myself working hard for these ungrateful start-up founders? Even when I did everything right, Bob would defend them and scold me. I was much better off half-assing it around the office, prioritizing JerkAlert and making it the best it could possibly be. That's the only way I'd ever found a start-up of my own.

For the next couple of hours, I focused on optimizing my code, reconfiguring my server settings, and restructuring my database. It was the most I could do without upgrading my web hosting to a more expensive plan—which was definitely something I could *not* afford to do right now (or anytime in the foreseeable future). But it was more than sufficient, because as soon as I uploaded my changes, response times and page loads improved almost instantly.

Take that, Gene Steinbach and Michael McCarthy.

Feeling confident and accomplished, I moved on to the mind-numbing task of cleaning up Josh's infected laptop.

While the scanner searched for contaminated files, I read the BuzzFeed article for approximately the millionth time. And because I apparently enjoy making myself miserable, I went back to the comments section. Part of me had hoped to find people saying how speedy the site suddenly seemed, and berating Gene and Michael for their asinine remarks.

Of course, that wasn't happening. Instead, I found this gem:

Frankie Fanning—New York, NY
I'd say some frigid bitch made this website, but we all know girls can't code for shit.

My vision went blurry around the edges and my breath became ragged puffs of air.

We all know girls can't code for shit.

It's the kind of thing I always suspected men were thinking when they looked at me. Like when the guys at tech meetups told me I didn't look like a developer, or spent their time hitting on me instead of inquiring about my credentials. I'd even been aware of it back in college, when my classmates would ignore my suggestions during group work, and my professors would tell sexist jokes like I wasn't in the lecture hall.

To see it here, typed out in black-and-white, confirmed my worst fears: in this industry, I'd always be viewed as inferior, and it had nothing to do with my actual skill, and everything to do with my gender.

What I wanted right now, more than anything else in the world, was to tell everyone out there that a girl *was* responsible for creating this site. A girl had designed it, a girl had coded it, a girl was keeping it going through a period of tremendous growth.

And a girl was going to get rich off it.

My fingers flew to the keyboard, ready to type up a response to this asshole, Frankie Fanning. He was going to know exactly who he was dealing with: a woman who was no longer interested in taking anyone's shit. But as I sat there, stringing angry words together in a text box, I quickly realized that outing myself in the comments section of a BuzzFeed article was a terrible idea. Nothing good ever came from reacting in a moment of rage, and it certainly wouldn't reflect well on me as a woman, who already suffered the stigma of being "too emotional."

I needed to stay calm, to think this through, to devise a deliberate and effective plan for revealing my identity to the public. Closing my web browser and ignoring the comments section was a good first step.

The second step: consult Whitney. With her PR expertise, she'd know exactly what to do.

15

"Don't do it."

Whit's feelings about my desire to go public were unambiguous.

This was not the response I had hoped for. I'd envisioned squeals of delight, enthusiastic high fives, publicity plans plotted out on cocktail napkins. Instead, Whitney shook her head with disdain, as if I should've already known it was a stupid idea.

"Anonymity is part of the allure," she said. "Nobody knows who's posting what, or where JerkAlert even came from. Keeping your identity a secret will help generate buzz."

"Hasn't enough buzz already been generated?" Dani chimed in.

"This is nothing." Whit waved her hand dismissively and brought her wineglass to her lips. "Investors aren't gonna come running with cash in hand over one measly BuzzFeed article."

"It doesn't feel like nothing," I said. "Do you know how many unique visitors JerkAlert had yesterday? Three thousand, six hundred and fifteen."

"Is that more than you usually have?"

"Yeah. Like fifty times more."

"Wow," Lia said. "Do you know how that #JerkAlert hashtag got started?"

The smirk on Whit's red lips was all the answer we needed.

"It was you?"

"Hashtags are one of the best ways to launch an organic marketing campaign."

"But how did you get it to trend like that?"

"It wasn't hard. I picked some of the more heinous JerkAlert profiles and tagged a few influencers who I know are single and dating. They tagged their friends, who tagged their friends and so on, until it exploded." She sipped her wine. "I also hooked into #DickInTheDark."

"What?" That damn hashtag was just beginning to fade from the collective memory. The last thing I wanted was for Whit to resurrect those awful memes and connect them to my burgeoning tech venture.

"Calm down," she said, "it's no biggie. I just said things like, 'Avoid a #DickInTheDark with #JerkAlert.' It helped to increase visibility. Then I shot a casual email off to Kirra and said she might consider covering it for BuzzFeed. The rest is history."

Our server dropped by with a tray of sliders ordered off the happy hour menu for five bucks a pop.

"Here you are, ladies," he said, as he placed the dishes down in front of us. "Three beef, three veggie, and two crispy fish."

"Oh my God, these look amazing," Whitney said.

"My personal favorite is the fish." He crouched down slightly and leaned toward Whitney, as if she was the only person at the table. "But watch out for the jalapeños."

Never one to turn away from blatant flirtation, she bit back a smile. "Thanks for the warning, but I can handle the heat."

Dani didn't even try to contain her laughter at that cheesy line. It didn't faze Whit or the waiter, though. They held each other's gazes, steady and smoldering, until the woman at the next table loudly demanded more bread. As the waiter turned away to fetch a new basket, Whit's eyes stayed glued to his backside.

"The thing is," I said, "I've decided that I'd like to take credit for JerkAlert."

"And you will," Whit said. "Just give it a little more time. We need to draw out the suspense for as long as we can."

"Why?"

"The longer people don't know who's behind JerkAlert, the more people will offer up their own theories. That means more people posting about it on blogs and social media, more press coverage, more excitement. Speculation can work people up into a frenzy."

"Like with the iPhone," Dani said. "They always release as little information as possible before the official product launch."

"Exactly," Whit said. "There are literally hundreds of articles written about each new iPhone before anyone has any idea what it looks like or how it functions. And you see what those sales are like. People love a mystery."

Wasn't the whole point of JerkAlert to demystify the dating process? Anyone who spent their time researching a guy before they right-swiped most likely did not love a mystery. I must've looked skeptical, because Whitney sighed in that way she always did when she thought I was being, as she called it, a "philistine."

"How do you think Fluttr got so popular?" she asked.

"Word of mouth?" I shrugged and sank my teeth into a beef slider.

"In a way, yes. But it was all fueled by leads from the Fluttr marketing team. They planted rumors about a revolutionary new dating app that was coming soon. They created an artificial waitlist to make people feel special when they were granted an invite. They sent out vague emails and teaser tweets for weeks beforehand. By the time it went live, there were already thousands of users who were dying to get access. And what's so incredible about the whole thing is that there's absolutely nothing unique about Fluttr. It's exactly like every other dating app out there. It's only popular because of the buzz.

"But," she added, "you have a leg up, because JerkAlert really *is* unique. Now you just have to craft an image that will make investors hungry. Then you cash in."

Dollar signs danced before my eyes. Solid financial backing would change my life, dramatically.

Goodbye, help desk.

Goodbye, student loans.

Hello, start-up success.

"How are those sliders tasting?" The waiter sidled up to Whitney, interrupting my daydream.

"Delicious." Whit seductively sucked a drop of sriracha mayo off the tip of her finger. "Can we get some more napkins?"

"Absolutely," he said, and dashed off toward the service station.

Lia pulled her phone out of her purse. "So, I need your opinion, guys. It's about Cabo."

"We already told you," Dani said, sounding mildly exasperated. "Jay is not going to bail."

"Oh, I know that." She laughed, like the mere thought of him bailing was absurd. "I was totally overreacting the other night. I blame the champagne. Anyway, the resort we're staying at has this beautiful spa on the premises."

She swiped through her phone and showed us the photos from the Villa de Oro Resort & Spa's website. Massage tables lined up on beachfront platforms, gentle aquamarine waves battering the shoreline in the background.

"It looks incredible," I said, tamping down that familiar pang of jealousy.

"Well, since he's been so busy lately with work, I was thinking it might be nice for him to unplug completely for a little while, and I was planning to surprise him with a gift of a day at the spa. Do you think that's too cheesy?"

"No, not at all. It sounds really romantic."

"Great! So, my question is—should I do a couple's massage *and* a facial, or just stick with the massage and that's it?"

"Um..." I exchanged glances with Dani and Whit. "It's hard to say without knowing what he likes."

"It's really a bummer we couldn't meet him on Saturday night," Dani added.

"Yeah," Lia said, "he was really sorry he missed it."

Whit pursed her lips. "Sounds like he's the one who should be treating *you* to a spa day, and not the other way around."

"Well, he's treating me to an entire tropical vacation." When Whit rolled her eyes, Lia took a deep breath and calmly said, "Look, he apologized. I was completely honest with him about how disappointed I was and how he hurt me. He listened, he said he was sorry, and I've forgiven him. We've moved on. Relationships don't work if you hold on to grudges."

"Suit yourself." Whit polished off her crispy fish slider right as the waiter returned with a six-inch stack of napkins.

"Here you are," he said, placing the whole pile in front of her. "Anything else I can get for you?"

Whitney touched the tip of her tongue to her top lip. "I don't know. Is there?"

"I think we're good," I said, probably a little too loudly. Normally, I found Whitney's sex kitten act amusing, but tonight I didn't have the patience.

"You know what," I said, turning to Lia, "you can't go wrong with a massage. I say stick with that."

"Thanks." Lia smiled and tucked her phone back in her bag. "How are things going with Alex?"

"Yeah, he's super nice, Mel," Dani said.

"And hot," Whit added. "Good job snagging that one."

Alex had really charmed my friends, hadn't he? They all looked so impressed, so happy for me. It almost pained me to sully their image of Mr. Wonderful.

"Things are not so great with Alex."

Their mouths fell open in shock. "What happened?" Lia asked.

"I found him on JerkAlert. Apparently, he's got a reputation as a liar." I loaded his profile on my phone and passed it around for all the girls to see.

"Oh, that's bad," Lia said.

Dani and Whit weren't as concerned.

"That seems a little vague," Dani said. "I'm not sure you should dismiss him over one nebulous accusation."

"Yeah," Whit said. "You can't believe everything you read on JerkAlert, anyway."

"But why would anyone lie about what they post there?"

"Why would anyone lie about what they post anywhere? The internet is filled with people making shit up for the hell of it."

Whit had a point. I thought about the comments I'd read on that BuzzFeed article. All those men posting garbage opinions like they were facts, when in reality, they had no clue what the hell they were talking about. Was JerkAlert nothing more than an elaborate comments section?

"If you can't trust what you read on JerkAlert," I said, "then isn't it pretty much worthless?"

"Of course not," Whit said. "Its value isn't in the legitimacy of its reviews. It makes no promises of authenticity, or guarantees about finding a trustworthy partner. JerkAlert is valuable because it provides a safe, communal space where women can vent about their shitty interactions with men. It's purely about catharsis."

Catharsis. That's what had driven me to create it in the first place, wasn't it? I'd wanted so badly to tell the whole world about the guys who'd done me wrong. Brandon from Brooklyn. Joe from Murray Hill. Alex from FiDi.

Except it turned out I was wrong about that last one.

"For what it's worth," she continued, "I really liked Alex. And you know I don't ever like anybody."

"I liked him, too," Lia said.

"So did I," added Dani. "He really struck me as a straightforward kind of guy."

"You could always talk to him about it," Lia said. "Tell him how you're feeling and ask him what's going on."

"I'm not going to tell him I found him on JerkAlert," I said. "That's just...weird, isn't it? Like I was spying on him or something."

No one answered. Which was an answer in itself.

Dani reached into her purse and dropped some cash onto the table. "Well, ladies, it's been real, but unfortunately, I need to cut out a bit early."

"What're you up to?"

"I've got a date."

"Ooh!" Whitney clapped her hands together. "With who?"

"Her name is Yvelise, she's twenty-eight, she lives in Astoria, and she's getting her PhD in Neural Science at NYU."

"Sounds like a match made in heaven," Lia said.

"Hopefully. We've been talking for a while now. I have high expectations for this one."

"Did you meet her on Iris?" I asked.

"Nope. Iris shut down."

"Oh, no. What happened?"

"Who knows," Dani said, shrugging one shoulder. "You know how it is with these start-ups—here today, gone tomorrow. So I'm back on Fluttr."

Of course.

"Wish me luck," she called, before heading out the door.

We crossed our fingers and said, "Good luck!" As soon as she was gone, our waiter materialized. "Are you ladies leaving already?"

"Not just yet." Whit looked at us. "Want another round?"

"Sure. And maybe one more plate of those beef sliders?"

"You got it." He winked, a gesture I usually find cheesy and repulsive. Whitney didn't mind, though. She returned the wink and wiggled her fingers at him as he walked away.

The three of us lingered awhile, enjoying the cheap eats and the conversation. Soon, Whitney's flirtation started paying off; the waiter brought us warm chocolate donuts, free of charge, and when he finally brought our check at the end of the night, he'd slashed at least half the drinks from the bill.

We placed our cards in the leather folder, and as he swung by to pick it up, the waiter knelt down next to Whitney and murmured, "My shift ends in ten minutes. What're you up to tonight?"

"Actually," she said, "I might hang around until you get off."

"Cool," he said. "And then, hopefully, I can return the favor."

Barf.

With a quick hug and a promise to text us when she got home to make sure this waiter didn't do something shady, we said our goodbyes. Lia and I walked down Stanton Street, lamenting how early we had to wake up in the morning, and cursing ourselves for agreeing to that last round of drinks.

At the corner of Delancey and Essex, we parted ways; I was heading underground to catch the F train, while she was going to walk the rest of the way toward her apartment in Chinatown.

"I'll see you on Thursday," I said. "What are we doing this week?"

"Krav Maga. It looks intense."

"Why do we only ever pick intense workouts?"

"Because they're cheap."

We laughed and hugged, and before I ducked into the subway station, Lia said, "Mel, I really think you should talk to Alex. You don't have to tell him you found him on JerkAlert, but at least let him know what you're thinking. He has no idea what's going on. And honestly, you have no idea what's going on, either. This review could be a total fake. And even if it isn't, people do change."

"I know," I said. "You're probably right."

"I'm definitely right. He really seems like such a great guy. Let him at least give you a chance to prove himself."

The whole ride home, I mulled over Lia's words. I was giving far too much credence to the words of an anonymous stranger. Which was crazy, considering I already knew you should never trust anything you read on the internet. Why was I ignoring this tried-and-true advice, simply because the words appeared on JerkAlert?

When I emerged from the train station in Brooklyn, I sent Alex a text:

Hey. I know you're probably working right now, or maybe you're sleeping, but I wanted to tell you something. So whenever you have a sec, let me know.

Almost instantly, he responded: I'm free now.

Oh, no. It was too soon. I hadn't had enough time to compose my thoughts. I typed out a text, then deleted it and tried again. Over and over, trying to find the perfect words to camouflage the real question I needed to ask: *Can I trust you?*

Then I realized, this wasn't the time for pretense, or for perfectly worded questions. It was the time for honest, raw connection.

My finger slid to the call button.

"Hey." His voice was warm and thick like honey.

"Hey." *Take a deep breath. Don't think so hard. Just say what you're feeling.* "I'm sorry I was so…weird today."

"It's okay. I'm sorry I didn't text you last night. I know how it must look, especially after you caught me trying to sneak out in the morning without saying goodbye. I'm completely preoccupied with work right now. But I promise, it doesn't mean that I don't really like you. Because I do."

"I really like you, too." *But can I trust you?*

"Let me make it up to you," he said. "They're upgrading the servers tomorrow night, so I won't be able to work. Come to my place. I'll cook us dinner, okay?"

If I went to his place and let him cook me dinner, I knew exactly where that would lead: back to bed. Which was a dangerous proposition. Did I really want to dig myself any deeper without first finding out if he was who he said he was?

Considering our chemistry between the sheets, though, the offer was mighty tempting. I thought of our last sexual encounter, the sheer ecstasy of it. And all I knew was I wanted to feel that way again.

"Okay."

"Great. I'll see you tomorrow."

"See ya."

I ended the call without asking the question I really needed to ask.

But it wasn't a question he could answer, anyway. The only person who knew if I could trust him was me.

16

Alex lived in a luxury apartment building on John Street. The lobby had white marble floors and wavy crystal chandeliers and abstract art on the walls. Compared to my dumpy walk-up in Brooklyn, this place was a palace.

After the doorman (a doorman!) waved me in, I took the elevator to the thirtieth floor, following the faint scent of bacon and onions until I reached apartment 3017. Alex had propped his door open, and when I entered, I found him standing behind the stove, midsauté. Soft background music filled the room, something rhythmic and heavy on maracas. He flipped the contents of the frying pan to the beat.

"Whatever you're cooking," I said, "it smells amazing."

"Hey, there." He set the pan down and fiddled with the oven dial. "I didn't hear you come in. How are you?" Wiping his hands on a dish towel, he came out from behind the breakfast bar and gave me a warm, drawn-out kiss.

"I'm good now."

"Can I interest you in a glass of wine?"

"Absolutely."

He pulled a bottle of red from a wine rack—an actual wine rack built into his cabinets; not an upcycled dresser drawer—and poured us two glasses. We raised them in a toast, and Alex said, "Thank you for coming tonight."

"Thank you for having me." The first sip went down smooth. I craned my neck to peer into the frying pan. "What're you making?"

"My specialty—*arroz con gandules*. It's rice with pigeon peas and pork." His face blanched. "You eat pork, right?"

I nodded. "I eat all the things."

"Good. I probably should've asked you about that before I planned the meal. I'm making a salad, too. Is that all right?"

"It's wonderful. Thank you."

Alex let out a breath and returned to his station behind the stove. "I hope it turns out okay." He seemed nervous, bouncing back and forth between the frying pan and the well-worn cookbook splayed open on the counter, *Puerto Rican Cookery*.

"Can I help with anything?"

"No." There was that dazzling smile again. "You just sit back and relax. Enjoy your wine."

I hoisted myself onto a barstool and watched as he selected a ripe tomato from the basket beside his refrigerator. With a shiny chef's knife, he sliced it into even segments and placed it in a bowl, repeating it over and over until all the tomatoes were gone. His movements were careful and precise, the same way he'd washed those lava rocks after the fire. The same way he'd touched my body.

"So, this dish is your specialty, huh?" I asked.

"Yeah. Well, kind of. My dad taught me how to make it,

but it's been a few years, so I'm a little rusty. Cooking isn't exactly like riding a bike."

"You didn't have to go to all this trouble, honestly."

"It's no trouble," he said, quickly. "I love to cook, it's just I don't have much time to practice. I always wind up ordering takeout. This is really a treat, to be able to cook for you."

"It's a treat to be served. I rarely ever cook for myself."

"Do you enjoy cooking?"

"Not in the slightest."

He laughed. "Well, then, I can do all the cooking in our relationship."

"And I can do all the ordering of the takeout."

"Sounds good." He poured a few ingredients into the pan and covered it tightly with a lid. "My parents are like that. Mom can't stand cooking, so Dad made us dinner almost every night. They've been happily married for almost thirty years, so if it works for them, it could work for us."

I sipped my wine, hiding my giddy grin behind the glass. Silly as it may have been, it felt good to hear him talk as if we had a future together, to divvy up imaginary household chores and compare ourselves to his parents who'd been married for years. Jokes like these were reserved for girlfriends, not for meaningless flings.

That is, if it wasn't just smooth talk.

He pulled his phone from his pocket and grimaced. "Goddammit," he muttered, tapping away at the screen. "Sorry, this'll only take a second."

"No problem." I continued to drink, but my excitement gave way to annoyance with every passing second he spent silently engrossed in his phone. Who could he be texting so fervently? It couldn't be about work—there was a planned outage tonight; he'd said it himself.

It was funny: modern technology could forge a connection between two people on opposite ends of the earth, but it could just as easily drive a wedge between two people standing side by side in the same room. The more Alex scrolled through his phone, the more disconnected we became. His body was only two feet away from me, but his mind was off somewhere completely unknown.

Eager to regain his attention, I tapped my fingernails against my wineglass in time to the music. Then I started to hum along with the tune. Finally, I asked, "Who is this?"

There was a pause, like he didn't hear me. A moment later, without looking up, he said, "What?"

"The music. Who's this playing?"

"Oh, I dunno. It's just some Spotify playlist."

"What's the name of it?"

A look of irritation splashed across his face. "Gimme a second and I'll look it up."

"Never mind." My voice was as sharp as a razor blade. "I don't mean to be a pain in the ass."

He looked at me, eyes wide and contrite. "No, no, I'm sorry." He winced. "You're right. I *do* say that a lot." He dropped his phone on the countertop in frustration. "It's just more of the same. Work."

"I thought the servers were being upgraded tonight."

"Well, someone has to monitor the upgrades, make sure everything's going according to plan. Greg said he'd do it, but I guess there's some error message that keeps popping up and God forbid he fucking Google it." He winced again. "Sorry." And again.

"It's okay. Things happen."

"I don't understand why he can't figure it out for himself. I told him you were coming over tonight, so he knows I'm busy."

"He knows I'm here?" I flashed back to last Thursday, when Greg was giving me that creepy stare. This explained why he'd noted my existence for the very first time: he knew Alex and I were...doing something. Though last Thursday we hadn't done anything yet, except have lunch. "What exactly have you told him?"

Alex shifted his weight from one foot to the other. "That we're, you know, hanging out."

Ugh. The dreaded "hanging out." It connoted any number of things in guy-speak, all of which were firmly in the realm of "casual."

Then again, we'd only been "hanging out" for a week. What did I expect, for Alex to announce to the entire office that we were involved in a serious, monogamous relationship?

I mean, it's not like I would've minded. But it was completely insane to think about a commitment this early on.

His phone buzzed against the countertop again. "Are you serious?" He stabbed at the screen and grumbled, "Just fucking Google it, Greg."

"This is the story of my life," I said. "I can't tell you how many times someone comes to the help desk with a problem that could be easily solved with a Google search."

"I'm sure it happens all the time. To be honest, I don't understand how half these Hatchlings got their funding. Aren't start-up founders supposed to be innovative and resourceful?" Alex shook his head and sipped from his wineglass. "Sometimes I wish I'd never quit my last job. It was soul-sucking but at least I worked with competent people. I wasn't harassed by idiots on my one night off." He gestured angrily at his phone. "And if I'd stayed there, I wouldn't be on the verge of losing my paycheck in six weeks."

"Are you really worried you guys aren't gonna get funded?"

"The way things are going? I don't know. I always thought I wanted to get in on the ground floor at a start-up, but the whole experience with Hatch is making me want to run back to corporate America."

I reached across the table and touched my fingertips to the back of his hand. "You know, you told me Hatch was just a stepping-stone to bigger and better things for you. So maybe it sucks right now, but it's not gonna last forever. Soon you'll be on to the next thing. And when the time is right, you'll create the perfect opportunity."

Alex looked at me, his eyes meeting mine, all traces of irritation gone. "You're right. My time at Hatch has its purpose."

"It does."

"If I'd never started working at Hatch, I'd never have met you." He covered my fingers with his other hand and gave them a gentle squeeze, sending a ripple of joy through my entire being.

"You never know," I countered. "Maybe we would've met on Fluttr."

"Do you think you would've swiped right on me?"

"It depends on what picture you used."

"See for yourself." He picked up his phone and loaded his camera roll, swiping through and selecting a photo. "This was my default profile pic."

One glimpse at his screen and my stomach dropped to my

feet. Because I suddenly remembered that I'd seen this photo before. On Alex's JerkAlert profile.

I opened my mouth to speak, but had trouble forming words.

"It's that bad, huh?" he asked.

"No. It's just..." I trailed off, unable to finish the sentence, afraid the quiver in my voice would reveal all my insecurities.

"Your silence speaks volumes." He smirked, then swiped through to the next photo. "Here's the one I used before that. Any better?"

This time, it was a different image of him looking like his usual gorgeous, dapper self—but he was standing beside an even more gorgeous hazel-eyed brunette. They looked like they'd just shared a hilarious secret. His arm was wrapped tightly around her shoulder.

"Are you serious?"

"What?"

"This was really the profile pic you used?"

He glanced at the phone and then back at me. "Yeah. Is something wrong with it?"

"You're canoodling with a beautiful woman."

"We're not canoodling." He looked aghast. "This is my sister! We look exactly the same. See?"

I snatched the phone from his hand and studied the screen. Upon closer inspection, they *did* look alike. Same dancing eyes, same disarming smile, same olive skin and curly black hair. He wasn't being rude or obnoxious with this picture; he was merely clueless.

"It doesn't matter," I said. "Fluttr users make split-second decisions. They're not going to take the time to figure out if she's your sister or your ex-girlfriend. A woman in the photo is almost always an automatic left swipe."

He pressed the home button to dim his phone screen. "Then we never would've met."

"Simply because of a picture."

"I told you, Fluttr's the worst."

"It is." I couldn't help but think about the dozens—or more like hundreds—of men I'd left-swiped because they were oblivious to the unspoken rules of Fluttr photo etiquette.

"Okay. I showed you mine," he said. "Now you show me yours."

All of a sudden, I felt shy, afraid of being judged. Even though countless men had already seen this picture and made the instantaneous decision to swipe left or right on my face, having Alex right here next to me, delivering his verdict in person, made me anxious. Especially knowing that I'd have swiped left on him without a second thought.

I didn't have much of a choice, though. He was standing there, eyebrows raised, waiting for me to hand over the goods. So I tapped my screen and showed him my selfie. I'd snapped it on a whim, a couple of months ago, while I was walking home from work at dusk. The light had been perfect, all soft and golden, and my hair was in an unusually cooperative state. I thought it was flattering.

Alex stared at it, silent and unblinking. *He hates it.*

"It's nothing special," I said.

"It's stunning."

Oh.

"Your lips are just..." His gaze traveled from the face on my phone to my face in the flesh. "They're perfect."

Instinctively, my fingertips went to my lips. Alex looked

hungry. Like he'd been starving for days and my body was a satisfying meal.

He moved closer, eyes still fixed on my quivering lips. Then his mouth was on mine and my hands were in his hair and we were wrestling frantically out of our clothes. We barely even made it to his bed.

When we were finished, he kissed me hard, then said, "Total fucking right-swipe."

I giggled, still dizzy from the sex. But as the world steadied itself around me, I tuned back into my surroundings—including the acrid smell emanating from the kitchen. "Is something burning?"

"Oh, shit. The rice!" Alex launched his naked body out of bed and yanked the smoking pan of *arroz con gandules* from the stovetop. One peek under the lid and his disgusted face said it all. "Maybe we should order in."

While he summoned a delivery from Adrienne's Pizza Bar, I threw on my bra and panties and went to the bathroom to freshen up. When I emerged, Alex was sitting on the couch in his boxers, already engrossed in his phone.

"Greg still bugging you?" I asked, settling in next to him.

"Nah. I wasn't responding to him while you and I were… you know." He glanced up and flashed a mischievous smile. "So eventually he stopped texting me."

"Maybe he finally figured out how to use Google."

"Miracles do happen," he said, adding, "It's Café con Leche, by the way."

"What?"

"The music. You asked for the name of the Spotify playlist before."

"Oh, right. Thanks."

Tossing his phone aside, he looked up at me, eyes shimmering in the dim light. No one had ever looked at me that way before, like I was adored. In that moment, I wanted to believe every word that ever came out of his mouth.

"Wanna watch something?" He pulled me close beside him, wrapping his arm around me as he turned on the TV and started scrolling through Netflix. Whether or not Alex was sweet-talking me, I still reveled in the tenderness of his touch, his affection, his lingering gaze. Having someone to cuddle with, someone so complimentary and kind, was a long-wished-for comfort. So I tried my best to lose myself in the moment, watching an Ali Wong stand-up routine and stealing kisses between sips of wine.

About twenty minutes later, the buzzer rang, and my stomach grumbled at the thought of artisanal pizza. I paused the show while Alex squirmed into his T-shirt, and the buzzer rang again. "Coming!" he yelled, as he ran to the door.

But there was no piping-hot pizza waiting on the other side. There was only Greg, standing in the hallway with that signature slack-jawed look on his face.

"S'up, man?"

In a flash, I yanked a cushion from the back of the couch and held it before me like a shield. Then I froze, thinking if I stayed perfectly still, Greg wouldn't notice me sitting there in my underwear.

"S'up, Melanie."

Too late.

Alex whipped his head around, panic in his eyes, before turning back to Greg. "What are you doing here?"

"You stopped answering my texts."

"Right. Because you said you had this upgrade covered tonight."

"Yeah, but all I thought I had to do was watch it. I didn't think anything was gonna, like, happen."

"Are you—" Alex stopped himself midsentence, then scrubbed a hand over his face and took a deep, cleansing breath. When he spoke again, his voice was calm. "Okay. What's wrong now?"

Greg barreled his way into the apartment, sliding his laptop out of his messenger bag and popping it open on the kitchen counter. "It keeps saying it can't connect."

"What can't connect?"

"The database."

"Did you run a traceroute?"

"A what?"

Alex raked his hands through his hair, clearly exasperated with his partner's ineptitude. After a moment of tense silence, he said, "Let me take a look."

Tapping furiously at the keyboard, Alex cursed under his breath. Seconds passed, then minutes, and eventually the two of them were so absorbed in whatever crisis was unfolding on the computer screen, it was like I had ceased to exist. So I took the opportunity to escape to the bathroom, holding the couch cushion in front of me with one hand and plucking my clothes up off the floor with the other.

Once I was safely behind the closed door, I buried my face in the cushion and bit back a scream. Why was this guy always showing up at the most inconvenient times? If he weren't so painfully stupid, I'd have thought Greg was intentionally trying to sabotage whatever Alex and I had going on. But clearly, he was totally incompetent. He couldn't even fix a simple networking issue without Alex holding his hand the whole way through.

Poor Alex. Stuck in a failing business partnership with the world's most useless start-up bro.

I got dressed and fixed my hair, allowing my blood pressure to return to a reasonable rate. As the sound of my pulse pounding in my ears began to subside, I tuned into the voices in the kitchen, so easily discernible through the cheap drywall of an overpriced Manhattan apartment.

"You're the king, man," Greg said. "Fucking Rico Suave!"

Alex shushed him. "Keep it down."

"Dude, you're so fucking smooth. I didn't believe you when you said she was coming over. But you did it. You won, man!"

You won?

I picked up the couch cushion, hugging it to my chest, waiting for Alex to respond. Surely, he would jump to my defense and tell Greg to get bent. Because I was more than some brag-worthy sexual conquest. I was not just some trophy to be won.

But all he said was, "Yup."

Yup?

What the hell was that supposed to mean?

Apparently, Alex didn't have a problem with Hatch's frat house culture, after all. Sure, he criticized it to my face, but when he was alone with the boys, he was more than happy to play along.

I pushed open the bathroom door and returned the cushion to its rightful place on the back of the couch. In my peripheral vision, I could see Alex watching me, but I couldn't bring myself to meet his gaze.

"Everything okay?" he asked.

"Yeah," I said, but the moment I opened my mouth, the buzzer rang, swallowing my lie.

This time, it was the pizza, and as soon as Alex set the box on the counter, Greg flipped it open. He grabbed a slice and crammed it in his gaping maw, snorting as he chewed, like some sort of zoo animal. My stomach turned.

"Let me get some plates." Alex's voice sounded weary, resigned to the fact that Greg was here, eating our pizza, disrupting our date.

"I think I'm gonna head out," I said, slipping into my shoes.

"What? Why?" Alex followed me to the door. "The pizza just got here."

"I'm not that hungry."

My gaze flicked toward Greg, whose sauce-smothered lips were curled in an infuriating smirk. "Smashin' and dashin', huh, Melanie?"

"Shut up, Greg," Alex snapped, eager to play Prince Charming now that I was here to witness it.

I slung my purse over my shoulder and opened the door, ready to flee, but Alex squeezed my arm and gently pulled me back toward him.

"Hey," he whispered, his breath tickling my ear. "I'm really sorry about this. This upgrade is completely screwed up now and if it bombs, Vijay's gonna flip."

"It's fine. I get it."

"I'll make it up to you, I swear."

I nodded, knowing full well this was just more of his insincere and meaningless smooth talk.

But when he kissed me goodbye, my whole body felt limp and tingly. And there was nothing phony about that.

17

On my way to the subway, I grabbed a slice of pizza from a hole-in-the-wall on Fulton Street. Despite what I'd told Alex, I actually was hungry. I just couldn't stomach the thought of staying there, pretending I hadn't overheard them discussing me like I was some sexual prize.

When I arrived home, Vanessa was sprawled on the couch, one hand clutching her phone, the other hand wrapped firmly around a bottle of rosé. As soon as I shut the door behind me, she asked, "Have you ever heard of this website called JerkAlert?"

My feet froze to the floor. "Um...yeah. How'd you find out about it?"

"It's everywhere. Don't you read BuzzFeed?"

"Right. Of course."

"Anyway, there are some seriously messed-up guys out there." Her thumb tapped and scrolled against her screen. "Including the guy I was supposed to go out with tonight."

She held it up for me to see:

Name: Justin
Age: 29
Location: Williamsburg
Review: Our first date was going great until he asked to "fingerbang" me in the bar bathroom. When I told him no, he called me ugly, then ditched me with the bill.

"Oh my God," I said.

"I canceled as soon as I saw the review." Vanessa took a swig from her wine bottle. "Why didn't Vilma know about this? She is so fired."

It pleased me to know that JerkAlert was of more use to women on the New York City dating scene than an overpriced, overhyped matchmaker. So much for Whit's claim that the site was purely about catharsis.

"You should demand your money back," I said.

"Maybe." She fiddled with her phone for another moment. "I looked up Ray, too."

Not Ray. He seemed like such a nice guy, so genuinely kind and helpful. Not to mention, he had the keys to our apartment. What if he was sneaking into our rooms and rifling through our underwear drawers when we weren't home?

Ugh.

"What does it say about him?" I asked.

"Nothing." Her lips turned up in a coy little smile. "He's not in there."

"Wow." I was shocked. Not because Ray's reputation was clear, but because of the way Vanessa looked right now: totally lovestruck. "He *is* a great guy."

"Yeah." She took another swig of wine, not bothering to

wipe the resulting dribble from her chin. "You were right about him."

"I'm glad to hear you say that."

"If he moved out of Bensonhurst, I would totally consider dating him."

Vanessa may have been lovestruck, but she was still Vanessa.

"I suppose it is less than ideal that he's still living with his mother," I said.

"It's bullshit."

"Okay, but—"

"I mean, he's pushing thirty. And I've discovered that being a building super pays surprisingly well, so it's not like he can't afford to move out on his own. Or in with a roommate. Or *anywhere* that isn't under his mother's roof."

"Have you ever asked him why he lives there?"

"To 'save money.'" She rolled her eyes, using sarcastic air quotes, as if saving money was a ridiculous notion. "He's waiting until he gets married to move out. By then, he hopes to have enough for a down payment on a house. Good luck in this market, am I right?"

"Well, that's kind of...cute, I guess. In an old-school way."

"It's kind of stupid," she muttered, scowling into her wine bottle.

"He's being responsible. Though I do think it's important to live with someone before you marry them."

Her face flushed pink, the furrow deepening between her brows.

"My point is," I continued, "if this is the only thing keeping you from pursuing a relationship with Ray, maybe don't let it."

"What do you mean?"

"Maybe dive in and start dating him, anyway. He can't live

with his mother forever. And, you know, he could change his mind."

"Men don't change their minds." Her hands tightened around the neck of the bottle, so hard that her knuckles turned white. "Men don't change, period."

"Sometimes they do."

"Well, I'm not gonna jump into something with him and get all attached and then discover he's one of the ones that don't. I already did that once. And it was horrible."

"Bad breakup?"

She tilted the lip of the bottle toward her mouth, paused, then said, "Bad divorce."

As she guzzled the wine, I struggled to hide my shock. "I didn't realize you were ever married."

"It's not something I like to advertise, you know. I prefer to pretend that phase of my life didn't actually happen. I was really young and really stupid." She sighed and looked up toward the ceiling. "The marriage only lasted for three months, anyway. At first, I was super happy, but he turned out to be a huge shithead. I walked away with a big lump of cash for all my troubles, but honestly, it wasn't worth it."

"I'm sorry," I said, because I didn't know what else to say.

"It's okay. I'm fine now. But I've learned my lesson. Don't expect guys to change for you. That's why I usually vet them so carefully before I get involved. Ray was…an exception."

Vanessa pursed her lips, staring off into space with doleful eyes. It all made sense now, why she had such impossibly high standards. She was understandably reluctant to commit to a man again, afraid of going down another dead-end road on her journey toward the happily-ever-after.

Surely, Ray was a thousand times better than whatever shithead she'd married. But it wasn't the time to try to convince her of that. Not when she was two-thirds of the way into a bottle of Barefoot Pink Moscato. So instead of talking, I patted her shoulder. Just to let her know that I was there, listening.

She took a deep, shuddering breath, then blinked at me. "Anyway, what about your man?"

"Alex? What about him?"

"Have you looked him up on JerkAlert?"

Ugh.

"Yes."

"And?"

There was nothing I wanted to do less than rehash this with Vanessa. But like Alex had told me, my silence spoke volumes. In a flash, she loaded the search screen.

"How old is he?" she asked.

"Twenty-six, but—"

"And he lives in FiDi, right?"

"Right." I buried my head in my hands, unwilling to look at the profile I'd already viewed well over a hundred times since Sunday.

"Oh." Her voice was ominous. I peeked through my fingers and saw her reading the screen with a disapproving grimace. "Well, that's not good."

"I know. At first, I wasn't sure if I should believe it. People lie all the time on the internet."

"But why would two different people lie about the same thing?"

"What?" I snatched the phone from her hand and scrolled through the page. To my horror, someone had posted a second review.

Review: lying scumbag.

"This wasn't there before," I said, panic rising in my throat. "I mean, there used to just be one review. Now there's two."

Vanessa clucked her tongue. "He's got a reputation."

"And it's so vague." I stared at the words on the screen, willing them to reveal some hidden meaning. "I wish there was more information. *Scumbag* is such a harsh word, you know? What did he do that was so bad?"

"Can you message the women through JerkAlert? Ask them what happened."

"No, I purposely didn't build that feature." *Shut up, shut up, shut up.* "I mean, that's not something you can do on the site. The whole point is that it's supposed to be anonymous, without a messaging system. Otherwise, guys would start sending harassing messages to women who posted stuff about them."

"Oh. That's too bad. It would be really helpful to get some more info." She chewed on the inside of her cheek, thinking. "Do you know anything about his ex-girlfriends?"

"No."

"Have you Google stalked him to get more dirt?"

"No!" I don't know why I acted scandalized by this question; it's not like every woman didn't occasionally Google stalk their dates. Or their boyfriends. Or their boyfriends' exes. "Not yet, anyway."

"If I were you, I'd get on that, ASAP." She swigged from her bottle and suppressed a belch. "But right now, *I* need to go to bed."

Honestly, so did I. It was creeping up on midnight, and I had to wake up early for work in the morning.

Sleep was hard to come by, though. My mind raced with panicky thoughts, trying to piece together all the bits of information I'd accumulated over the past few days. There was the JerkAlert profile, both the old review and the new one. There was his weird relationship with Greg and the Hatchlings—how he complained about the frat culture in private, but failed to publicly call it out.

Then there were the convenient excuses he had; work was always to blame for everything. You know who else always used work as an excuse? My dad. And look how well his marriage worked out.

Lying scumbag.

My jaw throbbed from clenching my teeth. It was painful, being in the dark like this. Not knowing if I was being lied to, or who was telling the truth. It felt like my life was completely out of my control.

There was only one thing left to do: just fucking Google it.

I pulled out my phone and started typing every combo of every keyword I could think of that might provide me with valuable information.

Alex Hernandez girlfriend.

Alex Hernandez New York girlfriend.

Alex Hernandez lying scumbag.

But nothing turned up. There were so many people named Alex Hernandez in New York City alone, it was virtually impossible to find out anything about him.

If only I'd built in a messaging system, like Vanessa had mentioned. Then I'd be able to contact these women and ask them exactly what they meant by these comments. I knew it would never work, though. The whole allure of JerkAlert was that it was a safe space for women. Introduce DMs, and it'd undoubtedly turn into a free-for-all of abuse and harassment.

Then it hit me: I *could* message them. Users who registered with JerkAlert were required to provide an email address. It was my way of preventing spammers from flooding the site with gibberish. Email addresses were hidden from other users, but because I owned the database, I had unfettered access to them.

Sure, it could've been construed as a violation of trust between a webmistress and her visitors. But honestly, wasn't that what the spirit of JerkAlert was all about? Women helping women to steer clear of lying scumbags. If they'd been wronged by Alex Hernandez, surely they'd want to help me avoid the same fate.

Once I'd convinced myself that swiping these email addresses would not only be virtuous, but essential, I flipped open my laptop and queried the JerkAlert database, pulling data for all users who'd logged reviews to Alex's profile.

My search returned exactly one record. Meaning the same woman had written both reviews, at different times. And her email address was jboogie2592@gmail.com.

Now I could find out the whole story.

With shaky fingers, I opened my browser and pasted the address into a new email. But when it was time to compose the body of the message, I froze. Because what was I actually supposed to say to this stranger?

Dear JBoogie,

You don't know me and I don't know you, but I happened across your email address…somewhere. Anyway, a little birdie told me you used to date Alex Hernandez, and that he treated you like crap. Care to elaborate on why you think he should never be trusted?

Thanks!
Melanie

No. This was a terrible, horrible idea.

There had to be a better way to find out the truth. Like, maybe, coming right out and asking Alex about it.

Or, better yet, Googling this woman's email address.

I deleted my draft and typed "jboogie2592" into the search bar. The first result was a Twitter account:

> **j*boogie @jboogie2592 nyc**
> 25 | sagittarius | nyu stern mba candidate | i tweet about beer, books, and bad dates

The profile photo was a Bitmoji avatar wearing a dragon costume.

It didn't give me much to go on, but it seemed like a promising start. I scrolled through the feed, passing right over the Goodreads reviews and Brew York retweets, looking for the latest news on JBoogie's bad dates. Finally, I found one from Sunday evening:

> is there anything more cathartic than logging some douchebag on #jerkalert?

No, I thought, *but I'd love to know why you did it.*

I continued to scroll, looking for clues. It turned out JBoogie was pretty funny, and her takes on the NYC dating scene were spot-on. She took screencaps of her cringeworthy Fluttr exchanges and chronicled her romantic disappointments in a way that was sharp, sincere, and totally relatable.

After ten minutes or so of reading her tweets, I felt a kinship with her. I wanted to take her out for drinks and commiserate with her about how shitty guys were and how much better off we were without them in our lives. We would've understood each other. In an alternate universe, I could even see us being friends.

When I happened across a tweet from a couple of weeks back, it was almost like she was speaking directly to me.

so sick of men and their empty apologies.

Without even thinking, I tapped the little conversation bubble and typed:

I feel this tweet hard.

After I sent the reply into the ether, I had a sudden twinge of regret. Should I really have been interacting with the woman I'd just Google stalked? As far as she knew, I was some random internet stranger who'd stumbled across her Twitter profile by following the #craftbeer hashtag. She had no idea that I'd hunted her down in a depraved moment of jealousy and paranoia. What I was doing was wrong and dishonest and, frankly, weird.

It felt even weirder when she liked my reply.

The right thing to do would've been to close the browser window, shut down my laptop, and go to sleep. To forget all about JBoogie and her Twitter account.

And I swear, that's what I was about to do.

But then my phone buzzed with a text from Alex: I'm so sorry about tonight.

Of course he was. He was always sorry.

I was so sick of men and their empty apologies.

Ignoring his message, I tossed my phone aside. Instead, I

went back to jboogie2592's Twitter profile and clicked Follow. Seconds later, a notification appeared: j*boogie followed you back.

I was officially Twitter friends with Alex's ex.

18

It took me a while to fall asleep. All told, I probably got about two hours of shut-eye that night. When my alarm sounded at 7:00 a.m. I snoozed it three times before forcing myself to face the inevitable: another shitty Wednesday at the office.

Before I dragged myself out of bed, though, I scrolled through my phone, checking up on all the important social media I missed out on overnight. There were photos of Dani's late-night writing session on Instagram, Snapchat videos of an art opening for one of Whitney's clients, and a couple of witty one-liners tweeted by JBoogie, including:

> just received the most offensive fluttr message ever sent in the history of offensive fluttr messages

I replied: More offensive than a dick pic?

Thirty seconds later, she DMed me the screencap of her exchange with Nick, 29, from Crown Heights, who'd composed a detailed description of everything he wanted to do to her ass. It included sushi, body paint, and a bow tie.

NYCTechGal: Wow. I've had plenty of offers for generic "butt stuff" but nothing quite so...specific.

jboogie2592: what's the worst message you ever got?

NYCTechGal: Hmm, lemme think. There's so many to choose from.

I switched to my photo app and swiped through my camera roll, looking for screencaps of old Fluttr conversations. Obviously, I hadn't saved every single message I'd ever received; just the ones that were super gross or shocking or hostile.

So maybe, like, half of them.

Finally, I selected a gem from last month in which Ryan, 34, from Jersey City had told me I was "a solid 7, but after a few beers, might be considered a 9." Then I sent it off to JBoogie with the message: This guy was a real charmer.

i hope you logged him on jerkalert, she replied.

My thumbs hovered over the screen as I contemplated my response. This was the perfect opening. A chance for me to ask her all about the guy *she'd* logged on JerkAlert. And why she'd logged him. Twice.

But I couldn't bring myself to do it. Google stalking Alex was one thing; all that info was out there, in the public domain. To come right out and ask JBoogie about her experience with him crossed a line, though. This was no longer research. This was betrayal. Wasn't it?

There wasn't enough time to decide. I'd already procrastinated enough this morning, and now I was running twenty minutes behind. I typed off a hasty **Not yet**, then launched myself out of bed, threw on the least wrinkled outfit I could find, and ran out the door. By some divine miracle, the A train was waiting for me when I got to the station, and I arrived at the office only ten minutes late.

No sooner had I sat down than Josh Brewster had materialized in the doorway of my cubicle.

"Nice of you to finally show up."

He was the last person I wanted to deal with right now. Or ever. But I needed that paycheck. So even though I already knew what the problem was going to be, I took a deep breath and asked, "How can I help you, Josh?"

"This piece of shit—" he held the laptop aloft "—is still not working. Since you're obviously incapable of fixing the problem, can you just give me a new one already?"

"A new laptop isn't going to fix your issue."

"What? Of course it will."

"No. It won't." My voice was steady, my mouth was a hard line.

"You really have no idea what you're doing, do you?" Then he sneered, "You must give good head or something."

"Excuse me?"

"Yeah, you've gotta be slobbing somebody's knob. Because there's no other explanation for how someone as incompetent as you are can manage to keep this job."

My cheeks burned. Even though I knew Josh was a moron, even though I knew everything he said was total trash, that glare he was giving me made me feel inferior. Like maybe I actually *didn't* deserve this job.

In a flash, I came to my senses. Because Josh had no idea I knew what he was up to. No clue that I was thinking two steps ahead of him. After all, I was just a girl who must've sucked someone's dick to get a shitty job at the help desk. A girl who could never outwit a Hatchling.

Well, fuck him.

"I know what you've been doing," I said, low and ominous.

He sucked his teeth. "What the hell are you talking about?"

"I think you know what I'm talking about." We stared at each other, not saying a word. Soon enough, his brow twisted in confusion, and I realized he really *didn't* know what I was talking about. So, I clued him in. "You need to stop going to all those shady websites."

"I'm not going to any shady websites."

"Stop lying, Josh."

His voice grew louder. "I'm not lying."

Clearly, Josh wasn't going to listen to me unless I provided irrefutable proof of his offenses. Which is why it was a good thing I'd never actually uninstalled that keylogger.

I snatched the laptop from his hands. Two quick taps of the trackpad and the keylogger interface filled the screen. An organized record of everything he'd done on this laptop for the past week and a half, on full display. Things he'd never thought anyone would see.

For once, Josh Brewster was speechless. But I still had a lot to say.

"Do you think we can't track everything you do on this computer?" I asked.

He squinted, trying to make sense of what was going on. I could hear the squeak of rusty gears turning inside his head. All this thinking was hard for poor Josh.

Taking pity on him and his feeble powers of deduction, I decided to walk him through the features of the keylogger.

"Here's a record of everything you did on this computer last night. See, this is where you disabled the virus scanner. And here's where you visited a website called GiganticAsses.xxx. It says you spent about fifteen minutes there before heading over to PokerParty.com. Two hours later, you deleted your browser history, and then turned the virus scanner back on."

Finally, understanding dawned on his face. "You're spying on me?"

"Very perceptive."

"That's illegal."

"Oh, but it's not."

I stood up and pulled a thick stack of pages from the cabinet above my desk. The other day, after Bob had told me to wipe the keylogger from Josh's laptop, I'd pulled a copy of the Hatch Code of Conduct from our corporate intranet, and reviewed the section titled Company Resources. In the second paragraph, I found the following statement:

> All members of the Hatch community, including full-time employees, part-time employees, contractors, and Hatchlings, shall use company resources only for legitimate business purposes. This includes, but is not limited to, Hatch-issued mobile phones and electronic devices, such as laptops and desktop computers. Hatch retains the right to monitor usage of said devices to ensure adherence to company policy at all times.

In other words, Bob was wrong. What Josh did on his own time on a Hatch-issued laptop wasn't his own business. Installing a keylogger wasn't against company policy. I'd been right all along.

I had printed out the whole Code of Conduct, all eighty-five pages of it. Then I highlighted the section on the use of company resources, as well as a number of pertinent passages about Hatch's policies against pornography, gambling, and offensive stickers. Now, I presented these to Josh, pointing to the sentences marked with neon yellow lines.

"See?" I said. "It says it right there. And there. And there."

He sputtered like a malfunctioning engine. I couldn't hide the satisfaction I felt, putting this jerk in his place, watching him struggle to find a rebuttal.

"You're not gonna get away with this," he said. What a sad attempt at a threat. As if he was capable of plotting some brilliant revenge. He couldn't even hide his porn consumption properly.

"It'll take me a couple of hours to fix this," I said, casually ignoring his threatening remark. "Just leave it here and I'll—"

"I'm not leaving this here, you crazy bitch."

With one beefy hand, he slapped the cover of his laptop closed and snatched it away. And then he was gone.

Too bad I didn't know how old he was or where he lived. If I did, I'd have logged him on JerkAlert as a precaution. *Don't date him, girls. He's a raging sexist douchebag. Also, painfully stupid.*

Regardless, I decided to check in and see how my baby was doing. According to the dashboard, I'd had over a hundred new visitors overnight, half of whom had logged new entries in the database. Profiles now numbered well into the thousands. Things were looking up.

Except for one tiny problem. The performance monitor on the server showed increasing signs of slowness: backlogged requests, delayed responses, pages that took forever to load. From a coding standpoint, I'd done all I could do to address performance. The only solution was to upgrade my hosting plan. Which I couldn't do until I got some more cash.

Out of desperation, I pulled up my existing code, searching for weaknesses I might have overlooked. Maybe a minor tweak somewhere could help the pages load a little bit faster.

I became so engrossed in my work, I didn't hear Alex sidle into my cubicle.

"Melanie."

At the sound of his voice, I shrieked and startled, spinning around to see him standing there, looking dapper as always.

"You okay?" he asked.

"Yeah. Yeah, totally fine."

He looked past me, at the computer screen. "What're you up to?"

"Nothing." My hand fumbled for the mouse, clicking furiously to close the working window.

"Are you coding something?"

"No. I mean, nothing interesting. Just some scripts to push out next Tuesday's updates."

It's not like he could tell I was working on JerkAlert. From his vantage point, the words on my screen were tiny and unintelligible. It could've been any programming language, for any piece of software.

"What's up?" I asked.

"Nothing. Just dropped by to see how you were doing."

"Um..." *I'm overtired, underslept, coming down off an adrenaline rush thanks to a fight with your fellow Hatchling, freaked out about the stability of my website, and completely unsure whether to believe a word you say.* "I'm fine."

He furrowed his brow. "Are you sure about that?"

Rather than lie, I looked down at my feet.

"I'm really sorry about last night, Melanie."

Again with the apologies. It was like Alex lived in a perpetual state of remorse. Did he even know what he was sorry for anymore? Or what he *should* be sorry for?

"It's okay, Rico."

I met his eyes and he flinched. "What?"

"Isn't that what Greg called you? Rico Suave?"

A flush crept up his neck. "Melanie, I can—"

"So how much did you win?"

"What are you talking about?"

"Last night, Greg said you won. Was there some kind of bet going on? Like which one of you Hatchlings was gonna be the first to get me in the sack?"

"No!" He looked genuinely horrified. "Of course not. Nothing like that happened at all. Greg's just an asshole." With a wince, he glanced over his shoulder, suddenly aware of how loudly he was speaking. In a softer tone, he said, "I would never do that to you. You know that, right?"

Funny thing was, I didn't. I didn't know what to believe. And now he was standing here, staring at me with those gorgeous brown eyes, waiting for an answer I couldn't give him.

Where was a mandated fire drill when you needed one? Or maybe an actual fire. I willed someone to burn a Hot Pocket in the office toaster oven to save me from this conversation I was in no mood to have.

But somewhere, my signals got crossed. Because instead of a kitchen fire, my interruption came in the form of Bob, who'd poked his bald head around the corner of my cubicle. He nodded toward Alex, then glowered at me. "My office, now."

Shit.

He disappeared, and Alex knotted his brow. "What was that all about?"

I shook my head. There wasn't enough time to explain, and

even if there was, I wasn't so sure Alex was the person to turn to for a sympathetic ear. I'd conspired to catch Josh in a lie, and it worked. In a way, wasn't I trying to do the same thing to him? Except instead of keyloggers, I was using JerkAlert and following his old girlfriend on Twitter.

"I've gotta go." Grabbing the Code of Conduct off my desk, I brushed past him and stalked down the hallway toward Bob's office, where he was already sitting at his desk.

"Close the door behind you," he said.

"I take it this has to do with Josh Brewster." There was no place to sit in the cramped, messy room, so I stood there, the thick stack of paper in my arms, shifting from one leg to the other.

"Why would you tell him you installed a keylogger on his machine?"

"Because I was sick of him lying about why it was always broken."

"I told you to uninstall it."

"But I didn't have to." I flipped open the Code of Conduct, pointing out the passages I'd highlighted. "See? We have every right to monitor their devices, especially when they're doing things that cost the company time and money. Think about how many hours I've spent wiping viruses off his laptop. We never would've gotten to the bottom of it without the keylogger."

Bob's whole head turned the color of a pomegranate. He placed both palms facedown on his desk and took a centering breath. When his face returned to its normal pallor, he said, "Melanie, I ask this with concern for your well-being. When's the last time you took a vacation?"

"What? I don't know." In truth, I hadn't taken an actual vacation since I'd started at Hatch. It's not like I had enough money to go flitting off to Cabo whenever I felt like it. The only time I ever took off from work was when Benny from HR phoned me up to tell me my paid time off was about to expire. Then I'd spend a week or so binge-watching Netflix in bed. Which wasn't exactly what I'd call a vacation.

"It would do you some good to have a break from the office," Bob said. "Take a few days off to relax and unwind. Book a trip outta town."

"Where is this coming from?"

"Look, it's okay. Everyone needs a break at some point. Burnout is a very real thing."

"I'm not burned out."

"Are you sure? Because I've noticed over the past couple of days that you've been slacking off around here. That's unlike you."

Shit. Bob had noticed my half-assing, and from the look on his face, he wasn't pleased. Don't get me wrong, I certainly wasn't happy at Hatch, but I also wasn't looking to get fired.

"I'm sorry," I said. "I'll make sure to focus my efforts from now on."

He sighed and tapped a pen against his desktop. "You know, maybe it's my fault. I've probably been giving you more responsibility than you can reasonably handle."

"I can handle my workload just fine. What I can't handle is being constantly disrespected."

He recoiled, like my statement caught him off guard. Like I hadn't alluded to it a thousand times before. "Who's disrespecting you?"

"The Hatchlings."

"Not this again." He scrubbed his hand down his face.

"Melanie, we've been over this before. They're all under an immense amount of pressure."

"That doesn't give them the right to be verbally abusive."

"No one's being verbally abusive. Let's not be dramatic."

I wasn't being dramatic; I was merely telling the truth. But Bob was rolling his eyes, so I decided not to contradict him. When a man whipped out the *D* word, it meant you were on shaky ground. Even if your argument was solid, you'd have to tread carefully, or else he'd dismiss everything else you'd say out of hand.

"My point is," I said, "that they come in my cubicle and throw around the f-bomb, they cover their laptops in offensive stickers, and they bad-mouth me to you behind my back. And they do it all with impunity."

"The thing you're not getting is that Hatch isn't about you and me. We're here to support the founders. They are the stars of the show. Vijay has made that abundantly clear."

"There's still a Code of Conduct. In that all-staff meeting the other day, he was going on and on about the importance of integrity and decency."

"You know as much as I do that it's all lip service. And I cannot have you giving the Hatchlings a hard time, all right? Because they'll go complain to Vijay, and then life will become very difficult for the both of us."

I snorted. "I'm sure it won't be that difficult for you."

"What does that mean?" He leaned forward in his seat and scowled. "You think these Hatchlings are any nicer to me than they are to you?"

"I do, actually. That is, when they can find you, since you have the luxury of hiding out in the server room while I'm out on the floor, dealing with their complaints and abuse."

His eyes narrowed and his nostrils flared and I knew I had taken it too far. After a stony silence that lasted seconds but felt like hours, he threw up his hands. "All I suggested was that you take a little vacation. I'm just trying to look out for you, but you do what you want. Now go fix that laptop—and this time, uninstall the keylogger."

"Fine." I flung his door open and stalked down the hall, boiling over with rage. How dare Bob suggest that the solution to my problem with Hatch's messed-up broflake culture was a vacation? A couple of nights in a hotel wouldn't help me "get over it." It would only plunge me further into debt, and at the end, I'd come back to the same terrible work environment.

Back in my cubicle, I tossed Josh's laptop into the corner and collapsed with my head in my hands. I was fighting an uphill battle here, one I had no chance of ever winning. I wanted out, but I couldn't afford to up and quit my job without a backup plan.

Whit had this master marketing scheme all sketched out for JerkAlert, but frankly, I was getting antsy. The proof of JerkAlert's popularity was in the numbers on my dashboard. Investors cared about facts and figures, not crafty sales tactics. How much longer did I have to wait to cash in?

My phone buzzed once, twice, waking me from my mind-wandering. I pulled it out of my purse and found a chain of messages from the girls:

LIA:

I can't even believe what is happening.

DANI:

What is it? Are you okay?

LIA:

I found out last night that Jay has been lying to me this whole time.

LIA:

He's married, guys.

DANI:

WTF

WHIT:

Fucker.

LIA:

He has two kids and a house in New Jersey.

DANI:

Holy shit.

WHIT:

Of course he's from Jersey.

That state is crawling with assholes.

LIA:

I don't even know what to do. I'm freaking out.

DANI:

Okay. Stay calm.

WHIT:

Don't stay calm.

Burn the fucker's house down.

DANI:

DON'T LISTEN TO HER.

DANI:

When do you get off work?

LIA:

I couldn't handle work today. I'm at home in my pajamas wondering how I could've been so stupid.

WHIT:

You're not stupid. Men are assholes.

DANI:

Let us come over tonight. I'll bring wine.

And edible cookie dough.

WHIT:

Ooh, from that place near NYU?

DANI:

Yes.

LIA:

Don't bother. I can't eat. I can't do anything right now but cry and stare at the wall.

DANI:

Just hang tight for another few hours.

We'll be there as soon as we can and we'll make this all better.

WHIT:

Mel, are you in?

As I read through the thread, I alternated between feeling heartsick for Lia and furious with men in general.

What I didn't feel, though, was surprised.

MEL:

I'm off at 5 and I'll come straight to your place.

MEL:

I'm so sorry this is happening, Lia.

My chest tightened, my jaw clenched. Of all the people this could've happened to, why Lia? She was ceaselessly optimistic, always assuming good intentions. She believed in happily-ever-afters, and she believed everyone deserved one. And now, her own happily-ever-after was in ruins.

Because sometimes the greatest man in the world could turn out to be a dirty, dirty cheat.

19

After work, I jetted to Lia's place in Chinatown, stopping along the way at a discount liquor store to pick up a cheap bottle of Cabernet. When I got there, Dani answered the door and whispered a warning. "She's kind of a disaster."

"Understandably."

"No, you don't get it. I've never seen her like this before."

I held out the bottle of wine. "Maybe this'll help?"

Dani shook her head. "I don't know. I can't get her to eat or drink anything. Not even the cookie dough."

"Ooh. What flavors did you get?"

"Chocolate Dream and Fluffernutter. I waited on a forty-five-minute line for that dough and she won't even taste it."

"I'll give it a good home." I gestured inside the apartment. "Shall we?"

We entered the living room, where Lia was on the couch, curled into the fetal position atop a nest of blankets and balled-up tissues. She stared at the wall, her eyes vacant and dull, not even turning to acknowledge me when I said, "Hey."

Dani was right; I'd never seen Lia so bereft. If I ever ran into Jay, I'd strangle him with my bare hands.

"How are you?" I asked, even though the answer was obvious.

She let out a heavy, hiccuping sigh. "I thought he was the one."

Her voice caught on the final syllable as she broke into a fit of sobs. I placed the wine on the coffee table and sat beside her on the couch, stroking her back and making soothing shushing sounds.

"What is wrong with me?" she wailed. "Why couldn't I see him for what he really was?"

Dani knelt on the floor in front of her. "This is not your fault."

"Yes, it is." She sniffled and unearthed a book from within her tangle of blankets titled *Why Men Marry Bitches*. "This book says I'm too nice. Too trusting."

"Fuck that book." Dani grabbed it from her and chucked it across the room. It landed beside the radiator, pages splayed. "It's pseudo-psychology written by an ignorant hack. Nothing you did or didn't do made Jay into a conniving liar. This is a hundred percent on him."

"Absolutely," I agreed, because it was the right thing to do in this situation. But secretly, I wondered if Lia actually *was* too trusting. She'd believed every excuse Jay ever gave her, forgave him every time he apologized. I bet she'd never even looked him up on JerkAlert.

The buzzer blared and thirty seconds later, Whitney busted through the front door clutching a bottle of tequila. When she spotted the dead-eyed look on Lia's face, she made a beeline for the kitchen. "Where do you keep your shot glasses?"

Lia didn't answer, but Whit found them, anyway. She lined them up on the countertop and filled them to the brim with Don Julio Blanco.

"I didn't have a chance to stop and get limes, so we'll just have to do them as-is." She balanced the shot glasses carefully between her outstretched fingers and walked into the living room, handing them off to us one by one. Lia waved hers away, prompting Whit to scowl. "Wallowing won't make you feel any better. Tequila will."

Unwilling to argue, Lia relented. Whit held her glass in the air. "Bottoms up, ladies."

It went down surprisingly easy.

"Where's that cookie dough at?" she asked. Dani procured two pastel-colored containers from the fridge, along with four spoons, and we all dug in.

"Oh my God."

"This is amazing."

"It was totally worth the forty-five-minute wait."

Whit nodded toward a pile of random stuff in the center of the floor. "What's all that?"

Lia groaned. "That's everything Jay ever gave me."

"Really?" Whit scooched next to it and began rifling through the mishmash of clothing, cards, and candy. A jewelry box fell off the top of the heap and she picked it up, turning it over in her hands. "David Yurman. Nice." When she popped it open, her eyes went wide. "Holy shit. These are diamonds."

"Ugh, I want to burn it all. Or give it away. I think the Goodwill on 8th Street accepts walk-in donations."

"No way." Whit slid the bangle onto her slender wrist and gave it a jiggle. "This stuff is worth a fortune. You should sell it."

"I can't even look at it anymore. I just want it gone."

"Let me take care of it for you," Whit said. "I've got a friend who sells stuff on eBay for extra cash. She takes a cut of everything, but you'll still make a killing."

Dani cleared her throat and glared at Whit, who reluctantly removed the bangle with a frown. Then she turned to Lia and asked, "So, what happened? How did you find out about this?"

Lia reached for a tissue and wiped her nose. "You know how I wanted to plan that spa day in Cabo? Well, I called the hotel last night, but they couldn't find any reservations under Jay's name. The only Roswell they could find was a Jeremy Roswell. I'd never heard him go by Jeremy before, but it was definitely him—the dates of our stay matched and everything. At first, I didn't think much of it. Like, maybe Jay is just a nickname he prefers or something. But the more I thought about it, the more upset I got. I mean, at this point in a relationship, you should know someone's real name, shouldn't you?"

"Definitely," I said, briefly wondering if Alex was short for something else, like Alexander or Alejandro or Alexandrios. I'd be able to Google stalk him more effectively if I knew his full name.

"Then I thought," Lia said, "if he hasn't told me his real name, what else has he been hiding from me? I don't know where he works or even understand what he does for a living. I've never met any of his friends or family members. Maybe I don't know him at all. So, I looked him up on JerkAlert, under Jeremy. And this is what I found."

She held her phone out for us to see. A picture of Jay splashed across the screen, looking the same as he did in all of Lia's Instagram photos. Same salt-and-pepper hair, same wrinkles around the eyes.

The three of us pressed our heads together to read the damning evidence:

> Name: Jeremy
> Age: 41 (but honestly, who knows if he's lying about that, too)
> Location: Has an apartment in Midtown but his full-time house is in Summit, NJ
> Review: This motherfucker is WIFED UP. That's right: he's got a whole secret family out in New Jersey. We dated for a month but then he started acting shady. So one night, when he was in the bathroom, I went through his phone. Found photos of his wife, his kids, his minivan. Tried to explain his way out of it but eventually admitted the truth.

What the fuck.

"It explains so much," Lia continued. "Like why he would never let me tag him on Instagram, or why he was always canceling at the last minute with some excuse about work."

"What did he say when you confronted him?" I asked.

"He didn't even try to deny it. He was just like, 'Yeah, that's me.' Like it was no big deal. Can you believe that someone could be so callous?"

Whit said what we all were thinking: "Yes."

"So that's it." Her voice warbled, threatening to crack. "I guess I'm not going to Cabo now."

"Fuck Cabo," Dani said. "And fuck Jay. Or Jeremy. Or whatever the hell his name is."

Lia's lower lip twitched and she crumpled forward in another sobbing fit. I resumed my patting and shushing, while Whit poured us another round of tequila shots.

"Let's plan our revenge on this asshole," she said, handing

out the glasses. "What if we called up his wife and told her what a dick her husband is?"

"I'm sure she already knows," Dani said.

"Ugh. Stuck in the burbs with two kids and a cheating husband. What a miserable life." Whit knocked back her shot.

"This is my own fault," Lia said. "I should've asked more questions. Demanded more answers." She turned to me with a mournful look. "You're lucky you found Alex on JerkAlert now, before you got in too deep."

Funny, I didn't feel lucky.

"How are things going with him?" Dani asked.

I downed my shot and wiped my lips with the back of my hand. "There's another review on his profile."

"What does it say?"

"Lying scumbag." A chorus of gasps erupted all around. "The thing is, I looked at the database, and it was written by the same woman who wrote the first review. So I'm not sure if I should even believe it."

"Why shouldn't you believe it?" Lia's question sounded suspiciously like an accusation.

"Don't you think it's strange that the same person posted two different reviews?"

"No. Not if she was hurt and wanted to warn other women about his despicable behavior."

I shook my head, more confused than ever. "I'm just not sure."

She rolled her eyes. "Please."

Man, Lia was really fired up. Tequila and heartbreak were a dangerous combination. I looked to Whit and Dani for backup, but they were suddenly regarding the ceiling as if there was a Michelangelo fresco up there.

"If you're really that unsure," Lia continued, "why don't you just ask him about it?"

"I can't."

"Why not?" Anger burned in her eyes.

"I told you—it would be too weird."

"So, you have all this information that he doesn't know about, all these suspicions and doubts, and you're just gonna keep them a secret?"

That was exactly what I'd planned to do. But hearing Lia articulate it like that made me think twice about whether it was such a good idea.

"Forget it," she said, pouring herself another shot of tequila and guzzling it down. "It doesn't really matter what you do. Your relationship's doomed either way."

Dani squeezed my thigh, an unspoken message: *Let it go.*

But I couldn't let it go. "What do you mean by that?"

"Have you told him you run JerkAlert yet?"

Ashamed, I muttered, "No."

"So, how do you expect him to be honest with you if you're not being honest with him?"

"It's completely different." Even as I said the words, I knew my argument was flimsy. "No one can know I run JerkAlert. It's the whole secret marketing plan, remember?"

"Okay. Fine. But eventually the cat's gonna get out of the bag. And if these reviews turn out to be phony, do you really think he'll want to stay in a relationship with someone who knowingly allowed people to trash him on the internet?"

A fierce pressure began to build throughout my body. My eyes stung, my throat tensed, my heart clenched. Because I knew everything Lia said was true.

In an instant, I was on my feet. "I should get going."

"You just got here," Dani said.

"It's laundry day. I'm down to my last pair of underwear." It wasn't laundry day, and I had at least three more clean pairs of panties in my dresser drawer. But I couldn't stay here when Lia was obviously so upset with me. I felt bad for everything she was going through with Jay, but that didn't mean I was willing to be her punching bag. Patting her on the back, I said, "If you need anything, just call me."

She nodded, avoiding eye contact. "Thanks."

Whit walked me out. In the hallway, she said, "Don't listen to her. She's a train wreck right now because of that asshole. Who, by the way, I hated from the very beginning. And it is taking every ounce of my strength not to scream, 'I told you so.' But I won't, of course, because I'm a great friend."

"What if it's true?" I asked.

"What if what's true?"

"All that stuff about Alex on JerkAlert."

"Honestly? I can't see it. He really seems like a stand-up guy."

I nodded, feeling relieved. Whit had killer instincts. If she thought Alex could be trusted, she was probably right.

"That being said," she continued, "you can never know everything there is to know about someone. And even if you did, there's still a chance you'll get your heart broken. Dating is always a risk, no matter how much you know about a person beforehand. Sometimes, you just have to cross your fingers and hope everything works out."

"Wow. That was profound, Whit. For someone who shuns relationships, you know a lot about the way they work."

"I shun relationships *because* I know a lot about the way they work. I do not have the patience for that bullshit." She squeezed my shoulder. "Anyway, don't let Lia make you feel bad about anything. Especially not about JerkAlert. You're doing good work with that site. And there's so much excitement building about it. I've been working a couple of my contacts, trying to score this amazing opportunity I heard about."

"Really? What is it?"

"I don't wanna jinx it. But if I manage to pull it off, you'll never have to work another day at your shitty job."

That was the best news I'd heard all day. Possibly all week.

With a hug and a kiss, Whit and I said our goodbyes. As I walked toward the subway, I lost myself in daydreams, speculating about this "amazing opportunity." Maybe there was an angel investor with deep pockets who wanted to sink some cash into JerkAlert. Or maybe the lead engineer at some tech company was impressed by my coding skills and wanted to offer me a high-paying job.

The whole way home, I was so preoccupied with my own fantasies that I didn't bother to look at my phone. It wasn't until I'd arrived back home that I pulled it from my purse to find a message waiting for me from Alex.

Got pulled into meetings all day but wanted to see how you were doing. Everything OK after that thing with Bob?

I forgot Alex had witnessed me getting pulled into Bob's office. That was embarrassing enough without having to tell him the whole story of what went down behind closed doors.

MEL:

Totally fine. It was just a misunderstanding.

ALEX:

Cool.

ALEX:

You free to talk?

Ugh. I'd had enough talking for one day. I knew what he wanted to talk about, too: he wanted to pick up where we'd left off earlier, when I'd called him out on his Rico Suave act with Greg. I was in no mood to deal with this right now.

I typed two letters—*N-O*—but hesitated before hitting Send. There was no avoiding this conversation; we'd have to have it sooner or later. And I'd rather have it in private, on the phone, than in my cubicle, surrounded by a bunch of eavesdropping Hatchlings. So I deleted my response and tapped the call button.

He picked up on the first ring. "Hey."

"Hey."

Silence ensued. He cleared his throat once, twice, then said, "I don't know if I should say I'm sorry again. I know I say it so much it's probably lost all meaning by now. But I really am sorry."

"Are you sorry for what happened, or are you just sorry I overheard it?"

"Both," he said. "But I hope you know there was no bet going on. Nothing like that happened at all. I only told Greg you and I were hanging out so he'd understand why I wanted the night off. Of course, he's so useless, it turns out I can't take a night off, but that's not the point."

"What's the point, then?"

"The point is, I like you, and I told him I liked you. But that was a mistake, because he's...well, he's a pig. So he started giving me a hard time, with all this 'Rico Suave Latin lover' shit. I've just been ignoring it because he's an idiot, and this whole thing is complicated, you know? I have to at least try to get along with him, for Fizz. Even though most of the time I really wanna punch him in the face."

"Well," I said, "I don't advocate for you punching anyone, but in that moment, it would've been nice to hear you speak up. To defend me, instead of just playing along and saying, 'Yup.' Because now, who knows what he's saying about me around the office? People are gonna start talking, if they aren't already."

"So let them talk. Who cares what they think?"

"I do." My voice was louder than I'd intended. "It's hard enough for me to be taken seriously by these Hatchlings as it is. I thought you understood that."

He let out a long, heavy breath. "You're right. You're absolutely right. I should've said something. I will in the future."

"Good."

"Look, Melanie, I am in this with you, a hundred percent. I know we've gotten off to a rough start, but I need you to know that you're not some meaningless hookup to me. I really like you."

"I really like you, too." The words practically fell out of my mouth, that's how true they felt. I was falling for Alex, hard.

Which is why I was so scared.

I'd seen the pain in Lia's face, the way her body convulsed with uncontrollable sobs. There was an emptiness in her now, a hollow where hope used to live. The same hollow my mother had formed after Dad walked out. I never wanted to end up like that.

Before I got in too deep with Alex, I had to find out what

was really going on. Was he the kindhearted supportive guy he presented himself to be? Or was he a smooth-talking scumbag who shouldn't be trusted?

There was only one way to find out.

20

I'm not saying it was the wisest decision to send JBoogie a Twitter DM as soon as I got off the phone with Alex. Without a doubt, it was shady. And looking back on it, a little unhinged.

In the moment, though, it seemed like I had no other choice. Like it was the only way I could avoid a potential catastrophe.

Granted, I was two tequila shots in and severely sleep-deprived.

But I wasn't hurting anyone, was I? No. I was merely requesting some important information to help me understand what I was dealing with here. Namely, I needed to know exactly what Alex did to this woman to inspire her to call him a lying scumbag on the internet.

All I did was ask a very simple question: How many guys have you logged on JerkAlert?

Then I stared at my phone, willing her to respond immediately. I paced the room, chewing my thumbnail, waiting to see the bouncing ellipsis appear on her side of the conversation. If only she'd known how urgent this was!

After a few minutes of silently refreshing my Twitter feed, I realized how ridiculous I was being. It was late. She was probably asleep by now. Or maybe she was out on a Fluttr date. Whatever she was doing, replying to a DM from an internet stranger was most definitely not at the top of her priority list. So I shut down the app and went to bed.

When my alarm went off the next morning, there was still no answer from JBoogie, but I tried not to despair; it was early. Instead, I grabbed my robe and headed to the bathroom, ready to start my usual morning routine.

Any hope of a hot shower was immediately dashed, though, because Vanessa was standing in the tub, holding a busted showerhead in her hand.

"It just fell off." Her expression was all big-eyed and innocent.

"What do you mean, 'It just fell off?' It was perfectly fine yesterday."

"You know these old Brooklyn buildings," she said, waving the nozzle around for emphasis. "Things fall apart all the time."

"Well, did you try putting it back on?"

"I can't figure out how. Can you?"

I stepped into the tub beside her, inspecting the pipe protruding from the tiles. There was no obvious mechanism for screwing it back on. "How did this even happen?"

"No idea." She gave an exaggerated shrug, a dramatic sigh. "Guess I'll have to call Ray."

"Vanessa," I said, slowly and carefully, to prevent myself

from screaming, "you didn't rip the showerhead out of the wall to have an excuse to call Ray, did you?"

She gasped. "I'm offended you would even suggest that."

"If you like Ray, just tell him. Don't tear apart our bathroom."

"You know, I don't have to listen to this." With her nose in the air, she stepped out of the tub. "I told you, that night was a mistake, and it won't be happening again."

"Fine, whatever." I called after her as she fled down the hallway, "But if you have sex in our shower, I expect you to scrub it out when you're done."

Her bedroom door slammed shut. With no other choice, I ran a bath.

Before I left, I grabbed my gym bag. It was Thursday, which meant Krav Maga class after work. In light of last night's debacle, I wasn't sure if Lia was going to show, and if she did, I wasn't sure how she'd react to seeing me. But the Groupon was nonrefundable, their cancellation policy was strict, and I wasn't about to throw away my hard-earned cash simply to avoid an awkward situation.

My morning shift at work was soul-destroying, as expected. I unclogged two paper jams, replaced a broken keyboard, and fielded at least a dozen emails from people who said neither please nor thank you.

Then, at 11:53, my phone buzzed with a Twitter notification. A direct message from jboogie2592: honestly, i've lost count, lol.

I responded immediately: Ha. Anyone that stands out as particularly heinous, tho?

jboogie2592: the most recent one would be alex, 26, fidi.

Holy shit.

This was it! The moment I'd been waiting for. Finally, I was going to find out exactly what she meant when she called Alex a "typical Fluttr douche."

My heart pounded in my ears, and suddenly, I wasn't so sure this was a good idea. Whatever I saw, I could never unsee, and as a result, my relationship with Alex could change, irreversibly. Did I really want to know all the details of her experience with him?

Yes. Yes, I did.

NYCTechGal: What did he do?

After a minute passed by with no response, I realized I'd probably pushed my luck. If what JBoogie had with Alex was more than some meaningless Fluttr flirtation—if Alex had really hurt her—she wouldn't be willing to pour her heart out about it to some random Twitter stranger. Not without a very compelling reason.

So I decided to tell a little lie.

NYCTechGal: Let me explain. I'm a PhD candidate in Sociology. The working title for my dissertation is "The Great Swiping Swindle: A Critical Examination of the Societal Impact of Dating Apps." As part of my research, I've been interviewing women from around the country about their varied experiences with online dating and how their lives have been affected, both positively and negatively. All your information will remain completely anonymous and your contributions could help improve online dating for future generations.

Like I said, it was shady.

But it worked. Almost instantly, the bouncing ellipsis popped up, and thirty seconds later, her message appeared.

jboogie2592: we dated kinda casually for a couple of weeks, then as soon as we had sex, he ghosted. he didn't answer my texts or emails. he let my calls go to voice mail. it was humiliating.

NYCTechGal: That's awful. I'm sorry.

jboogie2592: everyone's been ghosted at some point, right? but it was the way he ghosted that sucked so hard. i didn't see it coming. the whole time, he was like, 'i really like you' and 'you're so awesome.' then suddenly we do it, and he's gone.

A queasy sensation swayed through me, roiling my guts and leaving a bitter taste on my tongue. My thumbs quivered as they typed: Ugh.

jboogie2592: the worst part is there were so many signs that he was lying to me, and i just ignored them.

NYCTechGal: Like what????

jboogie2592: he had excuses for everything. always canceling at the last minute or getting pulled away by some work emergency. i get that he had a stressful job but there's no way it consumed that much of his time. looking back on it, i bet he totally had a side chick. or maybe i was the side chick. whatever his deal was, he was an asshole. and i'm pretty sure everything he ever told me was a lie.

This all sounded painfully familiar.

Except he didn't ghost me after the first time we had sex. On the contrary, he'd come back for more.

Although, maybe that was just because we worked together. He had no choice but to see me every day; ghosting wasn't an option. Maybe as soon as his time at Hatch was up, he'd pull a disappearing act.

"Hey, Mel."

Speak of the devil.

Alex was standing at the entrance to my cubicle. I did my best to keep calm, setting my phone facedown on the desk and smoothing my hair. "Hello."

"How's it going?" he asked.

"Fine. Busy."

"I know what that's like."

Of course you do.

He drummed his fingers along the top of the cubicle wall. "What're you doing for lunch?"

"No plans."

"Can I take you out?"

I cleared my throat. "No, thanks. I packed my lunch today."

Raising an eyebrow, he said, "You'd really prefer your peanut butter sandwich to a fresh *bánh mì*?"

In fact, I wouldn't, and it must've been obvious from the look on my face, because Alex added, "C'mon. It's a gorgeous afternoon. Let's spend it together."

The offer was tempting, but still, I was hesitant. "Can we expect another interruption from your business partner?"

He shook his head. "Don't worry, we'll go someplace he'll never go."

We walked down Water Street in the afternoon sun, making our way to the Banh Mi Cart in Hanover Square. I tried to keep my distance, afraid to get too close, but Alex gently took my hand, threading his fingers through mine. I should've had the warm fuzzies from such a tender act. Instead, my mind wandered to JBoogie and all those things she'd said he'd done. The sweet talk, the lies, the disappearing act. Would he do the same thing to me?

I wished I was more like Whit: exultant in my singlehood, unaffected by men and their bullshit. Then I could walk away from Alex, without thinking twice. There'd be no drama, no disappointment. No heartbreak.

No matter how much I'd try to deny it, though, I *did* want a relationship, even if it took a lot of effort. And maybe that made me pathetic, but it was a natural feeling, wasn't it? To want someone to share your life with. Entire industries were founded on that very premise. That's why Fluttr was created. That's why Vilma the matchmaker continued to make money despite her inability to actually make any matches. Because finding someone was hard, and we needed all the help we could get.

But I'd already found someone. Despite my fears, Alex was sweet and charming and funny and hot, and I didn't want to give up on him. I just needed to find out the truth.

When we arrived at the food cart, we ordered two special baguettes with iced coffees and crossed the street to sit in the tiny pocket park, shaded by towering buildings and leafy trees. While Alex tore into his sandwich, I decided to do some totally nonchalant and unsuspicious investigative work.

"So, when was your last relationship?"

He nearly choked on his slow-roasted pork.

"We're having that conversation already?"

"We don't have to," I said. "I don't know why I asked it. Just making conversation, I guess."

"No, it's okay. I was kidding." He wiped his mouth with a thin paper napkin. "I haven't really dated anyone very seriously since college, so it's been about four years or so. What about you?"

"Same. Nobody serious since college." I sipped my iced coffee. "Although there *was* one guy I got involved with last year who seemed really into me. We dated for a couple of weeks and I thought things might get serious between us, but..."

"But what?"

I locked eyes with him. "He ghosted."

Alex immediately broke my gaze and shoved his baguette in his mouth, biting off a giant chunk of bread and meat.

"Ghosting," I continued, picking at a cilantro leaf poking out of the side of my sandwich. "I've never really understood it."

"What's to understand?" he said, still chewing. "Sometimes things don't work out between people. If one person wants to leave before things get too serious, why shouldn't they?"

"It's fine to want to break up with someone. But disappearing into thin air and cutting off all communication without an explanation is really fucked up."

"Yeah, but then you don't have to deal with some long, uncomfortable conversation. It's just easier for everyone involved."

"Sure, it's easy. It's also cowardly."

He flinched. "I think that's a little harsh."

"No. What's harsh is completely abandoning someone after you've led them on and made them believe you could really care about them. At least have the common courtesy to say goodbye. To give them some closure. Otherwise, the other person is always left wondering, 'What's wrong with me?'"

My bottom lip started to tremble and I stilled it with my fingers. When it came to dating, I always liked to pretend I could play it cool. If a guy ghosted or stood me up or otherwise hurt me, I said it was his own loss. He was a jerk, a loser, and I deserved better, so there was no point in wasting my tears.

In reality, though, it was hard not to think that there was something inherently unlovable about me. That guys kept leaving because I was chasing them away. That I'd never find anyone who would love me the way I wanted to be loved. Alex included.

"Mel." He leaned toward me, arm outstretched. His thumb caressed my cheek and I looked into his big brown eyes. "I would never do that you. I told you, I'm in this a hundred percent. You and me—this is serious."

And though I wanted to believe every word that dripped from his beautiful lips, I couldn't help but wonder: How many women had heard that exact same line?

Of course, I didn't say that. I just nodded, then peeled back the wrapper on my *bánh mì* and ate my lunch.

After we finished eating, we walked back to the office, and I tried not to wallow in hopelessness. Instead, I grabbed Alex's hand, squeezing it tight, reminding him that I was still there. He responded by pulling me close, wrapping an arm around my shoulder and nuzzling my neck. When we stopped on the corner of Wall Street to wait for the light to change, he leaned down and kissed me. It was so slow and sensual and seductive, I almost forgot we were standing in the bustle of midday foot traffic.

Maybe I was simply being paranoid. Maybe it was all going to be fine.

"Ow!"

Alex jerked away and clenched his biceps, his face contorting in pain.

"Are you okay?" I asked, then quickly saw the source of his anguish: Greg, walking backward through the crosswalk with a smirk on his face. He'd punched Alex in the arm as he passed by. Because that's a fun thing to do to your coworkers, I guess.

"I'm fine," he said, rubbing his arm. "I just wasn't expecting it."

As Greg disappeared into the crowd across the street, I could hear him yell, "Rico!"

"What is his problem?"

"He's a dick," Alex mumbled, then grabbed my hand and led me across the street.

We parted ways in the elevator bank with a promise to text each other later. After that, my afternoon went by much the same way my morning had: tedious tasks, performed with a fake smile. Since I'd adjusted my attitude and stopped slacking off, Bob stayed off my back. As long as I got my work done and no one complained, he didn't have a reason to bother me.

Which gave me plenty of time to check in on JerkAlert. Ever since I saw those troublesome performance stats yesterday, I'd been logging in regularly to make sure everything ran without a hitch. I was still making minor tweaks to the code here and there to improve stability, and so far, I'd kept everything under control.

At 5:15, I changed into my gym clothes and headed uptown

to the Krav Maga Institute. The whole subway ride, I was a bundle of nerves, worried what was going to happen when I saw Lia. We'd never fought like this before. Would she still be mad at me? Would she even show up?

My concerns were put to rest as soon as I walked into the gym, though. Lia was early as usual, sitting cross-legged on the edge of the bright red mat. When she saw me, she waved, a sad little half smile on her face, and instantly, I knew she felt as sorry as I did about everything that went down last night.

"I'm sorry," she said, the moment I approached.

"No, *I'm* sorry."

"You didn't do anything wrong. I jumped down your throat and attacked you for no reason."

"It's fine. You were going through an unbelievably horrible thing."

"That's not an excuse."

"But it's really okay. Water under the bridge. All right?"

She nodded. "All right."

"How are you feeling?"

"Shitty."

"Well, I'm happy you came today, I wasn't sure if you would."

"I have to get on with my life. What better way to do that than by kicking a grown man's ass?"

As if on cue, a stocky guy strolled into the gym in his bare feet, slowly rubbing his palms together. He wore this smug grin, like he owned the place. Which he probably did, but he didn't have to be so cocky about it.

"Ladies, ladies, ladies." His accent was sexy, I'll give him that. "My name is Tal. I'll be your instructor today. Welcome to Krav Maga self-defense course."

About a dozen women sat in a semicircle on the mat. He studied our faces, making individual eye contact with each one of us. "It's hard being a woman," he said. "Men are disgusting. They prey on you, night and day. At any moment, you can be a victim, even in the middle of a crowded subway. Remember that thing going around the internet last week? The dick in the dark?"

Oh, God.

"If that woman from the video knew Krav Maga, she could've taken him out, no problem."

I begged to differ. There was no way I could've whipped out elaborately choreographed self-defense moves on that train. We were packed in like sardines. I could barely even turn my head. While Tal was undoubtedly skilled in hand-to-hand combat, he'd clearly never been held hostage by an unwanted penis on a rush-hour A train.

"When you walk away today," he continued, "you're going to have the skills to protect yourself out there. Now, let's get into a stance. Everybody on your feet."

For the next half hour or so, Tal walked us through basic Krav Maga techniques: jabs, kicks, blocks, that sort of thing. When he was done, he asked for a volunteer to help him demonstrate how to put it all together.

Eager to kick some ass, Lia threw her hand up in the air.

"You." He pointed to her. "Come here, join me."

She leaped to her feet, practically giggling.

Tal grabbed a target pad from the corner of the room and held it up in front of him. "Okay, to start, let's try some downward hammer fists. Go!"

Lia pummeled the pad with both hands.

"Get up on your toe," Tal said. She struck again. "Follow

through. You're not following through." His voice was hostile, and I knew why. He was trying to agitate her. To get her to fight with every ounce of her strength.

But I don't think Tal quite understood what he was dealing with.

"Is that all you got?" He taunted her while she continued to strike, harder and faster. Her cheeks grew bright pink, her breath became raspy. "Come on! Give me more! Pretend I'm that guy on the subway." She hit him again. "That's how you hit a predator? That's nothing! Okay, then pretend I'm your boyfriend, and you just caught me in bed with another woman."

Lia's eyes caught fire. She laid into the target pad with such force that Tal had to jump back.

"That was a good one, finally," he said. "I feel sorry for your boyfriend right now."

Wrong thing to say, Tal.

In a flash, she ripped the target pad from his hands and tossed it across the room, then lunged at him, limbs flailing. Tal's eyes went wide with surprise. For someone who was supposed to have catlike reflexes, he'd been caught off guard pretty easily.

It didn't take him long to subdue her, though. He wrapped her in a bear hug, pinning her arms to her side and catching her legs between his ankles. She cried, "Let me go, you piece of shit!" and then a burly guy emerged from the back office.

"Tal, what's going on?" he called.

"I got a hellcat on my hands, Robbie!"

"Don't call me a hellcat!" she screamed, and jerked her head back so violently that the two of them collapsed to the mat in a heap.

The room erupted in a collective gasp and Tal began to moan. I rushed over to Lia. "Are you okay?"

She panted, dazed. "I…I don't know what happened."

"Should we call an ambulance?" one woman asked.

"No," another woman replied. "Just stick a tampon up there—he'll be fine."

I turned around to see Tal looking out of sorts, blood rushing from one of his nostrils. Robbie stood over him, unconcerned. "You'll be fine, man." He pointed to Lia. "But you? Gotta go."

Twenty minutes later, we were hunched over the bar at El Cantinero, downing flautas and margaritas with impressive speed.

"I'm really sorry about that," Lia said.

"Don't be. Tal had it coming. I mean, 'hellcat'? Really?"

She laughed and licked salt from the rim of her glass. "Men are ridiculous."

"Yeah." I fiddled with a flauta. "Although, I've been behaving pretty ridiculously myself."

"Is this about what I said last night? Because I didn't mean any of it, really. I'm so sorry I said all those terrible things to you."

"No. There's something else."

And then I admitted to my Twitter exchange with JBoogie.

"Whoa." I couldn't tell if Lia was impressed or terrified.

"It's shady, I know."

"Yeah, it's definitely shady. But, really, what do I know? Look at the mess I'm in. I should've been more like you. Maybe if I'd Google stalked Jay early on in our relationship, I could've avoided all this drama."

"So, do you think this means I shouldn't trust Alex?"

She shrugged one shoulder. "Honestly, Mel, I have no idea."

Lia downed the rest of her margarita and hopped off her barstool to go to the bathroom. In her absence, I pulled out my phone. Without even thinking, I loaded my browser and went directly to Alex's JerkAlert profile. It was almost a reflex now, checking to see if any new reviews had been posted while I'd been busy living in the real world.

Turned out, there hadn't been.

So maybe things would be different this time. Maybe Alex *was* telling me the truth. Maybe he'd meant it when he told me he was in this a hundred percent.

Maybe all I could do was cross my fingers and hope everything worked out.

21

The next morning, I woke up feeling rested, refreshed, and ready to approach this whole Alex situation with a new attitude.

First, I would stop being so shady. I unfollowed JBoogie on Twitter and made a promise to myself that I wouldn't check Alex's JerkAlert profile ever again.

Second, I would stop being so paranoid. Sure, Alex checked his phone a lot, but that didn't mean he was screwing around with other women. He was launching a start-up, for crying out loud. Of course he was distracted.

Finally, I would start being direct. No more pointless speculating; no more Google stalking exes. Whenever something was bothering me, whenever I had a question or concern, I'd come right out and ask him about it.

Also, I'd fess up about JerkAlert.

Eventually.

Excited to start implementing my new strategy right away, I dropped by Alex's cubicle to invite him to lunch. He wasn't there, so I wound up eating my peanut butter sandwich alone at my desk. Later on, I swung by again, but he was still MIA. He never signed into Slack, either. Thinking maybe he'd called in sick, I texted with a quick, Hey, everything okay? No response.

Was I about to be ghosted?

A little after five o'clock, I shut down my computer. Time to go home and face the weekend. Alone. With no plans. One final burst of naive hope inspired me to take the long way out, though, and I was glad I did. Because I finally found Alex, hunched over his laptop, looking totally defeated.

"Hey," I said. He startled at the sound of my voice, gaping at me as if I was the last person on earth he'd expected to see. "Everything all right?"

"Yeah, yeah." His gaze traveled back to his computer screen. "No, not really."

Apparently, Fizz was facing a crisis.

"I've been in meetings all day with Greg and Vijay," he said. "We are so behind schedule, I don't think it's possible for us to catch up. And Greg is so fucking useless, I—" He stopped abruptly, rubbing his jaw. "I should just give up now. There's no point."

"No, don't say that." I knelt beside his chair and gave his arm a reassuring squeeze. "It always seems impossible before it's done. How can I help?"

He turned to me with a somber smile. "You're wonderful, you know that?"

My heart softened like warm butter. "Seriously. What can I do?"

"Nothing." Alex gestured at his laptop with irritation. "There's this major bug that's existed for days. I keep trying to fix it, but at this point I'm only making it worse. It has a work-around, but that ruins the whole user experience. I feel like I've stared at it for hours and I am no closer to coming up with a solution."

"Well, sometimes when I'm having a hard time solving a problem, I step away from it for a little while. Give my brain a break. Then, when I come back to it with fresh eyes, it's like I magically find a way to fix it." I stroked his wrist, the soft skin peeking out from beneath the cuff of his shirt. "Why don't you go for a walk or something?"

With a deep breath, he said, "You're right. I need to step away." He slapped his laptop closed and shoved it in his bag. "In fact, I'm gonna bring this home with me. Maybe a change of scenery will help."

"Great. Mind if I join you?"

He knitted his brow. "Um…"

That was not the reaction I'd been hoping for. I was thinking he'd give me an enthusiastic "Absolutely!" Or at the very least, a lukewarm "Sure." Instead, he was hesitating, chewing the inside of his bottom lip, thinking it over as if this was some thorny problem to be solved. Like I was a bug in his code.

Then I thought: *Stop being so paranoid*. Obviously, he was very busy. He probably just wanted some peace and quiet so he could work.

"I'm sorry." I stood up and brushed off the front of my pants. "Forget it."

"No, Mel, I—"

"Really, it's totally fine. You need your space to work. I understand."

"I do have to take care of this, but I'd still love to spend time with you. Are you okay with watching me code?"

"Of course," I said, beaming. "You can bounce ideas off me if you need to."

"Great." He stood up and kissed me. It was quick, even a little chaste, but the contact was enough to leave a shivering sensation on my lips that traveled straight through to my toes.

We headed out, hand in hand, and the moment we walked into his apartment, he was already reaching for his laptop.

"You were right about stepping away." He stood at the breakfast bar, waiting for his system to load. "On the walk over here, I got a couple of ideas for how to get this thing working again."

"That's awesome." I put down my purse and popped open his fridge. "Can I get you something to drink while you're working?"

"Uh, sure." He focused in on the computer screen, and while his hands flew across the keyboard, I poured us two glasses of wine. After a few minutes of silence, he let out a frustrated roar.

"Not working?" I asked.

"Nope." He gulped down half his glass of merlot in one swallow.

"Would it help to talk it through with me?"

"Couldn't hurt." He slid closer, so I could see his screen, then explained the crux of the problem, walking me through his code line by line. We ran through a few test cases, checking values in the debugger.

"I just don't understand why this keeps happening."

"It's because of this." I pointed to a function call. "On line two fifteen, you're passing this value by reference—it's getting modified within the procedure."

His eyes bulged. "Oh my God. How did I miss that?"

"I told you, there's something about a fresh set of eyes."

"No, there's something about *your* eyes." He kissed my forehead. "I love this big, delicious brain of yours."

Love. He'd said it in a playful way, yes, but men so rarely played around with that word. Not unless there was a hint of truth behind it.

He tapped a few keys before letting out a triumphant whoop and shoving his laptop aside. "Now that you solved that problem for me, we can hang out properly."

"You mean you're done with your work?"

"Technically, I'm never really done. If I wanted to, I could work all night, all weekend, and still have more to do."

Anxiety darted through his eyes and his mouth turned downward. And suddenly, I realized something that should have been crystal clear from the very beginning.

"You really are always working when you say you are."

"What do you mean?"

"When you're distracted with your phone or get up to leave first thing in the morning or forget to text me or whatever, you're not lying when you say it's about work. You really *are* working that much."

"Of course I am. Haven't I been telling you what a nightmare this whole thing has been?"

"You have. I've had a hard time believing it, though. A lot of guys say they're working when they're not. It's a convenient excuse, you know what I mean?"

He raised his eyebrows. "Not really. You sound kinda paranoid."

"Well, I *am* kinda paranoid. But it's because I've been through this before."

"Did your ex lie to you about working when he wasn't?"

"No. Not my ex. My dad."

Alex leaned toward me and caressed the back of my hand. His expression was an open invitation. Fully focused, no distractions. "What did he do?"

I told him what I knew about my mother and my father and the demise of their marriage. Which wasn't much, admittedly, but it was enough to make me question men and their motives for the rest of my life. The whole time, Alex listened intently. When I was done, he pulled me into an embrace.

"I'm sorry that happened to you." He stroked my hair with what could only be construed as love. "And I want you to know that I would never do that to you. I promise, I'll never give you a reason to doubt me."

His lips touched mine, and in that moment, I knew it could be so easy to surrender to his words. To give up this burden of suspicion I carried around with me all the time. To believe him, and in so doing, allow him to lighten the load.

I deepened the kiss, and he responded in kind. His hands slowly worked their way down my shoulders, my breasts, my stomach, before diving beneath my waistband. And when I felt his fingers between my legs, I could no longer control myself. We did it right there on the breakfast bar.

Like feral beasts, panting and growling and clawing at each other's bodies. Our friction could've set the kitchen on fire. When we were finished, he collapsed forward, holding me in his arms, breathing heavy against my neck. He looked spent, satisfied.

"That was the hottest thing ever," he muttered.

Once we caught our breath and disentangled ourselves from one another, I went to the bathroom to clean up, feeling more confident than ever. Alex and I were solid. He wasn't gonna ghost me the first chance he could. Like he said, he was in this a hundred percent. I was his one and only, and we were in this for the long haul. I was sure of it.

Until I had a good look around the bathroom.

I swear: I wasn't snooping. It's just that while I was washing my hands, my eyes started to wander and I noticed a hot-pink razor in the corner of the shower stall. A woman's razor. Right next to a travel size can of raspberry-scented shave gel.

Funny, that wasn't there last time. Was it?

Naturally, my curiosity was piqued. I pulled back the shower curtain to see what else was in there. A bar of soap, some shampoo, a damp washcloth hanging off the showerhead. Nothing else particularly girlie.

But what might've been in the medicine cabinet?

A little voice whispered in my ear: *Stop being so shady.* But I easily ignored it and swung open the mirrored door to find a half-empty bottle of Prada Candy. The fragrance. For women.

So, of course, then I had to look under the sink, where, crammed behind a bottle of Liquid-Plumr and a six-pack of toilet paper, I found Alex's secret stash of Tampax Pearls. The variety pack, for the varied degrees of his monthly flow.

Was this why he'd hesitated when I'd asked to come over? Because he hadn't yet had a chance to clean up the mess his last girl had left behind?

Okay, okay.

I was not going to freak out. Freaking out would not solve anything. Instead, I was going to calmly and rationally ask Alex what the fuck was going on.

After two deep, centering breaths, I returned to the bedroom. Alex was on the bed, engrossed in his phone, not even looking up as I sat down next to him. His eyes were wide, his thumbs were tapping furiously. He muttered, "Oh man," under his breath.

"What's going on?" I asked. Totally calm, totally rational.

"Nothing," he said, turning off his phone display and resting it on the nightstand. "I'm getting hungry. You wanna order dinner?"

"Sure. Whatever."

He reached out and stroked my arm. "Is something wrong?"

Start being direct, I thought. This was the perfect opportunity to come right out and ask him about what I saw in the bathroom.

"No, I'm fine."

Nice work, Mel.

"Okay." From the lilt in his voice, I could tell he wasn't totally convinced, but he didn't press the issue. "Why don't you check Seamless and pick out something good?"

"What're you in the mood for?"

"I leave the decision in your capable hands." With an elaborate flourish, he bowed before me, then bounded off for the bathroom.

I was fine.

This was all fine.

I was merely overreacting. All that girlie stuff in the bathroom had probably been there before and I just hadn't noticed it.

Maybe it was leftover from JBoogie. You know, the girl he'd ghosted after sex.

But if he was never serious about her, then why did he let her store a stash of tampons under the sink?

Was there someone else he'd been serious about who he hadn't admitted to?

Or was I really just the side chick?

No more pointless speculating. I pulled up the Seamless app and scrolled through available deliveries in the neighborhood. As I tried to decide between poke bowls and pad thai, Alex's phone buzzed, and I looked up to see the screen lit with a text notification.

And I swear: I wasn't snooping. His phone was lying there on the nightstand, faceup, clearly visible to the world. Was I expected to turn away from it? To will my eyes not to see and my brain not to interpret the words displayed so plainly on the screen?

Of course, I wish that's what I had done. Instead, I got closer and read the damning evidence.

From: Jenny
i never heard from you. did you like my little surprise?

Somewhere in the distance, drums pounded. Steady, unrelenting, getting closer and closer by the second. Then I realized they weren't drums at all, but the surge of my heartbeat, thumping in my chest, reverberating in my ears, flooding my body with adrenaline and fury.

I had heard the name Jenny before. This was the woman I'd met that first night at the bar. The woman he'd said was his first Fluttr date that didn't work out. Why the fuck were they still texting each other?

Alex came out of the bathroom and I couldn't even look at him. With my eyes on the floor and my voice calm and even, I said, "I think you got a text."

He picked up his phone, unlocking it with a swipe of his thumb. The room filled with palpable silence as I watched him read the message, lock the screen, and drop the phone back onto his nightstand. His face betrayed nothing. He didn't even flinch.

"Who was it?" I asked, giving him a chance to tell me the truth. "Was it work?"

"Nah. Just spam."

Liar.

Alex had accused me of being paranoid like it was some kind of flaw. But obviously, it was a strength, because my suspicions were right on target. He'd been lying all along.

"Are you sure that's what it was?"

"What do you mean?" He pinched his brows together, miming confusion. Trying to paint me like the overly paranoid girl.

"What was the surprise?"

He cleared his throat. "I don't know what you're talking about."

"Stop playing dumb. Just stop it." I felt my voice getting louder but had lost all control over its pitch. "I saw the text, okay?"

"What? Why were you going through my phone?"

"I wasn't going through your phone. It was sitting there on the nightstand. The text popped up and I looked over at it and—"

"So you admit to reading my texts."

I crossed my arms against my chest, holding on tightly. "Is that the same Jenny from the night we met at The Barley House?"

Alex breathed in deeply, his bare chest expanding, his eyes focused on the ceiling. "Yes. But I haven't seen her since then. She just texted me today."

"Right, I'm sure. What was 'the surprise'?"

"Do you really want to know?"

"I asked, didn't I?"

He snatched his phone, swiping through it while working his jaw. "I can't believe this," he muttered, then held the screen out for me to see.

It was a close-up of a nude woman's torso. Two gigantic swollen breasts with pert pink nipples. The sensuous curve of collarbones. Above that, her lips, curled in a smile and painted berry red.

"Why is this on your phone?"

"She sent it to me!" He hurled his phone at his mattress, where it bounced off and landed on the floor. "I have no control over what she sends or doesn't send. I certainly didn't ask for it. Aren't you the one who was always saying how men send you unsolicited dick pics all the time?"

Ignoring the logic in that statement, I pushed forward. "Are those her tampons under your sink, too?"

"What?" His hands went to his head, pulling at his curls. "Why were you snooping around my bathroom?"

"I didn't have to snoop to see the evidence. Her razor and shaving cream were sitting in plain sight on the edge of the tub." He squinted, like he was trying to envision the state of his bathroom. "You forgot it was there, didn't you?"

"I don't understand," he said. "Why are you doing this?"

"You said I could trust you." I was warbling now, but I couldn't stop. "You said you would never give me a reason to doubt your words, and you lied."

"I didn't lie. What did I lie about?"

The audacity of this man, to double down on his deception.

He was trying to make me think it was all in my head, to get me to drop it. Well, I wasn't dropping anything.

"So Jenny sent you a picture of her tits, out of nowhere? After two weeks of no communication, she just randomly decided to text you today."

His cheeks flushed and he scratched the back of neck. "Well, I actually texted her first. But it's only because of what we talked about yesterday."

"What?"

"About ghosting. I wanted to apologize to her. See, Jenny and I had dated for a couple of weeks—nothing serious, but I think maybe she had a different idea of what was going on between us. And the way I left things… I wasn't very nice and so I apologized. But then, I don't know, I think maybe she took it like I was trying to get back together with her, so she sent me this picture out of nowhere, and then—"

"Wait a minute—I thought you told me that was your first date with her."

His mouth fell open as he realized I'd caught him in a lie.

And then it hit me.

Jenny was the *J* in JBoogie.

"When I asked you if Jenny was your girlfriend, you told me no."

"She wasn't my girlfriend. She never was. Like I said, we'd been out a few times, it was never serious."

"Right. You guys weren't serious. That's why she just happened to have a stash of tampons in your bathroom."

"They're not hers, they're—"

"Oh, so there's *another* woman I should be worried about?"

"What? No! I'm telling the truth. Melanie, I swear to you."

"I'm not sure why I should believe that."

"Because as soon as I walked into the bar and saw you sitting there, I realized *you* were the woman I wanted to be with. I stopped talking to Jenny the very next day, before you and I ever started anything."

"Then why weren't you honest with me in the first place? Why did you tell me it was a first date when it wasn't?"

"I was afraid it would scare you away."

"It probably would have. And I'd probably have been better off." I yanked my shirt off the floor and pulled it over my head. "Jenny said you were a liar and she was right."

He cocked his head. "Wait a minute. You've been talking to her?"

I zipped up my pants and slipped on my shoes, ready to leave without an explanation. But when I grabbed my purse, I realized: Alex needed to know. He needed to be aware that he no longer lived in a world where he could lie with abandon. From now on, women would hold him accountable for his actions.

It was time to fess up.

Grabbing my phone, I loaded Alex's JerkAlert page into the browser. Then I handed it to him and let him scroll, to see the truth printed out in pixels.

"I don't understand," he said. "What is this?"

"It's JerkAlert. It's this popular new website where women can go online and post about all the shady shit men have done to them. So they can warn other women not to get involved."

He looked up at me, his face twisted in pain, like I'd punched him in the stomach. "All this time, you've known about the stuff that was written here, and you haven't said anything to me? You've just been keeping it a secret?"

Without a word, I took my phone back and tucked it in my purse.

"That's pretty dishonest, isn't it?" he said.

"Don't even."

Pushing past him, I rushed toward the front door, eager to be anywhere but here. As I flung the door wide, he called after me, "What kind of terrible person would make a website called JerkAlert, anyway?"

I stopped short, turning around with daggers in my eyes. "*Me.* I did it. Because of lying men like you."

The whole building shook when I slammed the door.

22

The worst part about breaking up with someone isn't the initial shock of betrayal, or the ensuing loneliness, or the humiliation of having to admit you snooped underneath their bathroom sink.

It's the death of hope. The idea that you'd staked your faith in someone, grown comfortable in their continued presence, daydreamed about a possible future together, and then it was all ripped away, suddenly and painfully.

With Alex, I'd had something to look forward to, and now it was gone.

Though I had to look on the bright side: at least I hadn't gotten in too deep. Since we'd barely been dating two weeks, I hadn't even had the chance to put a picture of him on my Instagram yet. Not like Lia, who'd spent days deleting all traces of Jay from her social media accounts, only to have random people from high school ask her, "Hey, what happened to your boyfriend?"

The internet is a terrible place.

Then again, my apartment was a terrible place, too. Oh, the bathroom was looking pretty snazzy; Ray had installed one of those luxury rainfall showerheads to replace the broken one, and while he was at it, he'd thrown in a heated towel rack for post-bath coziness.

But these upgrades came at a price. Namely, listening to Vanessa and Ray engage in athletic sex at all hours of the day and night. It was hard hearing the soundtrack to their burgeoning love affair while I was busy licking the wounds of my shattered one. Which is why I barely left my bedroom the whole weekend. Instead, I lolled around in my dirty sheets, eating junk food and watching *Gossip Girl* and definitely not tearing up whenever I thought about how Alex sort of looked like Dan Humphrey.

It was almost a relief to go to the office on Monday morning. Of course, I wasn't too thrilled about the idea of running into Alex, but since we'd barely had reason to talk to one another at Hatch before we'd started dating, I was sure it'd be easy enough to avoid him now.

Truth be told, I wasn't as worried about running into him as I was about him running his mouth. Aside from the girls, he was the only person who knew I was responsible for JerkAlert. I wasn't concerned that he'd spill my secrets out of spite. More that he'd carelessly let it slip without even thinking. After all, this was a man who had no idea his ex-girlfriend's razor was still hanging out on the ledge of his bathtub. Prudence was not his strong suit.

Everything was going fine so far, though. Just a typical Monday at the help desk: answering emails, unlocking frozen user accounts, battling an existential crisis. At noon, I took my scheduled lunch break, eating at my desk to avoid a potential encounter with Alex. Or with anyone, for that matter.

When I reached into my bag to pull out my peanut butter sandwich, I noticed a missed call on my phone. It was some random 415 number; a quick Google search told me this area code was from somewhere in northern California. Nobody I knew lived in San Francisco, so I figured it was a robocall. Especially when they called again, thirty seconds later. I sent it straight to voice mail and unwrapped my sandwich.

As I ate, I surfed the internet, scrolling through the news and catching up on the latest celebrity gossip to distract myself. Halfway through reading a juicy blind item, my phone buzzed with a new email notification.

From: The Fluttr Executive Team
To: Melanie Strickland
Subject: CONFIDENTIAL

Dear Ms. Strickland,
We've been provided with your contact information as the primary owner of the website JerkAlert.biz. We have unsuccessfully attempted to contact you by phone, and would like to discuss some urgent confidential matters with you.

Please call us at (415) 555-2493 at your earliest convenience.

Regards,
The Fluttr Executive Team

Oh, shit.

My first instinct was denial. Maybe this wasn't from Fluttr at all. But if it wasn't really from Fluttr, then who could have possibly sent it? It wasn't like the girls to play a prank on me like this, and I doubted Alex had the time to be screwing around. Unless he opened his big mouth and told someone who does.

On the other hand, it was pretty easy to forge an email, but to spoof phone calls from a 415 area code takes a lot more effort. So maybe this actually *was from* Fluttr. But if it was, how did they get my contact information?

To make matters worse, the wording of this email wasn't particularly promising. *Urgent confidential matters.* Were they going to try to shut me down? Was this the precursor to some sort of cease-and-desist motion? Because I could not afford to hire a lawyer that would be tough enough to go up against whatever powerhouse legal team Fluttr employed.

I was in a full sweaty panic when Whit's text popped up on my screen: Did someone reach out to you today?

So Whitney was behind this.

At this point, I wasn't about to put anything potentially damaging in a text message. Those were admissible in court, and I was already at a strong disadvantage without digging myself into a deeper hole.

Grabbing my phone, I stalked through the halls, deliberately avoiding the Fizz area, and heading toward the row of conference rooms situated against the north wall. Most of them were occupied, but I spied one open door at the far end of the corridor. I broke into a run, dashing inside and turning the lock, before dialing Whitney's number.

"Isn't this exciting?" She sounded positively bubbly.

"I don't know. Is it? The email they sent sounded like a veiled threat."

"Look, they're not gonna give anything away in an email. But trust me, this is huge."

"Huge how? I don't even know what they want from me."

"Mel, this is the amazing opportunity I was talking about. Fluttr is impressed with what you've got going on, and they are willing to pay big bucks for it."

"Oh my God." This was it. The reward for all my hard work. "How did you make this happen?"

"A friend of a friend of a friend is a Content Strategist at Fluttr. She passed it on to someone on the design team, who passed it up the chain to someone on the board, who apparently flipped his shit when he saw it. You're welcome."

"Thank you so much, Whit. This is unbelievable."

"You deserve it, girl. All I ask in return is that you invite me to those parties in Silicon Valley when I come out to visit. I heard they're nuts."

"Slow down, I'm not moving to Silicon Valley." *Yet.*

"The hell you aren't. Go, call them back and see what they have to say. I wanna know all the details, immediately."

I hung up with Whit and pulled up the 415 number in my call history. While listening to the digital click of the ringtone in my earpiece, I stared out the window, at the East River, the Brooklyn skyline, the two bridges connecting the boroughs. The only thing I'd miss about working at Hatch was this breathtaking view.

"Fluttr Corporate Offices. This is Sheila. How may I direct your call?"

"Um, hi." I cleared my throat, affecting what I believed to be a professional tone of voice. "Hello. My name is Melanie Strickland. I'm returning a call that—"

"One moment, please."

Apparently, my name was recognizable enough that I didn't even need to finish the sentence. This was good. Very good.

The hold music cut out and a man came on the line. "Melanie?"

"Yes. Hello."

"Hey, it's great to hear from you. My name is Johnny Holder." An echo rang through the line. It sounded like he was on speakerphone. "I'm the CEO of Fluttr. I'm joined here in the room by my Chief Strategy Officer, Will Hertz, and my VP of Product, Mitch Lansford."

A chorus of faceless men said, "Hi."

"Uh, hi. Nice to…meet…you all," I said.

"You're probably wondering why we've contacted you. So let's cut right to the chase. JerkAlert is hot. We want it, we want you, let's do this."

This was moving faster than I'd anticipated.

"What do you say?" This guy was insistent. What did he say his name was again?

I opened my mouth, hoping one of the five thousand questions floating around in my brain might come sailing out. But all I managed to say was, "Okay."

"Okay, great! Listen, let's get you out here to the office to discuss logistics…" He trailed off, his voice lowering as he addressed his colleagues in the room. "When are you guys free? What're your schedules like?" After some unintelligible mumbling, he came back with a forceful, "Tomorrow at noon."

"Um…that sounds good, but you know I'm in New York, right?"

"Yeah, no problem. Sheila will hook you up with a flight out of JFK tonight."

Wow. So this is what life was like at a big Silicon Valley tech firm. Cross-country flights booked hours in advance. No biggie.

"Sound good?" he asked.

I wasn't sure; I hadn't had a chance to think about it. This guy was asking me to make a tremendous decision in a matter of seconds. Almost like the Fluttr app itself.

But I couldn't keep him waiting. What if he had second thoughts, and realized JerkAlert actually wasn't all that hot? I had to pounce, now, before this opportunity passed me by.

"Sounds good," I said.

"Fantastic. I'm gonna shoot you over to Sheila now—she'll help you work out all the travel stuff, the flight, the hotel, the whatever. We're looking forward to seeing you tomorrow."

"Likewise."

While hold music chimed in my ear, someone started pounding on the conference room door.

"The room is occupied," I called.

Muffled yells resounded from the hallway, followed by more pounding. I tried my best to ignore it as Sheila came back on the line, telling me she'd booked me on a direct flight to SFO at 7:25 p.m., with a reservation at the Westin in Union Square for the evening.

"Feel free to charge whatever meals or services you'd like to the hotel room. A car will be by to pick you up at 11:30 tomorrow morning."

"Thank you so much," I said. "See you then."

I ended the call and ran to the door, flinging it open to see Greg on the other end, one meaty fist balled up and ready to pound. "What are you doing?" I said. "I told you, the room was occupied."

"It's 12:30. We booked this room for the next two hours. Check the office calendar."

At his mention of the word *we*, I glanced over his shoulder.

Alex was standing behind him, looking in every direction but mine. Instantly, I was overcome with regret for breaking the golden rule of dating: never shit where you eat. Not that it mattered all that much, since I wouldn't be eating at Hatch much longer.

"Sorry," I said. "It's all yours."

"No harm, no foul," Greg said, then winked and twisted his lips into a sickening pucker. Was he trying to make a kissy-face at me? Because it looked like he just had bad gas.

I walked away, not looking back, clenching my fists to keep my hands from shaking uncontrollably. This was all too much. The call from Fluttr, the trip to California, the unexpected hallway meeting with the one person I'd been trying to avoid. Frankly, I was impressed with myself for keeping it together.

Instead of going straight back to my cubicle, I turned left, toward the server room, where I swiped my access card and hunted down Bob. I found him in his usual spot, on the floor, looking as surly and shabby as ever.

"What are you doing in here?" he said, by way of greeting.

"Remember when you said I needed a vacation? Well, I'm taking tomorrow off."

"You can't. It's Update Tuesday."

Shit. "I need the day off. And maybe Wednesday, too."

He made a patronizing face, sucking in his lips and raising his eyebrows. "Boy trouble got you down?"

My stomach dropped to my feet, which had somehow become soldered to the floor. How did Bob know about my breakup with Alex? How did he know I'd been involved with Alex in the first place?

"It has nothing to do with that," I said. "I just need the time off."

"Sorry. You can't have it." His eyes were already on his laptop. I'd been dismissed.

Well, fuck him.

No one was going to stop me from getting ahead. I planned to be on that plane tonight, whether Bob liked it or not.

23

I didn't bother to finish out the day. My flight took off in less than seven hours, and there was a lot to do beforehand. Like pack a suitcase, and take the A to Howard Beach before switching to the AirTrain. Plus, the security line at JFK would undoubtedly be a nightmare. I had to hustle if I wanted to get on board before they closed the cabin doors.

After leaving the server room, I went straight to my desk to enable my out of office message, then ran for the elevator. I made it home in under twenty minutes, which was some kind of record, and found Ray inspecting our kitchen countertops.

"Hi, Melanie, how you doin'?"

"Good." I moved toward him, but stopped abruptly when I noticed that our kitchen looked completely different. And much, much nicer. "Did you install new countertops?" I ran my hand over the cool, smooth surface. "Is this granite?"

"Nah, it's not real." He held up a roll of what looked like thick, shiny wrapping paper. "It's called 'Instant Granite.' Pretty cool, huh? Found it on Pinterest. It's an easy upgrade.

Makes the place look nicer without spending a fortune or pissing off the landlord."

"It's awesome. Thanks a lot."

Vanessa emerged from her bedroom. Still engrossed in a full day of virtual assisting, her Bluetooth headset flashed in her ear. "What're you doing home?" she asked.

"I have to catch a plane tonight," I said, remembering how much there was to do and how little time there was to do it all.

"Where are you going?"

"San Francisco. I've got a…job interview tomorrow."

Her bottom lip protruded in a tragic pout. "Are you moving away?"

"No. I don't know. I'm not really sure what's gonna happen. But I have nothing to wear."

She held up her hand. "Say no more. I can help." Turning to Ray, she said, "Everything okay out here?"

He smiled as if he worshipped her existence. "Everything's great, baby."

In my room, Vanessa closed the door and clapped her hands together, surveying the tangled mess that was my tiny closet. "This is…" She trailed off and sighed. "We can work with it, we can. Where are you interviewing?"

"A tech company in Silicon Valley."

"Which one?"

"Fluttr."

From the look of horror on her face, you'd have thought I'd said "Hell."

"Like I said," I continued, "I don't know what's gonna happen. If I can score something with them, though, it'd be huge for my career." *And my debt pile.*

"No judgment." She turned back to my closet, picking

daintily through my clothes. "You need something that says 'girlboss.'"

"I don't have much." As a help desk analyst, my wardrobe consisted mainly of outfits I felt comfortable wearing while crawling around on the floor behind a malfunctioning printer. And that one discount blazer.

"We'll find something," she said, then pulled her phone out of her back pocket. "I've got a Pinterest board for this."

"For what?"

"How to shop your closet. Basically, how to take pieces you already own and mix them up to make something different. I know I pinned something in here about creating stylish ensembles from comfy basics." She scrolled up, squinting at her screen. "Aha! Here it is."

We spent the next half hour going through my stretchy pants and billowy shirts and garbage bag dresses. Miraculously, Vanessa came up with two separate options for interview outfits that looked not just presentable, but totally chic.

"The key is to accessorize," she said, pulling out belts and earrings and something called "statement necklaces" from her own stash to pull the looks together.

"You're so good at this," I said.

"It's fun." She cinched a thick braided belt around my waist and smoothed the fabric above the buckle. "There, that's perfect."

I assessed my reflection in the full-length mirror bolted to the back of my door. "Thanks. You saved me."

"No problem. Where are you staying in San Francisco?"

"The Westin in Union Square."

"That's a nice hotel. Fluttr must really be trying to win you over. While you're there, you should grab a drink in the lobby at the Clock Bar. It's super cute and they have the best cocktails."

"You've been to San Francisco?"

"I used to live there." She gathered my discarded clothes and hung them back up in the closet. "My ex worked at a tech start-up. He got in on the ground floor before they blew up really big."

That explained why she walked away from the marriage with a huge lump of cash. "Is he still there?"

"Last I heard, he got fired. I'm not surprised—he's a total cokehead." She took a deep breath and closed my closet. "I actually looked him up on JerkAlert the other day. He's one of those losers that sends out dick pics."

"No!"

"Yeah. Obviously, I'm much better off now."

"Obviously." I took off my shoes and tossed them into my open suitcase. "So, are you and Ray, like, officially an item?"

She shrugged. "We're taking it slow. I'm not thrilled about the fact that he's living with his mother, but like you said, he can't live with her forever. And who knows? Maybe he *will* change his mind. In the meantime, our apartment is getting some serious upgrades."

"I know. Those countertops are amazing."

"He's got some ideas for an easy backsplash, too. Which reminds me, I wanted to show him this pin."

With her nose in her phone, Vanessa left the room, and I got to work packing the rest of my stuff. In addition to the outfits we'd assembled, I also made sure to bring my laptop, as well as all the handwritten notes I'd taken while JerkAlert was under development. The six-hour flight would be the perfect time to put together a PowerPoint presentation all about my motivation for creating the site, a brief high-level code walk-through, and some stats about web traffic and performance.

Of course, I didn't want to spend *too* long discussing performance, since it was clearly JerkAlert's main weakness. My tweaks had helped, but the hosting service had its limitations, and it couldn't handle much more in terms of load. Fortunately, this problem could be solved easily with an influx of Fluttr cash. Moving JerkAlert to a spendy but spacious server farm would speed things up significantly. I'd make sure they understood that.

Packed and ready to go, I wheeled my suitcase out the door, waving goodbye to Ray and Vanessa, who were taking measurements in the kitchen. "Good luck," they said in unison.

"Thanks," I called, and let the door close behind me.

Between signal problems, congestion, and the general clusterfuck of New York City public transportation, it took about an hour and a half for me to get from my home on State Street to Terminal 4 at JFK Airport. As suspected, the security line was out of control, nothing but a disorganized clump of angry travelers, barely contained by a handful of apathetic TSA personnel. I meandered to what appeared to be the end of the line, but when I showed my boarding pass to the ticket agent, she shook her head.

"You want Priority Boarding," she said, gesturing to a much shorter, much calmer line of people. Happy people, who strolled through the metal detectors with their shoes still on their feet and their laptops still safely stowed in their bags.

"I'm not TSA PreCheck," I said.

She glared at me. "You're First Class. That gets you in over there. Unless you'd *like* to wait in this line."

First Class?

I'd never flown First Class in my life. I hadn't flown all that much, to be honest, but when I did, I was always crammed into those tiny coach seats in the back of the airplane, like a pleb. Things like free food and legroom and short security lines were completely foreign concepts to me.

But, I guess, they wouldn't be anymore, now that I was entering this new phase of my life. The high-tech, high-flying, Silicon Valley start-up phase.

Sauntering through the Priority Boarding lane, I reveled in my new status, thinking about how different things were going to be. Daily lunch would no longer be a sad peanut butter sandwich; it'd be an overpriced organic salad packed with non-GMO superfoods. And forget fitness Groupons, because now I could afford my very own gym membership, at a fancy gym.

Most important, I'd no longer be drowning in debt. Because once I got my big payday, the first check I'd write would be to my student loan servicer. I couldn't wait to get the notice that my obligation was paid in full. I'd frame it and keep it on my desk, right next to my college diploma. Finally, this computer science degree was going to prove its worth.

After flying through security, I made my way to the Sky Club, also known as the First Class Lounge. It was even more beautiful than I'd imagined it would be. A smiling woman greeted me at the front desk, confirming that yes, I belonged here, before handing me a complimentary glass of white wine. She directed me to a room filled with ambient music and plush seating, framed by glass walls overlooking the bustle of the runway. I loaded a plate up with munchies from the free snack bar, and settled into a comfy chair.

This was the life.

As I feasted on tomato basil flatbread crackers with a peppercorn parmesan spread, I connected my phone to the Sky Club's WiFi. With the commotion going on all day, I'd barely had time to check in on social media. I started by loading my Twitter feed, where, to my delight and surprise, #JerkAlert was trending again.

It took a minute to scroll through an interminable number of retweets and replies before I finally found the source of the drama: an article on BrosBeforeHos.com. At which point, my delight disappeared.

JerkAlert: Where Trash Girls Talk Trash

By Anony-bro

Posted: Monday, April 23, 1:28 p.m.

Fellas, we've all been there: you meet a chick on Fluttr, you hit it off, and you wind up banging. The next day, while you're chilling at home trying to complete a mission in Mass Effect, she's blowing up your phone, asking to see you again. What gives?

Everyone knows Fluttr is a hookup app. By design, it encourages superficial, split-second decision-making—not the smartest way to go about meeting the love of your life. Yet so many people (read: women) insist on treating it like a matchmaking service.

Now these birdbrains have formed a support network in JerkAlert (that's .biz, not .com…someone in marketing didn't do their branding homework before coming up with that name), a crowdsourced directory of men whose Fluttr hookups expected a whole lot more than just a one-night stand—and when they didn't get it, they got even.

We get it. These girls are hurt. But, in some cases, the

stuff they're posting is downright cruel. So if you've ever swiped right and had it turn sour, you might wanna check out JerkAlert to see if you're listed. Then change your name and move to a different neighborhood, pronto.

With my heart in my throat, I texted the link to the girls:

MEL:

Whit, have you seen this?

WHITNEY:

Jgh, yes.

DANI:

VTF is BrosBeforeHos.com?

WHITNEY:

It sounds like some
men's rights activist bullshit.

LIA:

've heard of it before.
ay subscribed to their newsletter.

WHITNEY:

hat should've been your first clue
hat he was an asshole.

LIA:

MEL:

Okay, but what about this article?
I'm in the airport waiting for a flight to SF right now.
What if Fluttr sees this? Should I be worried?

WHITNEY:

No. It's publicity. You know how
much traffic this'll drive to your website?

LIA:

This article is garbage.

DANI:

Yeah, it's garbage…but there's some
truth buried in there, too.

WHITNEY:

What the hell is that supposed to mean?

DANI:

Have you looked at the Reddit thread
the author references?

WHITNEY:

Don't have time. Running to SoulCycle.
Give me the two-second summary.

DANI:

Basically, most of it's a bunch of dudes
whining and being sexist, but there were a few
posts in there that gave me pause. JerkAlert was
designed to out the most egregiously offensive
Fluttr users, right? Cheaters, harassers, etc. But it
seems to be turning into, for lack of a better term,
a slam book.

WHITNEY:

Whatever.

Dani sent permalinks to a few comments she felt exemplified her point. Like DJZellyZell, who said:

> Some girl I had a one-night stand with six months ago told everyone on JerkAlert I have a "teeny weenie." But it's not! It's a fine size.

Or SlimTheSlug, who said:

> Yeah, I made mistakes with my ex, I admit it. I was a bad boyfriend to her, but I was also a lot less mature than I am now. With this site, though, it's like I'll never be able to prove I'm a changed man. I'll always be judged by my relationship with her, for the rest of my life. I can never just wipe the slate clean.

I wasn't sure why this comment made Dani second-guess the merit of JerkAlert. We all had to live with the choices we made for the rest of our lives. Who knew how SlimTheSlug had hurt his ex-girlfriend, or what he did to her? Maybe she was left with scars that would never heal.

MEL:

I'm not sure I agree with you.

DANI:

Fair enough. Take a look at this one, though.

She sent one more comment, posted by Piquete92:

> I got dumped because of my JerkAlert profile. The stuff written there wasn't even true, but she wouldn't believe me. JerkAlert is terrible, Fluttr is terrible. The whole inter-

net is terrible. It feeds our worst fears, incites paranoia, turns the past into the present, and ruins the magic of an unknown future. Sometimes I wish we would all unplug from it completely.

There was hurt in those words. Pain, disappointment. At once, my thoughts went to Alex, the look on his face when I showed him his JerkAlert profile. His eyes were so sad. Like he couldn't believe I'd betrayed him like that.

But I hadn't betrayed him. I was merely protecting myself, and I was right to do it. Maybe if he'd told me the truth from the very beginning, none of this would've happened. Maybe then, we might still be together.

Or maybe not.

Either way, now was not the time to play a game of what-if. It was time to get to work. So I put away my phone, took out my laptop, and started planning a kick-ass presentation.

24

If Vanessa was right, and Fluttr was trying to win me over, I'd say they succeeded in their endeavor.

Nothing says "you're special" quite like a trip in First Class. There's no fighting for overhead space. Flight attendants are constantly smiling at you, offering hot towels and complimentary prosecco. You get a hot meal, and it actually tastes good. You can practically *lie down*.

But the wooing didn't end when the plane parked at the gate, because Fluttr sent a car to pick me up at the airport. As I descended the escalator to the lower concourse, I spotted a man standing there at the bottom, a placard in his hand reading M. STRICKLAND. He carried my bag to his Tesla Model S and delivered me comfortably to the Westin, where the seduction of the high life continued.

The hotel suite was easily twice the size of my whole apartment. There were leather chairs, a Jacuzzi tub, a marble slab fireplace. On the dining table there was a bouquet of huge expensive-looking flowers, with a note:

Looking forward to our meeting tomorrow. Hope you enjoy your stay.
—The Fluttr Team

With these views, how could I *not* enjoy my stay? From this vantage point, I could see Alcatraz, the Golden Gate Bridge, the light of the full moon twinkling off the bay. Too bad I was in town for less than twenty-four hours; I would've liked the chance to tour around the city a bit. Maybe I could squeeze a little sightseeing in after my meeting and before my red-eye the next night. Although, if Fluttr hired me and I moved out here, I'd have all the time in the world to explore San Francisco.

For now, I ordered up dinner—flat iron steak, a glass of merlot, a chocolate *pot de crème*, all on Fluttr's dime—and reviewed my PowerPoint. I was more than ready for this. Tomorrow would be the first day of the next phase of my life.

Which is why I turned in early, skipping that drink at the Clock Bar that Vanessa had recommended. When I showed up at Fluttr HQ, I didn't want to be hungover. I wanted to be refreshed, and fortunately, sleep came easy on that luxurious California king. In the morning, I ate a light breakfast and dressed in one of my carefully curated outfits, cinching the belt around my dress exactly the way Vanessa had shown me, slipping into stack-heeled Mary Janes and a silver beaded statement necklace.

I looked hot, I felt hot, and I was gonna take the tech world by storm.

A Tesla pulled up to the curb of the Westin at 11:30, just as Sheila had promised. The drive from Union Square to Mid-Market was short, and in under ten minutes, I was standing in front of a seven-story art deco building, with relief sculptures and geometric columns and a gigantic Fluttr signboard hanging from the side. I pushed through the heavy glass doors and into the immense, echoing lobby, where a smiling security guard asked to see my ID before sending me up to the executive suite.

Sheila met me at the elevator. "Hello, Ms. Strickland. How was your flight?"

"It was great, thank you."

"Wonderful." I followed her down a wood-paneled corridor with slate floors and antique sconces. "Can I get you anything to drink? Water, coffee?"

"No, thank you. I'm good." Nerves were starting to kick in. If I drank anything now, I'd have to interrupt my meeting with a bathroom break.

She opened the door to a sunny space that looked more like a lounge than a conference room. There was a massive sectional and matching tub chairs, a glass coffee table atop a color-block carpet. The high-definition TV mounted to the wall showed a steady scroll of Fluttr profiles, which were being swiped in real time. Across the top of the screen, the familiar slogan shouted: Don't Let the *One* Get Away.

"They'll be with you in just a moment," Sheila said, then closed the door, leaving me alone.

With anxiety building inside of me, I focused outward, on the TV screen. It was almost meditative, watching Fluttr users fly by, the images so fleeting I could barely focus on one before it disappeared, replaced with a new one.

Minutes passed that felt like hours, until eventually, the door popped open and in walked three men. Their outfits were almost identical: ripped jeans, sneakers, and Fluttr hoodies. I leaped out of my seat, feeling supremely stupid for spending so much time worrying about what to wear.

"Melanie!" The guy in the lead held his arms out, like he wanted to give me a hug. Not wanting to make things awkward, I complied, holding my pelvis a good six inches away from him as our torsos embraced.

Fortunately, the other two guys just shook my hand.

"I'm Johnny," he said, then pointed to his colleagues. "This is Will and Mitch."

"Hi, it's so nice to meet you all. Thanks for bringing me out here."

"Oh, it was our pleasure." He surveyed me from head to toe, then gestured toward the chair I'd been sitting in. "Please, make yourself comfortable. Did Sheila get you something to drink?"

"I'm fine, thanks."

"Good, good." The three men sat in a line on the couch, directly across from me. Mitch and Will sat back, crossing their legs, while Johnny leaned forward with his elbows on his knees. "It's wonderful to finally meet you. We've heard good things. Honestly, when I got your contact info, I was shocked to hear this was a solo project. You really don't have any partners or anything?"

"Nope, it's just me."

He made a little sound of surprise, then said, "Well, JerkAlert. Amazing concept. Truly. Just love it."

The guy to Johnny's left—I couldn't remember if it was Mitch or Will, they looked the same—tapped the tablet in his hand, and the Fluttr profiles on the flat screen disappeared, replaced with the JerkAlert home page.

"This is disruptive technology at its finest. In fact, it's so disruptive, it disrupts disruptive technology." Johnny cackled at his nonsensical statement. "Tell us how you came up with the idea."

"Um, actually..." I pointed down at the laptop bag beside my feet. "I put together a little PowerPoint explaining it all. If I can just connect to your TV, I'll walk you through it."

Mitch (or Will) snickered, and Johnny bit his bottom lip. "We don't really do PowerPoints here."

I blinked. "You don't *do* them."

"No, they're counterproductive. I'm sure you worked hard on it, but let's just chat."

"Okay." I cleared my throat, trying to remember what I'd typed into those slides. Being put on the spot like this always made me nervous; I'd been hoping to use the bullet points on the presentation to guide me safely through this discussion. Now, with these three guys staring at me and no notes to keep me on track, my mind was a total blank.

Will and Mitch exchanged self-satisfied looks, but Johnny squinted, patiently waiting for my response. And suddenly, I remembered: Fluttr was trying to woo me. I had something they wanted, badly enough to fly me First Class across the country and put me up in a fancy hotel. There was no reason for me to worry about blowing this, because I was the one holding all the cards.

"Well," I said, "it all started one night after I'd had a really bad couple of experiences with Fluttr."

"Like what?"

"One guy stood me up. And then another one kept sending me dick pics."

"Yeah, that happens a lot."

"A *lot*. And I don't mean to sound critical, but it doesn't seem like Fluttr has an effective method of putting a stop to it. You can flag profiles, but they never actually get suspended."

"We don't really believe in account suspension."

"Even when people are using their accounts to harass other Fluttr users?"

"Harassment is a strong word." Johnny touched the tips of his fingers together and pursed his lips. "I don't think a man who sends a picture of his penis is trying to purposely make anyone feel uncomfortable. I think they're just inexperienced."

"Inexperienced."

"Yeah. Guys are nervous around girls. They don't know what to do or say. They see a pretty face and they act stupid. I'm not saying it's right, but I also don't think it's depraved, like some people try to make it out to be. Honestly, I don't think what women experience on Fluttr is any different than what they might encounter in a real-world singles scene, like in a bar."

"Interesting." I wasn't quite sure how to respond. Personally, I'd never had a guy whip his dick out on me in a bar. I was sure it had happened plenty of times to plenty of other women, though I was also sure it happened a lot more frequently on Fluttr. Flashing someone was a lot easier when you didn't have to look them in the eye.

But the man sitting across from me was a multimillionaire who ran the most successful dating app in history. Did I really want to have this argument right now, right here, in his executive suite? No. Especially not when there was a good chance he was about to offer me money or a job or both. There would be time to fix what was broken about this system after I'd successfully clawed my way out of debt.

His attitude certainly explained a lot about why Fluttr

worked the way it did, though. It also demonstrated why JerkAlert was a necessity.

Will/Mitch spoke up for the first time. "It cuts both ways, right? Did you see that Reddit thread about JerkAlert yesterday? Women can be pretty terrible, too."

"Yeah," Mitch/Will replied. "I felt bad for a couple of those guys."

"Like the 'teeny weenie' dude."

The three of them sucked air through clenched teeth, their faces distressed.

"I was disappointed to see that Reddit thread," I said.

Johnny laughed, like I was making a joke. "Nah, that thread was great. As of this morning, there were over nine hundred forty-four comments. You couldn't ask for a better advertisement."

"Yes, but I hadn't realized the negative ramifications of allowing women to post whatever they wanted on JerkAlert. To that end, I've given some thought to different methods of how to police the data to make sure only valid and relevant reviews get posted."

He dismissed me with a wave of his hand. "Let's not worry about that. Now, Mitch, can you bring up the search page for a minute? I have a question about how the JerkAlert profiles get linked to Fluttr."

Mitch tapped his tablet and we sat in silence for a few seconds, waiting for the page to load. It was awfully slow. Much slower than usual, even when accounting for recent performance issues.

Then, as if I was trapped in some hideous nightmare, an error message filled the screen: 504 Gateway Timeout.

JerkAlert wasn't responding. My app had crashed.

Shit. Shit, shit, shit.

"Web traffic must've increased because of the Reddit thread," I said. "The server is probably overloaded."

"Don't worry about it," Johnny said. "The code probably just needs to be refactored."

"The code is totally clean, I swear. It's a hosting issue. If the site was moved to a load-balanced environment, this would not be happening."

"Right." He exchanged sidelong glances with Mitch and Will and I resisted the urge to throw up. Because I knew what they were thinking: *Girls can't code for shit.*

Determined to prove them wrong, I reached for my laptop, flipping it open and turning it on in one movement. "Let me give you a quick code walk-through. You can see for yourself how it works."

Johnny held up his palm. "Melanie, that's not necessary. We're not interested in the code."

"You're not?"

He shook his head. I was completely confused. Clicking my laptop closed, I asked, "Then can you tell me why I'm here?"

"Fluttr would like to purchase the JerkAlert database."

"Just the database?"

"Yes. We're willing to pay five hundred thousand dollars."

"Uh..." It was a struggle to form words or to think coherent thoughts.

Half a million dollars.

They wanted to give me half a million dollars for something I'd created on an angry whim less than three weeks ago.

"That sounds..." I took a deep breath, slowly blew it out. *Get yourself under control, Mel.* "That sounds intriguing. And you're just interested in the database? Not the code?"

"Right. We're gonna chuck the whole front end and integrate it seamlessly with the Fluttr app."

"This data is just a starting point," Will/Mitch added. "Eventually, we'd like to align JerkAlert users with Fluttr accounts so that people can start leaving reviews directly on other people's profiles."

"So, the reviews would no longer be anonymous?"

"Well, they'd be anonymous to Fluttr users," he said. "But the important thing is *we'd* know who was writing them. That way we could track their activity more efficiently."

"Obviously," Johnny said, "we'd also be adding the ability for Fluttr users to review women."

"Really?"

I imagined the kinds of reviews I might find on my Fluttr profile: Snooped beneath my bathroom sink. Stalked my ex-girlfriend. Kept a huge secret from me then accused *me* of being the liar in our relationship. Horrifying!

Johnny snickered. "Of course. To allow women to rank men but not the other way around is reverse sexism, no? And let's not forget we have a tremendous number of LGBTQ users who would also be participating. We can't just narrow this down to a man-versus-woman thing."

"Right," Mitch/Will said. "Anyone on Fluttr would be able to review anyone else. No restrictions."

I swallowed hard. None of this felt right.

"What role would I be expected to play in this whole project?" I asked.

"Role?"

"Would I be joining the Fluttr team to assist with integration?"

He looked insulted. "Why would you want to join the

Fluttr team? We'd be giving you half a million dollars. Take the money and enjoy yourself. Go travel or something."

"Well, I feel like I could bring a lot to the team." Although, now that I realized what the team was going to be doing with this data, I wasn't sure I wanted to be on it anymore.

Of course, it's not like that had ever been an option.

"Listen," he said, slowly, as if he were talking to a child. "I'm not sure you're the right culture fit for Fluttr. To be clear, this isn't an offer of employment. It's a one-time business transaction."

I bristled at the words *culture fit*. What did that mean, exactly? Was he referring to the fact that I was wearing a dress and heels while they were decked out in hoodies and jeans? Or was he talking about something more deep-rooted, something completely immutable?

"So." Johnny clapped his hands together so loudly, I jumped. "Do you have any questions for us?"

There were lots of questions swirling around in my brain, but one of them stood out above all.

"In that Reddit thread yesterday, there was some debate over whether Fluttr was designed for finding hookups or for helping people find love. Which one is it?"

They all laughed. "Does it really matter? People use it for both, don't they?"

"Right. But what was the intention? When you first developed Fluttr, what problem were you trying to solve? How did you envision this app would help people?"

"Who said anything about helping people?"

I kept waiting for Johnny to say, "Just kidding!" but instead, the room filled with stony silence.

"You're serious," I said.

"We're not in the business of relationships here. We're in the business of data collection. Do you know how many people use our app every month? Twelve million. Every day, we average over a billion swipes worldwide. That's an incredible amount of information. Our databases are overflowing with locations, interests, behaviors, messages. That data is powerful and valuable. That's what matters."

"To who?"

"To advertisers. Personal data is what drives this economy. Not relationships. But, hey, if we help a few people get laid, all the better, right?"

"Right." I forced myself to smile, even though I felt like I was going to be sick.

It turned out Fluttr wasn't a hookup app, but it wasn't a way to meet the love of your life, either. It had absolutely nothing to do with human connection. It was all about gathering data, and trading that data for money. Counting swipes, tracking whereabouts, collecting statistics. Hooking into a person's most private moments and deepest desires purely for a profit.

"So, what do you say?" Johnny smirked. He was a man who was used to getting what he wanted.

"I need some time to think."

Even as I said the words, a panicked voice inside my head shouted: *You fool! What are you doing? Take the money! Now, now, now!* But I was too conflicted. Yes, I needed the money, but was this really how I wanted to earn it? I wasn't so sure.

Johnny's lip curled. A man who was used to getting what he wanted wasn't too thrilled when he heard the word *no.* Or even the word *maybe.*

"You're taking the red-eye tonight, right?"

I nodded.

"Then sleep on it," he said. "Let me know in the morning."

The three of them left the room without saying goodbye.

25

My desire to see the sights of San Francisco quickly vanished. Instead, I went straight to the airport and switched to an earlier flight, then spent the entire five and a half hours downing complimentary vodka sodas and spiraling into an anxious abyss.

I know, I sounded ungrateful. After all, I'd been offered more money than many people would ever see in a lifetime. I should've been whooping it up, bouncing around in this spacious First Class seat and planning a student loan payoff party. But I couldn't move. It felt like a cinder block had lodged itself deep in my guts, pinning me to the buttery leather.

As I stared out the window into the darkening sky, I kept thinking about how wrong I'd been. The flight, the chauffeur, the hotel—it all had me feeling so convinced that today was going to be the first day of the next phase of my life.

But it wasn't. It was more like a false start.

Don't get me wrong, half a million dollars would've changed my world significantly. It could easily get me out of debt, with enough left over to buy a small studio apartment in an uncool section of Brooklyn. I could even quit the help desk, remain funemployed for a little while.

Once I did that, though, what came next? I couldn't very well kick my feet up and do nothing for the rest of my life. Even if I wanted to, half a million dollars wouldn't sustain me forever. So where would I go from here?

I'd always said I wanted to create something of value. Not just monetary value, but a product or a service that would improve people's lives. With JerkAlert, I'd done that: I'd created a safe, communal space for women to vent about being harassed, to call men out on their inappropriate behavior, and to help find a trustworthy partner. To me, it wasn't just "data." It was one huge cautionary tale. It was catharsis.

If I accepted this offer, though, I'd be selling out to the very same man who'd created the problem I'd been trying to solve. A dick pic apologizer, who enabled Fluttr to become a free-for-all of harassment and emotional detachment. A man who reduced everyone's personal experiences to a bunch of data points. Handing this database over to him meant JerkAlert would be dismantled, the information would be sold to advertisers, and all that value I'd created would go away.

Then again, if I was being honest with myself, was JerkAlert really as helpful as I'd deluded myself into thinking it was? In the end, it had turned into a slam book, like Dani said. Sure, it had helped Lia discover the truth about Jay, but that was only after she'd caught him in a lie. JerkAlert merely confirmed her suspicions.

And then there was Alex. Every time I thought about what went down between us, a knot formed in my stomach. Because now that I'd had some distance from the whole situation, I realized JerkAlert hadn't helped me out. It had actually made things worse, feeding my paranoia. I had an almost obsessive need to catch him in a lie, and I didn't stop searching until I found one. I guess in that way, JerkAlert had helped me out.

But let's say I'd never found out the truth about Jenny. That I'd gone on believing she was an inconsequential first Fluttr date, and never thought twice about her again. Would it have changed the fundamental foundation of my relationship with Alex? I wasn't so sure.

Yes, it was a lie. But it was an inconsequential lie. It didn't impact our interactions, our experiences, our feelings for one another. At least, it wouldn't have if I'd simply let it go.

The truth was, I'd been far more dishonest with him than he'd been with me. Spying, snooping, keeping secrets. That's what ultimately led to the demise of our relationship. Not his little white lie.

When my plane touched down at JFK, my head was pounding. I'd achieved a new low: hungover at 10:00 p.m. Grabbing my bag from the overhead, I dragged myself down the Jetway and into the terminal, where there was no one waiting for me with a fancy placard or a Tesla. There was only the AirTrain, and the A train. On the walk home from the subway station, I saw a drunk man pissing on a pile of garbage bags, as if to say, "Welcome back to Brooklyn." This was my low-tech, low-flying lifestyle.

I fell asleep well after midnight, sleeping fitfully. By the time I woke up, the sun was already shining high. Light streamed in through the cracked blinds, illuminating the mess on my floor. Rumpled clothes, discarded Doritos bags, the crack in my phone that I couldn't afford to get fixed.

And I realized: Why on earth would I ever turn this Fluttr offer down?

By selling out, I would become part of the problem. But if I said no, it's not like the problem would magically disappear. Fluttr wasn't going anywhere. With millions of people and billions of swipes, it was only going to keep growing, getting bigger and more popular, collecting more data and earning more money. Why shouldn't I get a piece of that pie?

This was what the tech industry was all about. Johnny said it himself: the economy ran on data. To be successful meant to make some morally ambiguous decisions. Look at Hatch, and that farcical Code of Conduct. Vijay talked a lot about decency and respect, but when it came down to it, he didn't foster a decent or respectful work environment.

So instead of playing the martyr, I was going to pay off my loans. And fix this damn phone screen. Maybe I'd even take a proper vacation. But, perhaps most important, I was going to quit that miserable help desk.

I picked up my phone and shot off an email.

From: Melanie Strickland
To: The Fluttr Executive Team
Subject: re: CONFIDENTIAL

Hello,
After giving it considerable thought, I'm pleased to inform you that I gladly accept your offer to purchase the JerkAlert database.

Please let me know how you'd like to proceed with the transaction.

Sincerely,
Melanie Strickland

As I hit Send, I sighed, releasing ten pounds of pressure from my chest. This wasn't exactly what I thought my big break in the start-up world would look like, but it's what I had. And it wasn't bad.

With that decision made, it was time to head to Hatch and tell Bob to go shove it. I showered, dressed, and got back on the subway, grabbing a grande Flat White from Starbucks on the way in, simply because I could afford it now.

During the commute into the city, I entertained myself with daydreams, imagining the look on Bob's face when I told him the news. He'd be totally blindsided. The best part was, without an immediate replacement, Bob was going to have to take on the bulk of the help desk work. No more hiding out in the server room for him. Hopefully, he wouldn't give the Hatchlings a hard time.

I strolled into One Seaport Plaza with a smile on my face, my half-empty coffee cup still in my hand. Rather than going to my cubicle, I went directly to Bob's office.

"Knock knock," I said.

He smirked. "So nice of you to finally show up."

"We need to talk," I said.

"You're right, we do. But not here." He stood up from behind his desk and pointed into the hallway. "Follow me."

I imagined he had plans to chew me out for skipping work yesterday. Perhaps he wanted to take me into a conference room to do it. A place where we could both sit down, unlike his cluttered hovel of an office.

He led me down the corridor, through the open cube farm housing the Hatchlings. As we passed the Fizz area, I kept my eyes on the floor, hoping to pass by unnoticed. But I didn't have to look up to know Alex was staring at me. I could feel the heat from his gaze traveling all over my body.

Then it hit me: this could very well be the last time I ever saw him. Suddenly, I felt the urge to run to him, to talk about what happened, to suggest we wipe the slate clean and start over. I looked up, eager to catch his eye. It was too late, though. He was already looking away.

So I kept following Bob, who was walking toward an area of the floor I'd never been to. Where was he taking me? Was there some hidden conference room reserved for reprimands?

Then he stopped in front of a big blue door. The placard beside it read V. Agrawal. Bob had taken me to Vijay's office. As if the founder of Hatch cared about my illicit day off. He didn't even know who I was.

This was laughable. But if that's what Bob wanted, I'd just have to quit in front of them both.

The door opened, and there was Vijay. He nodded at Bob, then looked at me, a glint of recognition in his eye. "Melanie, Bob. Come in."

Since when did Vijay know my name?

As we entered his office and took our seats, I noticed the stark contrast between his drab brown surroundings and the colorful whimsy of the Fluttr executive suites. I'd always thought Vijay was such a big deal, but after seeing the Silicon Valley heavyweights in action, it became clear he was pretty small potatoes.

He had a great view, though.

"So," he said, clasping his hands on his desk blotter, "you're probably wondering why you're here."

"It is a bit strange." My eyes drifted out the window, following a helicopter as it flew across the river. "I've worked here for four years and I've never been called to your office before."

"Well, there's never been a reason to speak with you until

now. In short, I'm very interested in what you've been doing with JerkAlert."

I gripped the arms of my chair, afraid I might fall out, since Vijay's drab brown office seemed to be tilting onto its side.

Maybe I'd misheard. "Excuse me?"

"Your website. JerkAlert."

Okay, I hadn't misheard.

In that case, maybe I could just play dumb. "I don't know what you're talking about."

"Don't play dumb, Melanie," Bob said. "We've got all the logs. We know what you've been up to."

"Logs?"

"Do you think we can't track everything you do on our computers?" Vijay said.

At first, I didn't understand what he meant. I created JerkAlert at home, on my personal laptop. But, of course, I *had* logged in to the admin dashboard from work a lot to check up on stats. And there was all that time I'd spent tweaking the existing code to account for performance problems.

God, I was an idiot.

"After you started slacking off," Bob said, "I decided to start monitoring your web activity. I also installed a keylogger on your system to see exactly what you were up to. Since you pointed out that it was sanctioned by the Code of Conduct, I figured it was the most efficient way to ensure you were adhering to company policy at all times. When I found what you were doing with JerkAlert, it suddenly made sense. You were distracted by boy trouble."

"I wasn't distracted by boy trouble," I said. "I was building a website. One that's become quite popular, by the way."

"Yes," Vijay said, grinning. "I've noticed how much publicity it's received, which means traffic is increasing. However, I think performance would improve if it was moved to a load-balanced environment. We can make room on one of Hatch's server farms."

Unbelievable. Vijay had sat back for years, allowing the Hatchlings to treat me like garbage. Now that I had a successful side project going on, he expected me to jump on board and become a Hatchling myself, all so he could make a quick buck. Well, it wasn't gonna happen.

"I don't want to move it to one of Hatch's server farms."

His face was warm, his smile was kind. "I'm afraid you don't have a choice."

"Actually, I do. This is my website. I created it all by myself."

"Using Hatch's resources."

"No. Maybe I tweaked it here and there while I was at work, but I built the bulk of it while I was home. Using my own personal laptop."

He produced a thick stack of printed pages from his desk drawer, slapping it on the desk in front of me. "I suggest you read the Intellectual Property Agreement you signed on your first day with Hatch."

I vaguely remembered my first day. It was a whirlwind of introductions and instructions and, yes, mountains of paperwork. I'd been ushered into Benny's office and asked to sign contract after contract. I barely read any of it, and after a while I stopped even asking what it was I was signing. I was just so happy to finally have a paying job, I'd have probably signed away my firstborn.

Which, in a way, I guess I did.

"According to this," he continued, "we own any software

you've developed on a Hatch-issued device, at any stage of its development. Including small tweaks."

"Well," I said, "this is coming a little too late. Because I've already accepted an offer from Fluttr. They're purchasing the database. It's a done deal."

"I'm afraid it's not a done deal." Vijay's voice was so calm and good-natured, it was hard to believe he was threatening me.

"JerkAlert is mine." I shot out of my seat. "You can't steal it from me."

"It's not stealing, Melanie. You willingly signed that agreement. It's legally binding. If you don't believe me, consult your lawyers. You'll need them if you try to fight us on this."

Vijay smiled again. What an infuriating little man.

"This isn't over." I snatched the Intellectual Property Agreement from his desk and ran toward the door.

"Oh, Melanie?" Bob called. "One last thing before you go."

With my hand on the doorknob, I paused and turned back, hunching my shoulders against whatever bomb he was about to drop.

"You're fired for improper use of company resources."

Boom.

26

I was not going to freak out.

Freaking out would not fix this.

What would fix this was a time machine. Some way to go back and erase the moment I decided to make those tweaks to JerkAlert on my work computer.

Or better yet, to erase the moment I decided to make JerkAlert at all. Because honestly, what good had it done me? It had brought nothing but pain to my life: a pink slip, a breakup. The worst part was, Hatch would now reap all the benefits of my hard work, and I wouldn't see a dime.

Or at least, that's what Vijay said. Who knew if I should believe him?

Since time travel wasn't an option, there was only one thing left to do: sit down and read this Intellectual Property Agreement from cover to cover. I returned to my empty apartment, brewed a fresh pot of coffee, and curled up with the pages I'd swiped from Vijay's desk. I was sure I'd find a loophole in there somewhere.

Except I couldn't understand a damn thing I was reading. The entire thing was written in legalese of the highest order. There were some scary-looking terms in there, though, like the whole section referring to "Prior Inventions" and "Future Assurances." Did this mean Hatch owned anything I'd ever made or ever would make, in perpetuity?

The hell if I knew. The entire document was indecipherable.

I started wishing for that time machine again. Only now, I wanted to turn the clock back even further, to freshman year in college, to the moment I checked the little box on the form to declare my major. Computer science seemed like such a good idea at the time. It was fun (mostly) and I was good at it (mostly) and I thought I would make great money. I didn't realize I'd still be drowning in debt four years after graduation, or be dealing with an endless parade of douches hell-bent on making my life miserable.

Filled with despair, I tossed aside the paperwork and texted the girls: I'm fucked.

When Whit asked what happened, I told her the whole sad story—from my meeting with Fluttr to this unintelligible Intellectual Property Agreement.

MEL:

I should've majored in Communications.

WHIT:

Trust me, that's not a cakewalk, either.

LIA:

Nothing's a cakewalk. The ad business is one long douche parade, too.

DANI:

Ha. Try being a black lesbian in academia.

MEL:

I feel so stupid. I signed these papers years ago without even thinking.

WHIT:

And you're sure there's no way to get out of it?

MEL:

I have no idea. I can't understand a word the agreement says. I'm not a lawyer.

WHIT:

Okay. Check your email in 10 minutes.

Ten minutes later, a message appeared in my inbox.

From: Whitney Hwang
To: Melanie Strickland; Yumi Tanaka
Subject: Urgent Lawyerly Help Needed

Yumi, meet Mel. Mel's one of my best friends; a brilliant, funny, creative woman who's going to change the world one day with her badass coding skills.

Mel, meet Yumi. Yumi's a colleague of mine. She's sharp, insightful, meticulous—and she has a law degree.

I've given Yumi an overview of your situation, Mel, and frankly, she's just as pissed as I am.

Now, acknowledging that Yumi is in no way offering official legal advice, she's agreed to take a quick look at your Intellectual Property Agreement and help you translate some of the legal jargon into plain English.

You got this!
xo
Whit

Wow. The power of Whitney's network would never fail to astound me.

Using my phone, I scanned the contents of the agreement and emailed the document over to Yumi with a note of thanks and a few of my most pressing questions, all of which boiled down to: *Can you find me a loophole?*

In less than an hour, she responded:

From: Yumi Tanaka
To: Melanie Strickland
Subject: re: Urgent Lawyerly Help Needed

Hi Melanie,
I'm sorry to say, it looks like this agreement is set in stone. Hatch does indeed own your intellectual property, which includes all the code you've written, as well as the design of your database.

However, there is one important distinction that may work in your favor: by the terms of this agreement, data content is not considered intellectual property. While Hatch owns the database itself—meaning, the creative decisions you made in terms of what data gets stored, how it gets stored, how it is organized, etc.—they do not own the data contained therein.

Meaning, all the information inside the database is yours, to do with as you wish. You can keep it, you can destroy it, or you can sell that data to someone else.

Again, this isn't official legal advice. But, if I were you, I'd get a lawyer. Because if Hatch tried to come after your data, I bet they would lose.

Hope this was helpful,
Yumi

The data was mine. It was mine!

I didn't have to turn over a single name or review or email address to Hatch. Sure, they owned my code, but they could have it. According to Johnny, it was worthless, anyway. All Fluttr wanted was the data I'd collected. The names and reviews and email addresses. And if Yumi was right, I could still sell it to them.

That half a million dollars was as good as mine.

When my phone rang, I was still smiling. It was a 415 number, probably Fluttr calling to discuss the details of our transaction. I slid my thumb across the screen to answer, and heard Sheila's voice on the other end of the line.

"Hello, Ms. Strickland. How was your flight home?"

"It was perfect, thank you."

"Great." There was a pause. The rustling of papers. Sheila cleared her throat. "I'm afraid I'm calling with some bad news. Fluttr is rescinding our offer of purchase."

"What? Why?"

"We received a call from a Mr. Vijay Agrawal at Hatch Incorporated. He informed us of the terms of your Intellectual

Property Agreement and it's become clear you are not the sole proprietor of the JerkAlert business."

"No, that's not true. I reviewed the agreement with my lawyer, and she said that Hatch only owns the code and the database schema. The data is still mine. That's all Johnny wants to buy. He can still have it. I can show you—"

"Ms. Strickland." Sheila cut me off, her voice at once stern and resigned. "Intellectual Property Agreements are notoriously tricky. Fluttr is not interested in sustaining a protracted legal battle for this data. It would be far less costly to design a system to collect the data on our own. The offer is no longer on the table."

When she hung up, the click felt like a gunshot.

It was over, for real this time. There was no loophole to be found in the word *no*.

I opened my laptop and surfed over to JerkAlert, taking one long, last look at my creation before I handed it over to Hatch forever. The streamlined design, the faultless functionality: these were things I made from code I wrote, my intellectual property. It was an achievement I could be proud of.

What I wasn't as proud of? The data. Because no matter what that agreement said, this data wasn't really mine. It belonged to the people who wrote it, the users who added it to this database by hitting Submit on a web form without even thinking of where it would go, or what it would be used for, or who it would impact. Would they have been so quick to hand it over for free if they'd known how much money had been offered for it?

This data was a record of their hopes and their fears, their anger and their desire, their need for companionship and their failure to find it. It was messy and it was heartbreaking. It wasn't this disembodied collection of facts and figures. It was a story of the human experience.

Out of habit, I looked up Alex and scrolled through his profile, reading the reviews. How stupid and petty they seemed now.

I went to the dashboard and pulled up the database admin screen. I typed in a few commands. And when a pop-up message appeared with the question, "Are you sure you want to delete all the data from the JerkAlert database?" I answered, "Yes."

Hatch could take the schema, but they couldn't take the story.

As thousands of records disappeared from existence, I composed a letter, posting it on JerkAlert.biz, in place of the home page.

Dear JerkAlert User,

Things look a little different around here, huh?

Allow me to explain.

My name is Melanie Strickland. A few weeks ago, I created JerkAlert on a whim. I'd had a few bad days dealing with a few bad dudes, and I thought creating a website to get revenge on them would somehow make things better.

At first, I just wanted some catharsis. But as time went by, I realized this could be an opportunity for me to improve the online dating landscape. I envisioned JerkAlert as a safe space for women to avoid harassment, a way to weed out the liars and the frauds. I hid my true identity, thinking this would protect me, thinking I deserved it because I was doing something noble.

Well, I was wrong. About everything. Because JerkAlert wasn't a safe space. It was yet another online forum for harassment and bullying, allowing users to conceal themselves beneath the cloak of anonymity. It became the exact thing I was trying to fight against. It was anything but noble.

And hiding my identity didn't protect me, either. In fact, my life is much worse now than I ever could've imagined.

I'll spare you the details, but now JerkAlert is no longer mine. I'm sure it'll continue to exist in one form or another, but I won't be the one running things behind the scenes. Any reviews you added before today have been deleted. You can make the decision for yourself whether you want to continue to use this site moving forward. Before you do, though, let me offer some advice:

Never trust anything you read on the internet.

And never trust the internet with your heart.

If you're looking for love, stop swiping. Instead, look up. Look around. The love of your life could be working in your office, or sitting next to you in a bar, or standing right beside you on a crowded city street.

Get off the internet for a little while. Otherwise, you might let the one get away.

xo,
Mel

Before I could talk myself out of it, I sent the link to the letter to Alex, with a text that said: I'm sorry.

Then, even though it was barely seven o'clock, I pulled the covers up over my head, blocking out the setting sun. And I went to sleep.

27

I slept for eighteen hours. A deep, dreamless sleep, like my brain took a good look around and decided to peace out. If Vanessa hadn't knocked on my door shortly before one o'clock on Thursday afternoon, I probably would've kept on sleeping right through another night.

"Melanie? You okay in there?" she called.

When I opened the door, Vanessa jumped back in horror. I guess I must've looked pretty rough.

She didn't say anything, though. Just smoothed the front of her chiffon blouse and affected a smile. "I haven't seen you since you got home from California. How's it going?"

"Not so hot."

"Oh. Sorry. The interview didn't go well?"

I shook my head, too worn-out from the entire experience with Fluttr to form words.

"Listen," she said, "I saw what you wrote."

"What do you mean?"

"On JerkAlert. Your letter."

Right. I'd almost forgotten about that. But now that my brain was fully functioning again, it was all flooding back to me: the obliterated database, the confessional letter, the apology text I sent to Alex. The fact that I was now unemployed, with no job prospects, and the saddest little savings account the world had ever seen.

"I kind of just wanna go back to bed," I said, eager to lose consciousness as quickly as possible.

"Okay," she said. "But I want you to know, I'm super impressed with you. Not just for creating JerkAlert, but for everything you said in that letter."

"Impressed? What I did was supremely stupid. I'm a moron."

"No, you aren't. You're brave, you're creative, you're smart. And you have the best intuition. Like, if it wasn't for your amazing advice, I never would've given up my pointless quest for some ideal guy and given Ray a chance. And I am just so happy with him, Mel. He is really, really wonderful."

"That's great," I said, deadpan. At least one of us had found romantic fulfillment.

"My point is, all that stuff you said about getting off the internet and paying attention to the world around you, it was true for me, too. Even though I wasn't using the internet to find love, I was depending on some clueless matchmaker to set me up with someone who was supposed to be perfect on paper, instead of just trusting my heart and my instincts. You really helped me see that, and I think you have the power to help a lot of other people see that, too."

"Thanks." I was truly glad Vanessa thought I helped her, but on the whole, my insight into how to foster a healthy relationship wasn't particularly spot-on. JerkAlert was proof of that. So was the whole Alex debacle.

I closed the door and fell back into bed, grabbing my phone off the nightstand to check my messages. It was foolish to have expected to see a reply from Alex. Of course there wasn't one. Why would he ever accept my apology? We were over. End of story.

There was a text from Lia waiting for me, though.

Hey girl. Hope you're feeling better today. You know what'll help lift your spirits? Hot yoga! Class starts at 6:00 PM on St. Mark's.

Ugh. There was nothing I wanted to do less than stretch out in a sweltering room full of sweaty people and their smelly feet. Besides, then I'd have to get dressed, take the subway, face the world. Better to let my Groupon go to waste than deal with reality.

I replied: Not feeling it tonight. Sorry. Then I turned off my phone and dived back beneath the blankets, willing my brain to take another lengthy break.

Astoundingly, I managed to avoid the outside world for another two days. I subsisted on potato chips and frozen burritos, wearing the same filthy sweatpants round the clock and watching Netflix on my laptop with my headphones on to block out the sounds of Vanessa and Ray being happy and in love.

At some point on Saturday, there was another knock on my bedroom door. I figured it was Vanessa coming to check on me again, but when I opened it, I was surprised to see the girls. Whit, Lia, and Dani all glared at me from the hallway.

"Why aren't you answering your texts?" Dani asked.

"I turned off my phone."

They all groaned, and Whit spat, "It didn't occur to you that we might be freaking out?"

"You bailed on our Thursday night workout for the first time ever," Lia said, "then you went totally missing."

"Well," I said, "since I'm without a paycheck for the foreseeable future, I don't think I'll be buying any more fitness Groupons, so you might as well get used to going without me."

"Oh, lord." Whit barreled past me into my room and the other girls followed suit. "Spare me the pity party."

"When was the last time you showered?" Lia asked with concern.

"Is this how you've been living?" Dani plucked a soiled burrito wrapper from the end of my bed. "No wonder you're so despondent."

"I'm despondent because I lost my job, okay?" I snatched it from her hands, crumpling it in one fist and chucking it toward the garbage bin beside my closet. It bounced off the rim and tumbled pathetically to the floor. "I'm broke and I'm alone and my life sucks."

"Just stop it," Whit said. "You've had a few days to mope around in your own filth and feel sorry for yourself. Now it's time to rejoin the real world. Go take a shower and make yourself presentable. We're going out to brunch."

Pouting, I crossed my arms across my chest. "I can't exactly afford brunch right now."

"It's on us." She turned me around and shoved me out into the hall, in the direction of the bathroom. "Get clean. Our reservation's in twenty minutes."

After rushing through a shower and throwing on a pair of jeans, we crossed Atlantic Avenue and headed to Bar Tabac, a charming French bistro on Smith Street that was my usual go-to for brunch. Today, though, nothing looked appetizing. Not even the avocado toast.

When the waiter came, the girls ordered omelets and Bloody Marys, while I handed back the menu and said, "I'll just have coffee, please."

"You have to eat something," Lia said.

"I've been stuffing my face with junk food for the past three days," I said. "I could live off my fat stores for a week."

From the scowls on their faces, the girls didn't find my joke funny.

"Look," I said, "I'm sorry I made you guys worry. I just needed a little break from life."

Dani squeezed my hand. "It's okay. The important thing is you're all right."

"I don't feel all right." My voice wobbled. "I feel like I've screwed everything up, irreparably."

"In a way, you kind of did. But that's okay. Sometimes, you need to burn everything to the ground, so you can build something brand-new."

"Are you kidding me? I made a fool of myself in, like, ten different ways. No one in the tech world will ever want to work with me again."

The girls exchanged troubled glances. Finally, Whit looked at me and said, "You have no idea what people have been saying, do you?"

An ice block formed in the center of my chest. "God, don't tell me I'm trending again."

"Yes, you are." Whit whipped out her phone and loaded Twitter. "After you posted your letter, a new hashtag sprouted up."

She passed it over to me and I began scrolling through hundreds of tweets, all tagged with #GetOffTheInternet.

So sick of swiping. Mel Strickland said it best. #GetOff-TheInternet

Took this afternoon to #GetOffTheInternet. Totally refreshing. Will do it more often!

Fluttr sucks! #GetOffTheInternet

Would love to #GetOffTheInternet but I don't know any other way to meet single women who are actively looking for a man. Thoughts?

I even saw one from jboogie2592:

Taking a Twitter hiatus for a while. #GetOffTheInternet

"This is cool, I guess."

"You *guess*?" Whit was horrified by my lack of enthusiasm.

"It's nice that people have found inspiration in my letter, but it's not going to get me any closer to a job."

"This is a movement, Mel. Fluttr is shitty, everyone knows it, and they're hungry for something new."

"Hold on a second," Dani said. "Fluttr isn't *totally* shitty. I did use it to meet Yvelise."

"Oh," I said, suddenly realizing how out of the loop I had been, "you guys are still seeing each other?"

"It's only been a few weeks, but yes." She bit back a goofy smile and fiddled with one of her braids. "Things are getting serious."

"Watch out," Whit said, "you sound a lot like Lia did when she was dating you-know-who."

"Yeah," Lia added, "are you sure she isn't married?"

"Anything's possible, I suppose. But I've been to her apartment and it sure seems like she's single." There was that goofy smile again. "I met her cat. His name is Dendrite, but she calls him Denny for short."

Whit rolled her eyes, then turned back to me. "What I'm saying is, this could be an opportunity for you to help change the online dating landscape as we know it."

I barked a bitter laugh. "That's what I thought I was doing with JerkAlert, and look how well that turned out."

"JerkAlert wasn't changing anything. Not fundamentally. You were still centering Fluttr as the be-all and end-all of online dating, with JerkAlert as a supplemental tool. But what if you were to introduce something completely different? Something that helps people find love and get off the internet at the same time?"

Whit's words were like jumper cables to my brain, infusing it with much-needed power. Neurons fired. Ions flowed. And then, I had the seed of an idea. An idea for a service that would improve people's lives.

There was just one problem.

"I don't know how."

"That's what we're here for," Lia said. "Let's do what we always do—talk it out."

For the next hour, we sat in the corner at Bar Tabac and brainstormed my next big opportunity. Mostly, we talked about the problems with the dating status quo: how overwhelming it felt to swipe through thousands of people, making split-second judgments using only a photo and a few key pieces of identifying information. How impossible it felt to establish a human connection without the aid of body language or eye contact. And, of course, how frustrating it felt to be incessantly harassed, and never have anyone take your complaints about it seriously.

As we discussed the search for love in a digitally disconnected world, my appetite returned. I ordered avocado toast with a side of sausage. By the time our check appeared, my belly was full, and so was my brain. And that seed of an idea was beginning to take root.

"This is going to take some time to develop," I said. "This is way more complicated and involved than JerkAlert was. I can't just whip it up in a weekend."

"So?" Whit slapped her credit card down on the table. "You're unemployed. You've got all the time in the world."

"That's the problem. I need another job, immediately. I barely have enough in savings to cover this month's rent. Right now, I have to focus all my efforts on finding employment with a guaranteed paycheck and some health benefits. Not taking a chance on some project that may or may not find an investor."

Lia leaned forward. "I may be able to help. Remember that big pile of crap I had in my apartment? The stuff Jay gave me that I wanted to burn? Well, I took Whit's advice, and I sold it on eBay. And I made a fortune." Her eyes lit up when she said the last word.

"I'm not taking your money," I said.

"I'm not giving you my money," she said. "I'm investing it in your new start-up. When you get rich off your app, I expect to be repaid with interest."

"You're not serious."

"I am. Though I'm not giving you *all* of it." She smiled

triumphantly. "I'm setting aside a couple grand and booking a solo trip to Cabo."

Whit and Dani whooped. "Good for you!"

"Thanks. I'm pretty excited about traveling on my own." Lia turned to me with expectant eyes. "So, does that sound good?"

It sounded better than good. It sounded amazing.

"Yes, of course. Thank you. I don't know how to thank you enough. All of you." I looked around the table, at the faces of my very best friends. The women who pushed me to be the best version of myself I could be.

"You can thank us by changing the world," Whit said. "Go home, get started."

I practically flew out of my chair, propelled by the power of my flourishing idea. Running up Smith Street, my legs couldn't move fast enough. I needed to get back to my laptop, to dive in to the code. To seize the opportunity I'd created.

Finally, I was picking up speed. Someday soon, I might just take flight.

28

The Creator of JerkAlert Is Launching a New Dating App and We're Losing Our Minds

By Kirra Boyce, BuzzFeed Staff
Posted: Thursday, May 10, 10:32 a.m.

Single ladies everywhere shed a tear the day JerkAlert got wiped away. Without all that useful intel, it was like we were thrust back into the dark ages of Fluttr, never knowing if our next right-swipe would lead to a date or a dick pic.

Then again, Mel Strickland—the brains behind JerkAlert—had us thinking maybe Fluttr wasn't the best plan for finding a romantic partner, anyway. Her farewell letter gave us all the feels, and led to the #GetOffTheInternet movement that's still going strong two weeks later.

Meeting a mate in real life is a lot harder than it sounds,

though. How did people do it before the internet? The very idea of searching for love without the aid of our phones was enough to make us run crying back to Fluttr...

Until now.

Because Mel just announced that she's developed a new app, one that combines the convenience of internet dating with the intimacy of a real-world connection. She's calling it inPerson, and according to her spokeswoman, it's going to "change the online dating landscape as we know it."

So how can you get your hands on this amazingness? Right now, it's still in beta, but you can go to their website and get on their waiting list today. And as soon as you get your exclusive inPerson invite, you can delete Fluttr off your phone forever.

Developing JerkAlert had been an isolating experience. Apart from the girls, no one knew it was mine. I toiled in secret, hiding my work, hiding myself. I claimed to be crusading for the truth, but all I did was tell a bunch of lies. And in the end, it didn't really improve anyone's dating experience, or help anyone find love. Least of all, me.

Developing inPerson, though? I never could've done it alone. Sure, in the weeks following my departure from Hatch, I'd coded the whole thing myself, but creating a great dating app involves more than just code.

It requires a deep understanding of the human condition, and the ways in which people interact. Topics that, say, a PhD candidate in Sociology knows a lot about. So, in the weeks following my brunch-time intervention, Dani graciously answered my questions and gave me advice. Whenever I hit a roadblock, I'd take her out for coffee or lunch or edible cookie dough, and she'd happily talk me through my concerns.

Of course, I never would've been able to treat Dani to those working meals if I hadn't had such a generous investment from Lia. Aside from her monetary contributions, though, she'd also offered up her time and skill by designing a kick-ass inPerson logo. Something that made it look chic and professional. Something that screamed, "This is a serious business."

And, as always, Whit was instrumental in getting people to sit up and take notice. She'd dubbed herself my spokeswoman, and used the exact same marketing strategy Fluttr had used in the days before its launch to help build buzz for inPerson: vague emails, teaser tweets, and a gratuitous wait-list, which was currently at over two thousand five hundred sign-ups and counting.

Perhaps the most important thing Whit taught me, though, was the importance of having a network. People who step up and help you when you send out a distress signal. People who sing your praises when you've got something awesome to share. People who you can support when they're the ones in need of a favor or two.

Whit had successfully hooked me into her network, but I figured it was about time to start building a network of my own. Specifically, a network of tech-industry professionals who were looking for new opportunities, while at the same time looking out for one another. Coming from the toxic environment in which I'd been mired, it might've been an overly idealistic pipe dream. But that wasn't going to stop me from trying.

My goal was to organize a tech meetup that was different than the ones already out there. Ideally, we'd pack the room with women, and the men who showed up would have a clear understanding that it wasn't a meat market, and that harassment and sexist talk would not be tolerated. For example, anyone who told me I didn't look like a software developer would be tossed out and banned from subsequent events.

I envisioned attendance by a whole range of techies: coders, testers, engineers, founders, angel investors, even help desk analysts. All of them shaking hands, exchanging business cards, forming connections that could benefit them in their present situations, as well as far into their unknown futures. It would be respectful and uplifting and entirely devoid of dick pics.

At Whit's suggestion, I posted notices on Meetup, Craigslist, EventBrite, and about a dozen other forums frequented by New York City techies. Advertised as a "low-key, informal networking event to connect like-minded individuals in the tech sphere," the inaugural New York Techie Support Network meetup was held at 6:00 p.m., on Thursday, May tenth, at that unpopular FiDi watering hole, The Barley House.

Now, I know what you're thinking: I picked The Barley House for its proximity to Alex's apartment, and the fact that he told me he hung out there all the time.

And you're right. I did.

While I'd been tremendously preoccupied these past couple of weeks with developing inPerson and planning a tech meetup, I'd also experienced silent moments of sadness for everything that happened with Alex. They were fleeting, but still painful, knowing I'd wrecked what could've been wonderful because I'd chosen internet rumors over an honest conversation.

He still hadn't responded to my text message apology, and since I didn't want to seem like a pathetic loser, I never sent another one. Running into him in person was my only hope of a reconciliation.

But the venue had other perks, too. Like the fact that it was always half-empty, and therefore easily able to accommodate an influx of networking techies. Also, Alex said the Hatchlings never came here, so even if nobody showed, I'd at least be able to avoid an unpleasant encounter with one of my ex-coworkers.

Ten minutes before six, I installed myself on a barstool—the same one I'd sat in that night Brandon from Brooklyn stood me up, actually—and waited for the first guests to arrive.

At 6:15, I was still sitting alone, overcome with a sickly sense of déjà vu. Perhaps this barstool was cursed, sentencing whoever sat on it to an evening of humiliation and abandonment. A ridiculous notion, but at this point, I wasn't willing to take any chances. As casually as possible, I slid over to the next seat. And like magic, my curse was lifted.

"Melanie?"

A young woman was standing behind me, her big brown eyes shining with both excitement and trepidation.

"Hi there." I smiled and held out my hand. She shook it firmly.

"I'm Priya," she said. "It's so nice to meet you."

"Likewise. Have a seat." I pointed to the barstool beside me—the noncursed one.

"Thanks for organizing this. When I saw you were the one hosting this meetup, I knew I had to come. What you did with JerkAlert was so awesome. You're, like, my role model."

The idea that someone I'd never met looked to my sad little life as an example to be emulated was enough to make me burst out into a fit of giggles. Priya seemed crestfallen, though, so I quickly swallowed my laughter.

"I'm sorry," I said. "You don't understand how crazy that sounds to me. I'm not exactly cut out to be anyone's role model."

"Are you kidding me? You started your own website, by yourself, from your bedroom, and impacted thousands of people from all over the world in the span of a few short weeks. That's the kind of achievement I can only dream about."

When she said it like that, I guess it did sound sort of impressive.

"That's really nice of you to say," I said. "I assure you, though, it's something you can most definitely achieve. If I can do it, so can you. What's your story, Priya? Where do you work?"

"Right now, I'm a full-time student. I'm a comp sci major at NYU, and I just finished up my junior year. I came here hoping to make some connections in the industry. Ultimately, I'd love to find an internship to help build my résumé and gain some real-world experience before graduation."

"I'm so glad you came," I said, thinking that if I had attended a meetup like this when I was still an undergrad, maybe I wouldn't have settled for the first job offer I got. Maybe I'd have built a network that would've helped me chase my dreams from the very start.

Just then, a gaggle of women walked into the bar. They approached Priya and me with open smiles and extended hands, and as we exchanged introductions, even more people began to file in. Mostly women, but a few men, too. As the hours passed, the crowd continued to grow, slowly and steadily. Alex never did show, but it was hard to become too disheartened when I was surrounded by so much positive energy.

The focus of the event was networking, getting to know people and sharing contact information. But it also provided an excellent opportunity for me to perfect my inPerson elevator pitch. People kept coming up to me and asking me what the app was like, how it worked, or when it would be available, so there was plenty of time for me to practice what I'd already prepared and retool what wasn't really working. By the end of the night, I had all my talking points down pat. Which would come in handy when it was time to seek funding from investors.

I just hadn't been expecting that time to come so soon.

It was almost eight o'clock. The crowd was thinning and people were wrapping up, exchanging business cards and entering new numbers into their phones. I was paying my tab at the bar, credit card in hand, when I heard someone say my name.

"Ms. Strickland?"

I turned around to see a tall woman with a chic, short afro and striking red lips. She was a bit older than most of the other attendees, and a bit more sophisticated, too. From the tailored fit of her suit jacket, I could tell she was someone important.

"Yes, I'm Melanie Strickland."

"My name is Tisha Cole. I'm a managing director at FirstBrand Capital."

It took every last ounce of my strength to keep from collapsing in a fit of squeals. FirstBrand was a huge venture capital firm, famous for funding early stage start-ups, which they then ushered to untold heights of success. One of their first ventures recently secured an additional hundred-million-dollar round of funding, with a valuation of over a billion dollars.

A billion dollars.

"It's nice to meet you," I said. "Thank you for coming."

"I'm here tonight because I've read a lot about you and your work. I appreciate what you're doing with this meetup, and I'm interested in hearing more about inPerson. Can you tell me a little bit about where you got the idea from and how it functions?"

This was it. This was the moment I'd been waiting for. The chance to pitch one-on-one to a big-time investor who could change my life as I knew it.

I was not going to freak out.

Instead, I was going to knock this pitch out of the park.

"Well, I designed inPerson to solve a problem. Namely, the search for true human connection in a digitally disconnected world. Currently, internet dating reduces us to data points—single photographs, pithy taglines, labels to be categorized and filtered and parsed.

"But in real life, dating is more complex than a few pieces of data. It's about interaction and nuance and feeling. Body language is key in conveying our intentions. Eye contact is crucial in building empathy. Yet we think it's okay to begin a new relationship with an indifferent and hasty swipe of a finger.

"Now, we live in a world dominated by the internet and ruled by Big Data. And sometimes, that can be a good thing. In so many ways, access to all this information makes our lives better, fuller, easier, more convenient. So, I thought, why not harness that power to allow people to make more meaningful, personal connections?

"That's how I came up with inPerson. With inPerson, there are no pictures, no profiles, and no swiping. There are no direct messages, so there's no chance of targeted anonymous harassment. There's only a map, one that guides you to a secret location to a singles mixer organized and supervised by the inPerson team. When you get there, you'll be introduced to other single people who are in your age range, who share some similar interests, and who live in your general location. And you'll also be forced to give up your phone."

"Give up your phone?" Tisha raised a skeptical eyebrow.

"Yes. The whole point of inPerson is to encourage face-to-face interaction. We use technology to facilitate that, but when it comes down to the actual event, we want the focus to be on humans, not on screens—to really take the spirit of #GetOffTheInternet to heart. The phones are kept safe by members of our team, and at the end of the night, you get them back. And hopefully, you'll also get a new number or two to add to your contacts."

Tisha nodded, slowly. From the way her lips curled down in the corners, though, I wasn't sure if she was disgusted or intrigued.

"It's an interesting concept," she said. "But how do you intend to generate revenue? By selling the data you collect?"

"No. We're not interested in selling people's data. That's what all the big companies do—Fluttr, Twitter, Facebook—but we'd like to take a different approach, one that's more respectful of our users' privacy. To start, I envision a tiered membership model. Subscribers can pay more money to attend more events, and also to access special perks, like exclusive meetups in smaller venues. As we grow, I anticipate corporate sponsorships for our events, as well—I've already spoken with a rep at PointBreak PR who's expressed an interest in approaching some of her clients with this opportunity."

Actually, that was a little white lie; the idea for corporate sponsorships had only just occurred to me, so I hadn't yet cleared that idea with Whit. But I was certain she'd be proud of me for name-dropping her PR firm. Especially when Tisha's face morphed from skeptical to impressed.

"I'd like to see it in action," she said. "Do you have any events currently planned?"

"Yes." The word fell out of my mouth before I could even think about what I was saying. I just knew that whatever Tisha Cole was asking me for, the answer needed to be "Yes."

"When is it taking place?"

"Um…next week? It's a free event, since we're still in beta."

"I'd love to attend." Tisha plucked a business card from the front pouch of her Kate Spade and presented it to me. "Please let me know the where and the when."

"Of course. Absolutely."

As she walked away, I turned her card over in my hands, feeling the heft of the thick cardstock, running my fingers over the embossed lettering. Tisha Cole, Managing Director and Partner at FirstBrand Capital, would be coming to my first inPerson event.

Which meant I should probably plan it.

29

I arrived home to find Ray standing on a ladder in the middle of our living room, hanging a funky spherical light fixture from the ceiling. Vanessa stood at his feet, steadying his legs. When I opened the door, she turned to me, beaming.

"Isn't this lamp the cutest? I found it on Etsy."

"It's great."

Vanessa's face fell at the lack of enthusiasm in my voice. "You hate it."

"No, it's not that. It's adorable. I just have other stuff on my mind."

"Oh, right," she said. "I saw the article on BuzzFeed today. How was your meetup?"

"It was interesting. And kind of terrifying. A big investor wants to see inPerson in action."

"That's so exciting!" She clapped her hands together rapidly, releasing Ray's legs, causing him to wobble precariously on the thin metal ladder.

"Vee, I need help!"

Instantly, she returned to spotting him, and his body steadied. "Sorry, honey."

"It is exciting," I said, "but I told her our first mixer was next week and I don't have a venue. I need a private space with a place to store cell phones securely and check IDs at the door. This is New York—nothing's gonna be available on such short notice. Not to mention, I have about a million bugs to fix before the app can go live and I do not have the time to plan a party, too."

"Let me do it," Vanessa said, eyes shining.

"I can't ask you to take that on. It's way too much work."

"What are you talking about? You know I live for this kind of thing. I was hoping you'd ask me, anyway. I already started a Pinterest board specifically for inPerson parties."

I couldn't help but smile at Vanessa's generosity. "Thank you. That would be a huge help. But it doesn't solve the problem of the venue."

"We'll do it on the roof."

"Oh, no." Ray descended from the ladder, already shaking his head. "After what happened last time? No way."

"Everything was going fine until that hipster set his beard on fire," she said. "This time, we just won't have a fire pit."

"I can't do it, Vee. It's too risky. I don't wanna lose my job."

"Then stay home that night. Say you had no idea it was happening. And if anyone asks, I'll tell them I did it without your permission."

Ray looked at me. "How many people you expecting at this thing?"

"We're capping the guest list at fifty, plus there'll be a few other people working the event."

He pursed his lips and took a deep breath, probably doing

mental math to calculate how many people could safely fit on that tiny rooftop.

"There were definitely more than fifty people at the last party," Vanessa said. "I'll be super careful."

She squeezed his arm and he looked from her hand to her eyes, his mouth softening into a grin. "You better."

"I promise I will." She raised up onto her tiptoes, planting a kiss on Ray's lips.

With that problem solved, I still had about a thousand others to address. Like getting the mapping feature in working condition so people could find the venue the night of the party. Not to mention, testing out my algorithm to make sure I sent the right invites to the right people and kept an accurate count of RSVPs.

There was no way I was going to finish this all in a week.

I texted the girls: I'm fucked.

WHIT:

You say this shit so often the words have lost all their meaning.

MEL:

No, this time it's true. Big time investor showed up tonight. Wants to see inPerson in action. I lied and told her there was a party planned next week. Now she wants to come. So I have to actually put one on.

WHIT:

Oh, you're right. You're fucked.

LIA:

Stop. You'll get it done, you always do.

MEL:

There's too much to fix, though. Even if I stayed up all night, I'd never get it all finished.

DANI:

Can you enlist help?

LIA:

Yeah, did you meet any other coders at that networking event?

MEL:

Good call. I totally did.

I scrolled through my contacts and pulled up Priya's number, then sent her a text:

Hi Priya, it's Mel Strickland. I have an opportunity for an internship that I think you might find interesting. Give me a call whenever you're free to discuss.

Since it was ten o'clock on a Thursday night, and Priya was in the prime of her college life, I assumed she was out drinking somewhere on MacDougal Street and I'd hear from her tomorrow, after the worst of her hangover had worn off. To my surprise, though, she called me back almost immediately.

"That was fast," I said.

"Thank you so much for contacting me," she said. "I want first dibs on whatever it is you've got to offer."

"Well, as it turns out, we're going to be holding our first inPerson event next week. The problem is, the app isn't quite where it needs to be." *Translation: it's a broken POS.* "So, I was wondering if you'd be interested in taking on some extra work over the next few days, helping out with bug fixes and testing and stuff. I can pay you by the hour, and—"

"Yes!" Priya didn't bother to wait until I finished my sentence. "I would love to. Thank you!"

"Great. Right now, I don't have an office, but I feel like it would be beneficial for us to work in the same space. Would you be okay with coming to my place in Brooklyn tomorrow to get started? I'll provide food."

"Absolutely. I'll be there bright and early."

I hung up, wishing I'd been as ambitious as Priya when I was in college. If I had, who knew how much I'd have accomplished by now?

But playing what-if wouldn't get inPerson off the ground. I flipped open my laptop and got to work testing the algorithm for sending out those invites. I decided our first event would focus on straight couples, with dedicated safe-space events for queer users taking place at later dates. For now, that meant the algorithm would need to ensure a balanced selection of men and women, while keeping in mind similar age ranges, interests, and general locations.

After a few tweaks to the code, I found the perfect way to pick the guest list from the names on our waiting list. Then I composed the email:

To: inPerson Guest
From: Melanie Strickland
Subject: You're Invited to the First inPerson Singles Mixer!

Congratulations!
You've been invited to participate in the first ever inPerson Singles Mixer.

The event will be held in Downtown Brooklyn on Thursday, May 17 at 6:00 PM. An hour before it begins, you'll be provided with a map to the venue. Just open your inPerson app and let your GPS be your guide to love!

RSVP at the link below no later than Monday, May 14.

Can't wait to see you there!

xo

Mel

With a shaky finger, I hit Send.

There was no turning back now.

Coding with Priya was an unprecedented pleasure. Starting on Friday, we sat side by side on my living room couch, methodically working our way through the list of inPerson bugs and features that needed to be fixed. I ordered takeout for lunch, and provided an endless supply of junk food to fuel our coding marathons. We'd work for eight-to-ten hour stretches, sipping Cokes and staring at our screens until our eyes became dry and bloodshot. Then she'd head home for the night and I'd turn in, and we'd start the process all over again the next morning.

After so many years of sharing office space with people who talked down to me, doubted my intelligence, or told me to smile through a tirade, working with Priya was a breath of fresh air. We treated each other with respect, shared ideas openly and without fear, and handled disagreements in a mature and civil manner. It was unlike any working relationship I'd ever had.

While this was going on, RSVPs started to roll in for the

Thursday mixer. For every "No" received, the software selected another comparable person from the database and sent a replacement invite. I kept a close eye on responses, making sure it went according to plan. So far, so good. Eventually, we reached our fifty-person limit, with a shorter waitlist to account for any last-minute cancellations.

Then, on Tuesday night, at exactly 5:53 p.m., Priya and I closed out our final bug. After running through all our test cases, we confidently uploaded the official stable release of inPerson to the app store.

"We did it!" Priya squealed.

"I know. With a whole day to spare. I kind of can't believe it."

"I can. We worked our butts off."

I laughed. "Thanks for all your help."

"Oh, it was no problem." She zipped up her laptop bag and slung it over her shoulder. "Honestly, it was an honor to be included."

"Hopefully, this is just the beginning of much bigger things to come. For both of us." I led her to the front door, where we hugged our goodbyes. "I'll see you on Thursday night, right?"

"I wouldn't miss it."

After Priya left, I returned to my room and collapsed into bed, hoping to get a little bit of rest before the lead-up to the big event. Every time I closed my eyes, though, lines of code danced behind my lids. I picked up my phone, eager for some mindless distraction to wind down and de-stress.

Though I'm not quite sure why I thought I'd find respite in the blathering maelstrom that is Twitter. Particularly when I checked out the "Trends for You" section and decided to scroll through the #inPerson hashtag.

Most of it was positive. People had received their invitations and were excited for the big event. Others were speculating on venues and wondering who else was invited. Still others lamented their lack of an invitation and offered money to anyone willing to sell theirs. (Which was against our rules, and given our identification requirements, wouldn't have worked, anyway.)

But then I came across a troubling tweet, posted by a user who went by the handle BlitzkriegBoss:

> Why r u all creaming ur pants over this shitty app? Everyone knows the bitch in charge stole #inPerson from an ex-coworker.

I had to read the sentence a couple of times to understand it. Was this person really accusing me of stealing inPerson?

Against my better judgment, I clicked on BlitzkriegBoss's profile and discovered a litany of tweets aimed at discrediting me. He said I was a thief, and a liar, and a "thirsthound," whatever that meant. There was even a link to a Reddit thread, in which BlitzkriegBoss posted a lengthy diatribe explaining his stance in greater detail.

> I used to work with this bitch at Hatch before she got fired for being incompetent. She wasn't even a coder—she worked the help desk, and she sucked at it. You wanna know the reason she got fired? Because she installed keyloggers on everyone's laptop, including mine. She stole the code for inPerson from a qualified Hatchling, and now she's trying to make a buck off it. I hope she's exposed for the scam artist she is!

It was hard to read the words through the rage tears forming in my eyes. Clearly, BlitzkriegBoss was none other than Josh Brewster, the founder of that totally original fantasy football app, Blitz. I knew he was a liar and a scumbag, but if I told anyone the truth about why I'd really installed a keylogger on his machine, who would believe me? Obviously, I had a vested interest in protecting my reputation. And after the way things went down in my last days at Hatch, there's no way anyone there would have my back.

Especially Greg, aka FreakinFizz69, who had this charming anecdote to add to the thread:

> Don't forget she was hungry for the d. My partner banged her but dumped her ass when she went psycho. Heard she hacked into his computer to steal his code.

Oh, God. This just kept getting worse. The further I scrolled, the more horrid the accusations became, all of them generally boiling down to the same core message: girls are whores who can't code for shit. Most of the posts didn't even seem like they came from Hatchlings. They were simply random men who sniffed out a trollfest and jumped at the chance to pile on.

The internet is truly a terrible place.

Normally, I'd have tried to brush off these accusations. They were baseless and juvenile. Besides, it's not like people hadn't tried to slam me on the internet before.

For some reason, though, this felt different. This felt intensely personal. Because despite it being a bunch of faceless semi-anonymous commenters typing from behind the safety of a Reddit thread, they had a goal in mind: to smear me so badly that investors would run screaming away from inPerson. They didn't want my start-up to get funded. They wanted to bring my career to a standstill before it even got going.

Well, fuck them.

I clicked the comment icon to open the message box to post my own reply. This slander couldn't live out there on the internet, uncontested. I had to at least try to defend myself.

But as my thumbs hovered over the virtual keyboard, I struggled to find the right words. What could I possibly say to convince people I wasn't a liar and a thief? And why would anyone believe me over any of these other guys? I'd already had one big start-up deal fall through because my ownership of the code had been called into question. There's no way another investor would want to take a chance on me when I was surrounded by all of these rumors.

It was pointless.

This was the end of it: my career, my reputation, my future in tech.

At least, that's what I thought until I closed the message box, and found a new comment posted by Piquete92:

> This thread is filled with hateful garbage written by sad, jealous men. Melanie Strickland is a talented and intelligent woman, fully capable of developing her own kick-ass app. I've seen her in action, and trust me, she didn't need to be stealing anybody's code—especially not any of the mediocre coders pervading Hatch's noxious, bro-filled hallways. She's a good person, deep down, and she deserves all the success I hope inPerson brings her.
>
> (By the way, Greg, I didn't "dump her when she went psycho," as you so eloquently stated. Things between

us just didn't work out, and what happened is nobody's business—certainly not yours, and definitely not the internet's.)

Alex.

My heart swelled. He had jumped to my defense, publicly shaming his partner and bashing Hatch in the process. Words like this could put his job at risk. Why would he do that for me, when he didn't even bother to reply to my last text?

I pulled up our weeks-old message thread and typed: Thank you for defending me. But before I hit Send, I reread it. It looked so impersonal. Black letters on a white background, a bunch of lifeless pixels strung together. How could five disembodied words express everything I felt in that moment?

They couldn't.

With a stroke of my thumb, I deleted the sentence. Then I dropped my phone in my purse, slipped on my shoes, and ran for the door.

It was time to take this conversation off the internet and into real life.

30

If you want to smooth things over with your ex, working yourself into a frenzy before showing up at his apartment unannounced is generally not the best approach to take. But in my case, I didn't see another option. There was no way to properly convey my thoughts in a text message, and it's not like he was responsive to those, anyway. Plus, if I waited until I was less emotional, odds were I'd chicken out completely.

No. It was best to go now, while I was still flustered and verklempt.

On the A train into the city, I tried to think of the right thing to say. Some elegant way of expressing my gratitude and regret for everything he'd said, everything I'd done. "Thanks" and "sorry" just didn't seem to cut it. Not when what I really wanted to do was convince him to give me another chance. To give *us* another chance.

When the doors opened at Fulton Street, I jetted out onto the platform and flew up the stairs, rushing down John Street toward his luxury apartment building. As I sailed through the lobby toward the elevator bank, the doorman smiled at me, with what I thought was a hint of recognition. He'd remembered my face, even though it had been several weeks since my last visit.

Ugh. My last visit. I stepped into the elevator and memories of that evening flooded back to me: Tampons under the sink. Jenny's pert pink nipples. The accusations I'd lobbed like grenades, hoping to hit any available target, feeling a sick sense of satisfaction once I had. On the thirtieth floor, the elevator dinged, and I walked slowly to apartment 3017, weighed down by guilt and shame.

I raised my hand to knock on the door, then paused. It wasn't too late to end this. To turn around and go back and forget what I was about to do here. Which was, essentially, putting myself at risk of major heart-crushing humiliation. Because there was a good chance Alex would reject me. He could open this door, take one look, and say, "No, thanks." Sure, he may have wished me well on the internet, but that didn't necessarily mean he wished to be with me in real life.

But I'd come this far, and I couldn't back out now. I wanted this too much. Like Whit said, every relationship involves risk. Sometimes, you just have to cross your fingers and hope everything works out.

So, I knocked.

And a beautiful woman answered the door.

Not quite the specific humiliation I'd had in mind, but mortifying nonetheless.

"Hi!" She seemed awfully chipper and undisturbed by my presence. "Are you here to see Alex?"

"Um…yes?"

"'Kay, give him one second—he's in the bathroom." She

turned around, her flowing brown locks whipping a sensuous trail behind her as she sashayed into the living room. God, she was gorgeous. It made me wonder what Alex ever saw in me.

When I didn't follow her inside, she waved me over. "You can come in."

"Oh. Thanks." She must've thought I was a housecleaner. Or perhaps a delivery person. Carefully, I stepped over the threshold, but left the door open behind me. It wasn't too late to leave. All I had to do was take one step backward and I could make a run for it down the hallway. If I did it fast enough, maybe he'd never know—

"Mel?"

Shit. Shit, shit, shit.

Too late now. There he was, crossing the room toward me, his brow knotted in a question. I couldn't tell if he was annoyed or confused or just plain angry.

"I'm sorry. I shouldn't have come," I said.

"No, no. I'm glad you're here."

In the background, the gorgeous woman scrolled through her phone, completely indifferent to our conversation. I nodded my head in her direction. "I hope I'm not interrupting anything."

He looked over his shoulder, then back at me, and his eyes twinkled with amusement. "No, you're not. That's Gabby. She's my little sister. The one from the Fluttr photo, remember?"

Gabby glanced at me from over her phone and gave a little wave. I waved back, suddenly recognizing her hazel eyes and her curly hair.

"Also?" Alex leaned in, his lips so close to me I felt his breath on my neck. "Those are her tampons under the sink.

I tried to tell you they were hers that night, but you wouldn't let me get a word in edgewise."

God, I was an idiot.

"Come in," he said, "sit down. Gabby's staying with me for the night, but she's about to head out. Where are you going again, Gabs?"

"I'm meeting Ravi and Alana in the Village." She tossed her purse over her shoulder, kissed her brother on the cheek, and headed for the door. "Don't wait up. Nice to meet you, Mel."

The door closed behind her with a bang. Alex sauntered over to the couch and sat down. "Gabby goes to college upstate, but she's got a lot of friends in the city, so I wind up being her crash pad whenever she's down here. She just had her last final yesterday, so I'm sure she's gonna go nuts tonight."

"Right." I nodded, feeling like a fool.

"So that's why she keeps her tampons here, and the razor and shaving cream, and anything else you might've seen when you were poking around in my bathroom."

"I'm sorry about that." I was still standing, unable to move my feet. "I'm sorry about a lot of things."

"I'm sorry, too. I'm sorry I let my anger and pride get in the way of reaching out to you sooner. I'm sorry I didn't stand up for you when Greg was being a dick. And I'm sorry I wasn't up-front with you about Jenny. I never should've lied and said it was a first date when it wasn't."

"That doesn't mean I was right to contact her. I should've just asked you about it if I was concerned. And I shouldn't have kept you in the dark about everything she posted on JerkAlert. Or about the fact that JerkAlert was mine." I blinked back tears, refusing to garble this apology with sobs. "I made a mess of everything, and I'm sorry."

We looked at each other for a moment, speaking a silent language only our eyes could understand. A gaze could say so much, and with more honesty than the most perfectly crafted sentence. In Alex's eyes I saw remorse, I saw fear, I saw anger. But I also saw forgiveness. And that gave me hope.

He patted the seat cushion next to him, an invitation I gladly accepted. "So," he said, "JerkAlert's gone."

"JerkAlert's gone. I sent you a text when I wiped the database but…" I trailed off. We both knew how the sentence would end, anyway.

He took a deep breath and pressed his fingertips together, like he was thinking carefully about his next words. "I didn't know what to say. I started to type a reply, but when I read it back, it sounded too angry. I thought I'd let myself calm down before I responded. But I never worked up the nerve to send another one. I'm sorry."

"It's okay. You didn't owe me a response."

"No, I didn't owe you one, but I wanted to send you one, all the same."

In a bold move, I reached out to touch his hand. He didn't brush me away.

"Well, I'm here now," I said. "What did you want to say to me?"

He laughed a little, nervous to be put on the spot. It was a daunting prospect, to speak honestly from the heart without the benefit of time to come up with the ideal words, to reread them, revise them, and proofread. To second-guess them before putting them out into the world. There's no deleting the things that you say out loud.

But he said them, anyway.

"I wish things could've been different."

"Different how?"

"I wish we'd both been honest, right from the start."

"Yeah," I said. "But, to tell you the truth, even if you'd been a hundred percent honest about Jenny, I would've found some way to sabotage what we had going on. It was like I wanted to catch you in a lie. Like you said, I'm paranoid."

"To be fair, you're paranoid with good reason. Everything that happened with your dad—"

"My dad was my dad," I cut him off, so tired of letting my father's past actions impede my present. "I can't keep projecting his mistakes on to every man I meet. Some guys are shitty. Some guys aren't. You aren't. And I'm sorry I didn't give you a chance to prove that to me."

He interlaced his fingers with mine, rubbing the pad of his thumb gently back and forth across my knuckles. "It's okay."

"Anyway," I said, taking a deep breath, "the reason I came here tonight is because I saw what you wrote on Reddit."

"Oh." His cheeks flushed and he stopped stroking my hand.

"Thank you for defending me. You didn't have to."

"It wasn't about whether I had to. It was about setting the record straight. Those assholes at Hatch think they can get away with saying whatever they want. But I wasn't going to let them talk shit about you all over the internet."

"And I appreciate that so much. But, honestly, you need to delete that comment."

"Why?"

"Because you're putting your job at risk. Bad-mouthing the Hatchlings like that will get you kicked out of the program."

He huffed and raked his free hand through his hair. "I'm not exactly worried about getting kicked out of the program."

"You should be," I said. "Vijay's vindictive. I've seen it myself."

"I know he is." Alex swallowed hard and looked at me. "But I'm no longer working with Hatch."

"What? Why?"

"Fizz lost its funding."

"Oh, no!"

"Look, it's not like I didn't see this coming a mile away."

"What happened?"

Alex sighed, resigned. "We met with Vijay this morning. He said we weren't up to the task of presenting to investors on Demo Day, and he was stripping us of our Hatchling status effective immediately. So, as of a few hours ago, I am officially unemployed."

"I'm so sorry."

"Don't be—it's for the best. Greg was the worst business partner I could've asked for. I'll be happy to never see him again."

I looked around his apartment, a well-appointed studio in a luxury apartment building in the heart of Manhattan's Financial District. There was no way he could continue to afford this rent without a salary.

"What's next?" I asked.

With a shrug, he said, "I've got a bit of savings, thankfully. The old job may have been soul-crushing, but they gave good holiday bonuses. It's enough to tide me over until I can find a new gig."

"Are you still looking to work with a start-up?"

"Yeah, as long as the people aren't total jerks, like they were at Hatch." He shot me that dazzling smile. "Why, you got any leads?"

"Unfortunately, there are no job openings at inPerson right now."

A look of genuine disappointment appeared on his face. "That's too bad."

"But you could come to the next New York Techie Support Network meeting. I'm sure you'd find some totally unjerklike people there to connect with."

"That's a good idea. When is it?"

"It hasn't been scheduled yet. I'm too preoccupied planning the inPerson mixer right now."

"Oh, yeah. I read all about that. Are you excited?"

I nodded. "Excited, yeah, but mostly nervous. There are so many moving pieces and lots of last-minute stuff to take care of."

"Well, I've got plenty of free time right now, so if you need an extra set of hands to help with coding or whatever, I'm your man."

"Thanks, but the code's all done." I looked at his hands: strong, capable, wholly on offer. "I could use some help the night of, though. How do you feel about tending bar?"

"Never done it before, but I'll give it a shot."

"Great. That'll actually be a huge help."

"Great."

An awkward silence ensued, the kind where you're not only unsure of what to say next, you're unsure if there's anything left *to* say at all. Maybe there wasn't. Maybe there was nothing left for me to do now but go home.

I got to my feet. Alex followed suit.

"Listen, Mel, thanks for coming over. I'm really glad we cleared the air."

"Me, too."

The two of us stood there, staring, silently daring each other to move. Then I saw it, the flicker of hope in Alex's eyes, and I knew it wasn't too late.

I flung my arms around his neck, pulling him close, pressing my hips to his hips, my chest to his chest. And we let our kiss do the rest of the talking.

31

As expected, Vanessa worked wonders on the rooftop.

The fairy lights were back, as were the tin can lanterns. Instead of a fire pit, though, there was a cocktail table against the brick wall. It was a high-top, designed for standing. In fact, those high-top cocktail tables were scattered around the entire roof. There wasn't a single seat to be seen.

"Where are people supposed to sit?" I asked her.

"Nowhere," she said, as she arranged peonies in decorative pots. "This event isn't meant for sitting around in one spot all night. It's meant for standing and walking and mingling. It's a singles mixer. People need to mix!"

I still wasn't convinced. "Maybe you should bring out some of those floor pillows from last time?"

"Trust me. I know what I'm doing."

"But what if—"

"Stop right there." She pointed a peony at me. "If you want to run a start-up, you're going to have to learn to delegate. No one likes a micromanager." Popping the peony in a pot, she smiled. "Just let me do this. I promise I won't let you down."

Vanessa was right; making a business successful was a joint effort. I might've been in charge, but I still needed help from other people to get it off the ground. People like Priya, whose brilliant coding skills made it possible to launch the app ahead of schedule. She was here tonight, looking stunning in an embroidered minidress and gladiator sandals. If a guest so much as suggested to her that she didn't look like a software developer, I'd eject him from the venue myself.

Alex had pulled through, too. He looked like a natural behind the bar, stacking mason jars and popping wine corks like a pro. Every drink he poured, every lime he sliced, was handled with precision and care. Plus, his forearms looked particularly muscular peeking out from the rolled-up cuffs of that crisp button-down shirt.

And, let's be honest, inPerson never would've existed without the support of my girlfriends. If they hadn't forced me out of my self-pitying squalor, I'd probably still be lying in bed right now, drowning in nacho cheese and regret.

Whit was still busting her ass for me at this party, coordinating the media reps (media reps!) who were covering the event. There were reporters from Elite Daily and Refinery29, and of course, BuzzFeed, all clamoring for me to give them some sound bites.

But I couldn't do anything yet; I was too busy overseeing the guest list. As far as I could tell, the mapping software had worked perfectly, because people started trickling in through the roof access door forty-five minutes early. When they arrived, I scanned the QR code from their inPerson app to ensure their invitation was legit. Then, after they were confirmed, I held out my hand and asked them to hand over their phone.

Most people complied without a problem. I simply showed them the safe in which the phones would be kept, dropped their phone in a baggie with their name and number on it, then handed them a claim check and locked it away. But some people had full-on panic attacks at the idea of being separated from their devices. One woman was actually on the verge of tears.

"But how will I Gram it?" she whimpered.

"There are several inPerson employees wandering the rooftop this evening with phones." (By "employees," I meant Lia, Dani, and Yvelise.) "They'll be happy to snap your picture and tag you on Instagram to keep the memories of the evening alive."

For a moment, I thought she was going to turn around and leave. As soon as I waved two drink tickets in her face, though, she handed it over and made a beeline for the bar.

Of course, this wasn't some special concession. Everyone in attendance got two free drink tickets. I'd considered handing out wristbands and holding an open bar, but after talking it over with Vanessa, we both agreed it was too risky. We were trying to fly under the radar here on the rooftop to keep Ray out of trouble. The last thing we needed were a bunch of out-of-control drunks acting up and causing a scene.

At 6:34, our last attendee rolled in the door.

"Sorry I'm late," he said, as he pulled up the QR code on his phone. "I'm always late."

"It's no problem." This guy was hot. If I wasn't already committed to Alex, he'd be exactly my type: pouty lips, deep-set eyes, beautiful beard.

Wait, that beard looked familiar.

When I scanned his phone, his private inPerson profile came up on my screen, confirming my worst fears. His name was Brandon, and he was from Brooklyn, and this was the same guy that had stood me up all those weeks ago.

I was overcome with the impulse to chuck his phone off the top of the building, then run to the edge and watch it smash into a billion tiny fragments on the sidewalk below. But then I took a deep breath, regrouped, and reminded myself that the night Brandon from Brooklyn stood me up, I was a different person. I was suspicious and bitter and paranoid. And while that didn't erase the fact that what Brandon did was completely assholish, I had to give him the benefit of the doubt. Maybe he was a different person now, too.

Or maybe he wasn't. But the dating scene was definitely different, because I was making it different. And with any luck, his experiences with inPerson could inspire him to stop being such a flaky piece of shit.

"Welcome to the inPerson party," I said, with a smile. "Here are your drink tickets. Enjoy!"

"Thanks." He took the tickets and walked away.

Asshole.

With our last guest checked in, I was free from my post at the door. I locked up the safe, tucked the key in my pocket, and went to join Whit with the media representatives.

"Melanie, this party is amazing," one woman said.

"Where did you get those lanterns?" another asked.

"Oh, thank you, but I can't take credit for all of this. My roommate, Vanessa Pratt, is my event coordinator. She put this all together."

Their fingers tapped away at their phones, taking notes.

As their eyes fixated on their screens, I casually scanned the room in search of Tisha.

"There's been a lot of buzz on the street with regard to first-round financing," one of them said. "Is it true you're in talks with Hatch to join their next incubation period?"

Undoubtedly, Vijay had planted that little crumb. I laughed, loudly. "There is no way I would ever willingly go back to that office. Hatch is a terrible company run by terrible people."

I hoped they quoted me on that one.

"Are you looking for funding from other sources?"

Just as I opened my mouth to answer, I spotted Tisha. She was standing in the corner, studying the crowd, whispering to a man and a woman beside her.

This was it. The moment I'd been waiting for.

I'd better not screw it up.

"Excuse me," I said, "I'll be back in a minute."

The three investors saw me approach and abruptly ended their conversation.

"Ms. Cole, it's nice to see you again." I extended my hand and she shook it. "Thank you for coming."

"Thank you for inviting me. Ms. Strickland, I'd like to introduce you to two of my colleagues. This is Catherine Sokolov and Byron Yang."

"It's a pleasure to meet you both. Can I get you anything? Water or a glass of wine, maybe?"

They all said, "No, thank you," and I waited for them to say something else. To ask a question or pay a compliment or talk about how nice the weather was that night. Instead, I was met with stony silence as they exchanged uncomfortable glances. Like they were totally underwhelmed with what they saw, and wanted me to leave so they could ridicule me in private.

"Well," I said, "I've gotta get back to work here, so if there's anything else I can do for you, please let me know."

My stomach twisted in painful knots. I walked to the bar and asked Alex for a glass of club soda.

"Everything okay?" he asked, spooning ice cubes into a mason jar. "You look upset."

"I'm okay," I said. "Just nervous. I'm not sure this is going so well."

"What are you talking about?" He handed me a glass, then pointed over my shoulder. "Everyone's having a blast."

I turned around to survey the space, and found a sea of smiling faces. People were talking and laughing and interacting. No one had their nose shoved in their phone. They were experiencing the night for what it was, in the moment. No hashtags or filters or swipes. Just pure human connection.

"You're right," I said, but when I turned back to him, he was already busy fixing someone else's drink.

I wandered away, edging the perimeter of the crowd, watching people connect for a long while. It gave me a little thrill to think that people could be coupling up tonight—could potentially fall in love—because of something I'd created. Even if FirstBrand didn't fund inPerson, at least I'd accomplished this much.

"Mel." Whit had me by the arm. She was wearing her no-nonsense, get-shit-done, businesswoman face. "I think it's time for you to say a little something."

"What?"

"Give a little speech."

"I don't have a speech prepared." Sweat beaded under my arms. "Why didn't you tell me to prepare a speech?"

"You don't have to say anything big. Just, 'Welcome, thanks

for coming, blah blah blah.'" She cocked her head and lowered her voice. "It would look good to the investors."

My gaze slid to Tisha and company standing in the corner, still wearing their game faces. "Anything to please the investors, I guess."

Before I could change my mind, Whit said, "Great, I'll introduce you," and she was already pushing her way to the center of the roof.

"Excuse me, everybody! May I have your attention, please?" A circle widened around her and the crowd grew silent. "Thank you all for participating in the first ever inPerson mixer!" Hooting and clapping broke out, then quickly quieted down.

"We're so pleased you decided to come. I hope you're having a good time, drinking some good drinks, and hopefully, finding some good matches. I know I've already found a match of my own." She winked at some guy, who made a kissy-face back at her. Man, Whitney worked fast.

"But none of us would be here tonight if it weren't for the brilliant brains behind inPerson. So, without further ado, allow me to introduce you to the woman who is bringing Fluttr to its knees and changing the dating landscape as we know it—Melanie Strickland."

Applause started again. On wobbly legs, I walked over to Whit, who greeted me with a hug and whispered in my ear, "You got this." The clapping faded, and I cleared my throat, scanning the faces in the crowd. Everyone looked at me with eager eyes, as if I was someone with something important to say.

Well, maybe I was.

"Thank you, Whitney, and thanks to all of you. When I

first came up with the idea for inPerson, I was at a very low point in my life. I'd lost my job. I'd lost a great guy. I'd lost hope. But what pulled me out of it was the power of human connection. And as I look around this roof right now, that's what I'm seeing. Connections. Real, true..."

I trailed off when the men in blue uniforms emerged from the roof access door. One of them bellowed, "Is there a Melanie Strickland here?"

Shit. Shit, shit, shit.

Scandalized murmurs arose from the crowd. I glanced over at Tisha, who was grimacing with her colleagues. There went any chance of securing funding tonight.

"I'm Melanie Strickland." The crowd parted as I made my way toward the two police officers, standing at the door with their hands on their batons. "What seems to be the problem?"

"We've received several noise complaints about your little shindig up here." He scrutinized the gathering, scrunching up his nose like he smelled something foul. "Do you have permission to be on this rooftop, Ms. Strickland?"

"I...uh..."

"No, we don't." Vanessa was suddenly at my side.

"And who are you?"

"Vanessa Pratt. I'm the event coordinator for inPerson. This is all my fault. I told Melanie we were allowed to host the mixer up here."

"You knowingly trespassed?"

"I wouldn't call it trespassing," she said. "No one ever actually told us we *couldn't* be on this roof. The landlord has never provided us with any specific directions either way."

"How did you gain access to the roof, then?"

"I jimmied the lock."

"You what?"

"It's not like it's hard. All it takes is a butter knife and a bobby pin and boom! You're in."

The cops both winced, horrified by Vanessa's disclosure. At first, I didn't understand why she'd taken it so far as to incriminate herself. Then I realized: she was protecting Ray. If she'd said the door was propped open or not properly locked, he'd have gotten in trouble. This way, the fault was all hers.

The things we do for love.

One of the cops released an irritated sigh, while the other whipped out his notebook and started writing. "Okay, look, it's getting late and we've got more important things to do than deal with whatever it is you've got going on up here. We'll release you with a summons for a noise complaint, but we'll be contacting your landlord to follow up on this tomorrow."

"And," the other one added, "this party is over. Get everyone outta here now."

Vanessa took the ticket with a muffled, "Whatever," and the cops started escorting guests to the door. Whitney, Lia, Dani, and Yvelise quickly attended to the safe full of cell phones, exchanging claim checks for gadgets as people headed out. Despite the abrupt and troubling end to the evening, people were still laughing and smiling. A few people looked smitten.

This would make a great story for a first date.

Unfortunately, I wasn't in a smiling mood myself. Not with the way the investors were frowning. As they filed out the door, I shook each of their hands. "Thank you for coming. I'm sorry it turned out like this."

They looked at each other, then Tisha asked, "Was this party held illicitly?"

I nodded, ashamed, afraid to look them in the eye.

"Well," Catherine said, "I can't say I approve of that."

"However," Tisha said, "we are always looking out for founders who are resourceful and driven. And if the measure of this evening's success was whether human connections were made, I'd say it was a triumph." She pointed to a couple holding hands as they walked out the door.

"Let's meet on Monday to discuss this a bit further," Byron said. "I'll send a meeting invite. Does that work for you, Ms. Strickland?"

It was a struggle not to scream my answer. "Yes. Yes, of course."

"Excellent. Have a nice weekend," Tisha said, and the three of them disappeared into the building.

I'd done it. I'd coded an app, hosted a singles mixer, attracted investors, and narrowly avoided arrest. This was my big fat decadent hunk of the start-up pie. And, hopefully, it was only the beginning.

After the bulk of the crowd dispersed, the cops left, as well, too distracted by a real life-or-death emergency to make sure the final stragglers had cleared off the roof. Soon it was just me, the girls, Vanessa, and Alex, who produced a bottle of Moët from beneath the bar.

"Hey, I don't remember buying that," Vanessa said.

"You didn't," he replied. "I brought this one from home. I figured we'd have good reason to celebrate at the end of the night." The cork released with an ear-splitting pop, and he poured us a round of champagne.

"Congratulations, Melanie," he said. "You did it."

"I always knew you had it in you," Whit said.

"I couldn't have done it without all of you," I said. "Thank you all for everything."

We clinked our glasses and sipped our drinks. Alex wrapped his arm around my shoulders, holding me close as we looked out over the Manhattan skyline. It looked postcard-perfect from up here. Not like the reality of living in the city, which was messy and flawed, and full of unsolicited dick pics.

My life in New York was far from postcard-perfect. But it was getting better every day, starting now.

EPILOGUE

The bad news is we got evicted.

Our landlord did not take too kindly to us using his rooftop for a public gathering of internet strangers. He also wasn't thrilled to hear about Vanessa's lock-picking skills. Ray (who got to keep his job) posted a huge, unambiguous sign on the top floor—No Roof Access—and added a high security padlock to the access door. But as of June first, all those gorgeous upgrades he gave our apartment went to some other lucky winner of the New York City real estate game.

The good news is we found another apartment. A bigger, nicer one, with all those gorgeous upgrades preinstalled. There was even a doorman! And I no longer had to commute on that miserable A train. Instead, I could walk to work, since our new place was a stone's throw away from inPerson HQ.

We called it HQ because it sounded cool, but really, it was a modest open office space in Chelsea, just big enough to hold our small, but growing, staff. Priya sat right next to me, since I figured it was important to work in close proximity to my chief technical officer. Vanessa had a desk, too, but she was rarely ever in it. Which was fine by me, considering an event coordinator does most of her work in the field.

Whitney got a new office at her job, too—a corner office, with a view. It came along with a sweet promotion and a massive raise, all for bringing a client as edgy and buzzworthy as inPerson to PointBreak PR.

As for Lia, she spent a week in Cabo by herself, replacing all those deleted Instagram photos of Jay with smiley solo selfies on the beach. Meanwhile, Dani filled her feed with increasingly mushy couple photos. But I couldn't really fault her; Yvelise was her perfect match.

Alex wasn't unemployed for very long. Once inPerson took off, I didn't have time to devote to growing the New York Techie Support Network anymore. So, he grabbed the reins, and transformed it from an informal, haphazard get-together to a full-blown business, designing a companion app to help connect underrepresented voices in tech with companies that value inclusion. Basically, it's a way to help start-ups hire a more diverse staff and, in time, eliminate toxic work environments like the one we had at Hatch. After BuzzFeed ran a feature on his new app, an angel investor snatched it up, and he's currently in the process of taking it from New York to other cities around the country. Eventually, he plans to take it around the world.

And yes, the two of us are still going strong.

In case you're wondering, Fluttr is still the most popular dating app in the city. All that swiping is kind of addictive. But inPerson continues to grow. And I'd like to think it's part of a bigger movement. The movement to #GetOffTheInternet.

Because, you know, you can't trust anything you read there.

★★★★★

ACKNOWLEDGMENTS

So much of this story revolves around the power of women and the importance of female friendships. I'm beyond grateful to have so many strong, intelligent, supportive women in my corner—both professionally and personally.

Thanks to my super-agent, Jessica Watterson, for being a badass advocate and an all-around wonderful person—and thanks to Elise Capron for playing matchmaker. Thanks to my editor, Brittany Lavery, for believing in this story and bringing out the best in it. Thanks to Laci Ann and Gigi Lau, the talented artist and designer who created the beautiful cover. Thanks to the publicity and marketing dream team of Steph Tzogas, Lisa Wray, and Heather Connor. And thanks to everyone at Sandra Dijkstra Literary Agency and Graydon House for the support.

My girlfriends have all helped me through the difficult task of writing this book. Whether you offered to read my half-finished manuscript when I was a panicky mess, or bought me a drink at the Craftsman when I needed to vent, or talked me through my writer's block, or hung out with my son so I could get some work done, or simply offered words of encouragement, you've helped me more than you probably know. For all of this and more, my thanks go to (in no particular order): Margaret Chantung, Christa Gallego, Kate O'Brien, Lisa Pannek, Jordan Pascoe, Erica Jo Gilles, Rosy Catanach, Mandy Tang, Elizabeth Salaam, Gauri Savla, Cathy Atkins, Lauren McFall, Sarah Apuzzo, Kathleen Barber, Chelsea Resnick, Suzanne Park, Laura Heffernan, Helen Hoang, Renée Carlino and, of course, always and forever, Marci Blaszka and Jessica Schwarz.

Finally, thank you to the two guys who make my life complete: Emilio and Andrew. I love you both more than words can say.